Her life was spiraling downward. She needed to do something to change it, and fast...

When the phone rang at four-thirty p.m., it could only be her boss, Marvin. She could feel the vibrations of his personality across the miles.

"Hey," he said flatly. "How's it going?"

Marvin was an extraordinarily, often irritatingly cheerful sort, so his coldness took Jo by surprise. She pushed her wineglass behind the computer as if he could see it. "You know—good days—bad days. What's up Marvin?"

"The bad days," he said.

"That doesn't sound good."

"Jeep," he said, using the nickname he'd favored from their first meeting. "You know you've been my girl for years, and I wouldn't be saying anything unless I thought you could do something about it—"

He had paused. Probably to take a drag from the cigar she knew was in his hand.

"Something about what?"

"Trouble in my little corner of paradise."

"Good grief, Marvin, what's with the drama?"

"You're losing it, Jeep. You're a jingle writer. You're supposed to convey upbeat, positive, cheerful messages."

"And?"

"And nothing, sister," he said. "Frankly, your work stinks. I don't like it, clients don't like it, and the sponsors are ready to pull the plug. You've lost *it*." He paused for another drag. "I'd like to believe you still have *it* somewhere."

Raising teenagers is hard enough. But when a single dad has to deal with a bi-polar daughter, it can be a recipe for disaster. Fortunately, the cosmos has a way of evening things out, and introduces a lonely young widow into their lives. Set in rural Maine, *Lonely Hearts Cry* is the parallel love story of one such father and his headstrong daughter.

KUDOS for *Lonely Hearts Cry*

In *Lonely Hearts Cry* by Anji Nolan, we are treated to two love stories. Jingle writer Jo Weston is recently widowed and wants to move to rural Maine. But the house she wants to buy belongs to an eccentric widower who has a bi-polar daughter and very firm ideas on who should be living in the house that he is selling. Once Jo makes it through the interview and actually buys the house, she has to acclimate to being away from everything she has ever known as well as the difference between city and country life. Her first night there, she freaks. It's too quiet. As the seller, Mark Newcombe, understands what the new widow is going through, he takes her under his wing, and soon a budding romance blossoms. But Mark's bi-polar daughter, Dani, is a handful, and at eighteen, very hard to control. Mark frets constantly about her, whether she has taken her medicine, and whether he is doing everything he should as a single father. Dani, however, is also in a romantic relationship with her childhood sweetheart, Nick Brewster, but that relationship is also challenged as Dani's bi-polar disorder makes everyone's life difficult. Giving us a glimpse or what it is like to both be bi-polar and to have someone you love who is, Nolan treats these subjects with sensitivity and compassion, crafting a moving and heartwarming tale of love, loss, and starting over. An excellent read. ~ *Taylor Jones, The Review Team of Taylor Jones & Regan Murphy*

Lonely Hearts Cry by Anji Nolan is the story of a young widow whose life is in a downward spiral. Jo Weston has lost her husband recently and the spark she once had for both life and her work as a jingle writer for an advertising agency. Determined to pull herself out of the funk and get her life back on track, Jo moves to rural Maine, where she meets long-time widower Mark Newcombe. An old hand at the grieving game, Mark helps to draw Jo back into the light, but their romance is fraught with problems. Mark's daughter, Dani, who is bi-polar, has her own share of problems. Her boyfriend, Nick, plans to be a doctor, and Dani wants to be a vet. Dani, who is now eighteen, is striking out on her own, and Mark finds it difficult to relax and let go, especially when Dani cannot really be trusted to take her medicine like she should. Told with compassion and skill, *Lonely Hearts Cry* is both a romance and a story of overcoming loss and starting over, when moving on seems to be the most difficult thing to do. I think it's a book everyone should read. `

Regan Murphy, The Review Team of Taylor Jones & Regan Murphy

ACKNOWLEDGMENTS

Many thanks to my long-suffering friends and beta readers, Susan Permenter, Kay Norris, Rosalie Pszenny, Doug Combs, and R.T. Anders. Special thanks to Doctor Jennifer Waara for her invaluable medical expertise and endless gratitude for all she has done to keep me well. And to Reyana and Faith my super Black Opal editors, thank you for polishing my rough diamond.

Lonely Hearts Cry

Anji Nolan

A Black Opal Books Publication

Black Opal Books

BECAUSE SOME STORIES JUST HAVE TO BE TOLD

GENRE: ROMANTIC SUSPENSE/COMING OF AGE

LONELY HEARTS CRY
Copyright © 2019 by Anji Nolan
Cover Design by Jackson Cover Design
All cover art copyright © 2018
All Rights Reserved
Print ISBN: 9781644370636

First Publication: JANUARY 2019

Published by Black Opal Books http://www.blackopalbooks.com

DEDICATION

For Dad,
who gave me wings.

For Mum,
who let me fly.

And for Booj,
who was always there to pick up the pieces

xoxoxo

FROM HER DIARY – A LAMENT
Emiline Pete Lord – 1865 – 1882

It might be, that you leave this place
But never from my heart
If one day, you crave another's embrace
It will never happen, on my part

Over time, like shooting stars we fall
Love endures, leaving traces behind
And whatever Journeys we may take
You'll never be far from my mind

Cherish love in good times
To sustain you through the tears
Because when Angels call,
And they will, for us all,
Lonely hearts cry…

Chapter 1

Deja vu moments always puzzled Jo, and first impressions hadn't always worked out well. But as she pulled to halt, the log house in the distance had an inescapable and comforting familiarity. It had been a long drive from her house in Salem, Massachusetts, and it wasn't that she didn't like living by the ocean. It was just that she never felt like the house was *theirs*. Chris had it when they got married, and she simply moved in with her clothes. After he died, the unease she felt there had her whole world imploding.

Jo unconsciously clenched her jaw remembering that for a good while, she'd resided in a dark place where sorrow, guilt, and self-doubt lived. She had struggled with too much alcohol, too little food, and virtually no sleep. But how could anyone sleep, knowing so much had been left unsaid? Grief and those unresolved issues made her a work in progress. A tortured soul who needed to make sense of the years of emptiness. And she knew, that to get where she wanted to be, she needed a place of her own. A haven. A place of peace and solitude, where she could start afresh and exorcise the demons that plagued her.

As Jo let down her SUV's window, the sound of fast-moving water roared above the purring engine. She was atop a culvert into which a raging waterway flowed. She

moved slowly on, down a football field length drive, defined by a stacked boulder wall furred with moss. It held
back a majestic copse of pines and Jo wondered what ancient feat of engineering had maneuvered it there. She
could see decades of weather had stabilized the structure.
Nevertheless, its foundation surrendered in places to
damp spots, nurturing clumps of pink and white wild
flowers. And midnight blue Iris stood gracefully beside a
run-off ditch, glistening bright in the warm spring sun. At
the end of the drive, Jo stopped in a walled turnaround.
The house, its logs stained warm honey, was on a knoll
surrounded by birch and pines. She smiled. It was just as
she imagined. A storybook chalet painted in Christmas
colors.

She was daydreaming and lost in the moment when a
presence interrupted her thoughts. Looking down, she
found three Labradors, black, yellow, and chocolate, positioned in a line alongside her car. When she quietly said
"Hello," it set them to barking and whirling like dervish-
es. However, as soon as she switched off her engine, they
sat down, tails sweeping tiny dirt angels behind.

She remained in her car until a lady appeared on the
house's deck and beckoned her forward. Not wishing to
alarm the canine sentinels, Jo cautiously opened her door.
And as soon as she stepped out, the dogs sprang off toward the house.

Following on, up a sloping path, Jo took in deep
breaths of warm April air infused with the fragrances of
cut wood, pinesap, and the warming earth. And again, the
sound of water, lots of water, distracted her. She pin-
pointed the tumultuous roar to a waterfall at the bottom of
the knoll's slope. A pond was the source of the turbulent
cascade, and it was evident the spring thaw had surged
into a fast-moving brook that ran the length of the property.

"Hi, you must be Ms. Weston," said the lady. "I'm Sandy from Berry Real Estate. We spoke on the phone. Welcome to Maine. I hope you didn't have too much trouble finding us."

"Hi, Sandy. Nice to meet you. I used my GPS, which got me so far then sort of left me in the woods. I was about to call you when I came across a very nice old gentleman sitting outside the village post office. He knew exactly where I needed to be."

"That was Junior," Sandy said. "His father passed thirty years ago, but the name stuck. You'll always find him ready to help a pretty lady in distress. Besides, village folk are slow to change, and everybody knows everybody's business. Anyone could have directed you here."

Jo nodded. Growing up on a farm, she remembered the support of a farming community. "That's something I'll have to reacquaint myself with."

"You'll see the value of it especially in the winter," Sandy said. "Rural Maine can be a trial when you're under six feet of snow."

"Good grief. I'm so itching to get out of the city, I never gave it that much thought. But off the beaten track is what I want."

"Okay. So, we'll go ahead with the tour."

"You mentioned on the phone the seller wants to meet me," Jo said. She glanced around. "Is he here?"

"He'll be back in a few minutes. He had a family crisis." Sandy lowered her voice and leaned in close to Jo. "His daughter is a bit of a handful. He's probably up at the high school—again. What that young girl needs is a mother."

"Oh really," Jo said, surprised at Sandy's openness.

"He's the most eligible bachelor in the county. I can't think why he hasn't been snapped up. Now, I have to warn you, Mark is most assuredly a doting dad, but he's also a bit eccentric. He's refused several offers on the house."

"Might that just be a way to get more money?" asked Jo.

"Not Mark Newcombe. Money he doesn't need. He told me the other buyers didn't belong."

"Didn't belong? What did he mean?"

Sandy shrugged. "You'll have to talk to him about that. I have no idea. Frankly, his father died here a couple of years ago. I think he's simply having a hard time letting go."

"Did he die in the house?" Jo asked.

"Massive heart attack in the cemetery out back. Mark stopped by on his rounds and found him."

Jo frowned. "That must have been tough. But I think I understand where he's coming from. Not saying a proper goodbye does something to your soul." Jo vividly remembered seeing her husband Chris off to the airport, and the next time she saw him was in the morgue. Despite her restlessness living in his house, it had still taken her four years to summon up the strength to sell it. "Does Mr. Newcombe live around here too?"

"Mark owns all the land that-a-way." Sandy gestured across the entire horizon. "He lives in the big farmhouse a mile this side of Limerick. That's the nearest town with a general store and such. But enough of all that, come on into the house."

಄಄಄

After touring the house, Jo was more in love with the property than even she imagined. And when Sandy showed her the generator room under the deck, Jo realized whatever hardships the Maine winter might bring, she had everything she needed to survive. "Well, Sandy, I really want this property. Will you offer Mr. Newcombe full price for me."

Sandy nodded. "I'll draw up the offer as soon as I get back to my office. However, you have yet to meet with him. Money aside, he has definite ideas about who he wants here. City folk aren't his first choice."

"Oh," said a startled Jo.

"Don't get me wrong. He's not a bigot or anything like that. But we've all seen city people move here, thinking it's easy to manage a rural property. Land is cheaper than down south, so they buy acreage and fancy themselves landowners. But when the snow starts, being in the sticks is a whole different animal. Local resources are limited, and many from away end up selling because they can't handle things. You'll have to get used to doing a lot of land and property maintenance yourself. Fortunately, Mark is including everything you need in the sale." Sandy looked at her watch. "So, that's about it for the tour. When Mark arrives, he'll have a bunch of questions for you."

"So that's why he's interrogating potential buyers?" Jo asked. "Because he doesn't like folks from the city?"

Sandy smiled. "He simply wants to make sure you belong."

"My husband is—er, late husband—was a pilot, away a lot. I'm used to doing things alone, and absolutely not afraid to get my hands dirty."

"Good."

"Plus, I'm a substantial gal who's worked on a farm," Jo said. "I might be gussied up today, but I'm pretty much a jeans and tee-shirt sort."

"I'm just the real estate agent Ms. Weston. You don't have to convince me."

Jo blushed. "Sorry, but I really want this place. How

do I go about convincing Mr. Newcombe I belong?"

"I really have no idea," said Sandy. "Just go with the flow. He'll be here shortly. Don't be swayed by the overalls and Howdy Doody freckles. Mark is nobody's fool. I'll talk to you later."

"You're leaving me alone?"

"Sure. Help yourself to a glass of wine and some munchies. Sit on the deck and enjoy the peace and quiet."

The agent set off down the deck stairs.

"Wait," yelled Jo. "What about the dogs? They're still in the woods somewhere."

"They know their boundaries. Talk to you later."

Jo watched Sandy leave, wondering what she meant by "they know their boundaries," and exactly what she'd let herself in for. She'd heard jokes about people from Maine being "Maniacs." But being deserted in the middle of a real estate showing, to be interrogated by the property owner, gave a whole new meaning to the word.

ᑲᔭᥴᔭ

Once Jo was alone, the serenity of Maine brought back memories of her childhood in Ireland, surrounded by green and the smell of the earth. But the joy of those happy times was quickly overshadowed by the sadness of her marriage to Chris. At the time, it all seemed to be going along fine. But he was always flying off somewhere exotic, leaving her to become the stoic acceptor of a solitary life. And while he might have said, "Go out, join clubs, develop a circle of friends," she couldn't find motivation to do it alone. They'd had more than one conversation about the point of being married if you never saw each other. But his answer was always the same. "You knew what my job meant when we got together, it is what it is." Then, when he died, she realized her life was a series of unfulfilled dreams. She was thirty-nine, childless, with no family close, and she had nothing in her life that didn't revolve around work. Then the guilt hit. That unspoken menace that berated her for even thinking about abandoning Chris's house and starting afresh. He'd been a good provider. Didn't drink excessively, smoke, gamble, or chase other women. What more did she want? Was she the unreasonable one? Sandy had said, "Have a glass of wine and relax," and a year ago, she may have done that. But not today. She would be stronger. She would handle the emotional rollercoaster that was grief. An offer was in the works. She was making headway. She had to remain positive and believe time was the equalizer. And she couldn't forget what had prompted her to embark on a new life…

℮ℑ℮ℑ

It was three years after Chris died, and Jo was sitting on her porch in Salem. Her laptop was open, ready to re-work a loathsome jingle for an antacid she knew from experience was not that good. And she had just poured her second glass of Chardonnay.

When the phone rang at four-thirty p.m., it could only be her boss, Marvin. She could feel the vibrations of his personality across the miles.

"Hey," he said flatly. "How's it going?"

Marvin was an extraordinarily, often irritatingly cheerful sort, so his coldness took Jo by surprise. She pushed her wineglass behind the computer as if he could see it. "You know—good days—bad days. What's up Marvin?"

"The bad days," he said.

"That doesn't sound good."

"Jeep," he said, using the nickname he'd favored from their first meeting. "You know you've been my girl for years, and I wouldn't be saying anything unless I thought you could do something about it—"

He had paused. Probably to take a drag from the cigar she knew was in his hand.

"Something about what?"

"Trouble in my little corner of paradise."

"Good grief, Marvin, what's with the drama?"

"You're losing it, Jeep. You're a jingle writer. You're supposed to convey upbeat, positive, cheerful messages."

"And?"

"And nothing, sister," he said. "Frankly, your work stinks. I don't like it, clients don't like it, and the sponsors are ready to pull the plug. You've lost *it*." He paused for another drag. "I'd like to believe you still have *it* somewhere."

Jo wasn't entirely surprised that Marvin was complaining. She had missed a few deadlines, lately, and had to rework a lot of her stuff. However, she wasn't about to let him get away with pulling her to pieces. "Umm, so you've taken two long drags on that filthy cigar in as many seconds. What exactly is '*it*' and which 'somewhere' are we talking about?"

"Don't be a wise-ass, Jeep, I'm trying to help. You're festering in Salem. You have to get out of that house. Take a vacation and get your head together. Move for, Christ's sake. Seriously, I don't care what you do, as long as you do something. God knows you're still young. It's been over three years since Chris died, you have to make an effort to move on."

"What if I can't?"

"I don't buy that poor little me crap, and you know it. You were always the strong one, the loner. A feisty, do your own thing, piss in the wind sort of gal. You can't do a one-eighty and expect any of us to believe you prefer torturing yourself."

Jo took a swig of wine in defiance. "Maybe I'm comfortable with it."

"Bullshit, you're wallowing in self-pity, and it shows. I'm not gonna let it continue without saying my piece."

Jo heard him cough. Now he would pull one of those little bits of tobacco off his tongue and stub out the cigar.

"Look," he continued. "It wasn't like you two were joined at the hip. Chris was always leaving you to cope alone. And you got the job done."

"Are you trying to make a point, Marvin?"

"Hear me out, dammit. You're going down a one-way street to who-the-hell-gives-a-rat's-ass, and not even remotely getting it done. You're missing trends a mile high and sponsors can't relate to you anymore. Do something soon or they're gonna walk. And if they do, what will you be—just memories and an empty bottle of Beaujolais."

"What do you expect—my husband died."

"I expect you to get over yourself. You're not the only one who ever lost a husband. But for a woman who always rolled with the punches, you're letting Chris's death consume you. Jeep, believe me, I'm saying this for your own good. You've become more reclusive than is good for anyone, and I *strongly recommend* you get out of that house. Please, move away from Salem, take a year off, travel, Jesus, pick one!"

Jo felt an urge to bite back, hard. Tell him to shove his jingles and shove his job. She didn't need the money. Chris's investments and an insurance policy made sure she had plenty. But a little voice in her head said, *Listen. Marvin is your truest friend and is only doing what he feels is necessary.*

"I've worked at Bean Town for fifteen years," Jo said quietly. "Doesn't history and my loyalty count for anything?"

"It has, for the better part of two years. But I'm in business, and I can't protect you any longer. You know better than anyone, we are only as good as our latest campaign. Criticism isn't being whispered any more, it's being screamed. I need you to get it together."

Jo could almost see Marvin's face. Etched with concern and love. She had no doubt confronting her had been hard. And that every word he said was as painful for him as it was for her.

"Whatever you need I'll get for you," said Marvin. "Want help moving, need money for plane fare, I'm there. Think about it and get back to me—soon."

Jo couldn't prevent her tears from falling. "Thanks, Marvin, I will."

"Promise?"

"Umm."

"Say it, dammit."

"Okay, I promise."

"You've never let me down, don't start now. You're a huge part of why this agency is so successful. I'm counting on you."

When she hung up the phone, Jo knew the conversation was overdue. She'd simply convinced herself it wouldn't happen. And while she'd had a sense that their friendship had been keeping her in a job, hearing the truth from her oldest and dearest friend shook her to the core. She'd never been overly sentimental about her work because music and words were subjective. But in recalling how much of it had lately been rejected, she knew Marvin's admonition was different. This was personal. And it was loud and clear. His "strongly recommend" was not a request.

As she pulled her wineglass from behind the computer screen, Jo smiled. Marvin clearly didn't know her as well as he thought. She never drank red wine. But his words had struck a chord. She walked into the kitchen and poured the remains of the glass and the rest of the bottle down the sink.

$$\mathcal{c}\mathcal{s}\mathcal{c}\mathcal{s}$$

The encounter with Marvin had been some months previously. She rarely drank now. She was afraid it might set off a storm she couldn't weather. But he had been the catalyst for her moving on. Naturally, she had moments. Moments when plans for her new world collapsed, and she burst into tears, dropping right back to square one. But grief was unpredictable. An ongoing series of baby steps.

Now, as Jo looked out over the property, she drank in the beauty of the surrounding gardens. She made a mental note of plants she recognized, daylilies, peonies, and lilacs. Being late April, they sat quietly, a hundred shades of green, teasing her imagination with possibilities. However, she knew in a couple of months they would burst forth, and the beauty of this verdant island would become an uncontrived explosion of color. She had no doubt this little piece of Maine paradise, meticulously maintained to ward off the surrounding forest, was her new beginning. And as she settled on one of the deck's chaises, an immediate and unanticipated peace washed over her.

She'd been enjoying the tranquility for several minutes when she heard loud yapping from the woods.

Jo stood to find a beat-up truck turning onto the property. And as it rattled up the drive toward her SUV, the Labradors burst from cover. The vehicle was barely at a stop when the dogs hurled themselves at the driver's side door.

"Girls," the driver said, reaching out the window to pet them. "Behave. We have company."

They seemed to understand him and sat down. However, as soon as he stepped from the truck, they raced towards the house.

Jo assumed Mark Newcombe had arrived. At least six-three, with the sort of lean muscular build you only get from hard labor, his long, easy stride led her to believe he did a lot of walking. She couldn't miss the cell phone clamped to his ear, and by the look on his face, he wasn't happy with whoever he was talking to. As he saw her aloft, he nodded. Then he turned his back on her and continued his call.

Jo wasn't happy. She knew most people had a cell phone and used it as an extension of their consciousness. But she didn't like them and didn't have one. Moreover, she wasn't above telling someone to put it away if they were supposed to be talking to her. However, now was not the time for personal quirks. She had to focus on the job in hand. Feeling she was about to be interviewed for the most important job of her life, Jo waited until he put the phone away and met him at the bottom of the deck's steps.

"Hi, I'm Jo Weston," she said, extending a hand. His was solid and hard-worked, with an almost liquid sensuality. And when she felt its pressure, it gave her unexpected goose bumps. "Seems like it's just you, the dogs, and me. Is it usual for Maine real estate agents to desert a prospective buyer?"

"When they have me for a client," he said coldly. "Unless you were expecting someone else, you'll have realized I'm Mark Newcombe. Did you like the property?"

Jo bit her lip to stop from gushing. "As a matter of fact, I love your property, and I'd like to buy it. I know you have an agenda, but I have some questions too, do you mind?"

He raised an eyebrow. "I have forty minutes."

Jo wasn't sure whether he was being sarcastic or just plain rude. Ordinarily, she'd have called him out. But she didn't want to do anything to prevent her from "belonging," so she said nothing. "I'm a little worried. Is Sandy coming back for her dogs?"

Mark ran a hand through his hair. "They come with the house."

"You mean whoever buys the house, gets the dogs?"

"Is that a problem?" he asked.

"Well, I haven't looked after a dog in twenty years," said Jo, taken aback. "But I guess the drill is still the same. Sandy said they knew their boundaries. Do they live here alone?"

"Of course not. Nick Brewster, the doctor's boy lives here with them. Also keeps the house and grounds in order."

Once again, Jo bit her lip. It was becoming increasingly clear why Mr. Mark Newcombe was having a hard time finding someone who he felt belonged. "Well, he's doing a fine Job," said Jo, looking around. "Everything is perfect. Where will he go when you sell?"

"Harvard."

"Umm, bright kid," she replied. "So, you'll be selling by September?"

"More like July. He has a job at The Coop."

"I see. So, if I belong here—"

"If you belong?" asked Mark.

Jo's cheeks flushed. It appeared Mr. Mark Newcombe wasn't overly chatty about anything. So, she worried that Sandy may have spoken out of turn. "Yeah, sorry, bit sneaky to mention it. But I really like this place and am not above a bit of cheating to get it."

"Don't need to cheat on my account," he said, nodding toward the dogs that were impatiently milling around.

"The decision is theirs." He dropped his hand casually to the head of the chocolate lab.

The smiling dog wagged her tail deliriously, causing the others to close in for some attention. But when one of them heard a noise in the woods and took off, the others gave chase.

"So, if the dogs don't like me, you won't sell me the property?" asked Jo.

"Eccentric, right?"

"I've known worse. However, being one of those need-to-know gals, I'm assuming you and the dogs have a way of judging prospective buyers?"

"We do," he said, finger swiping across an eyebrow.

"And you would determine my acceptance how?"

"Did they bark when you arrived?"

"Furiously."

"Did they scare you?"

"Sort of," said Jo. "But not in a, we're-going-to-bite-you way, more like a we-might-slobber-you-to-death way."

Mark fought back a smile. "Did they sit down by the car?"

"They did, and it was very odd, because as soon as I opened the door, they ran up to the house."

"They were inviting you in," said Mark.

"Excuse me?"

"Will you indulge me with a little test?"

Jo grinned. "As long as it's not weird or perverted."

Mark whistled for the dogs, and they hurtled from the woods. "Do you think a gal like you can handle all this land and three rambunctious dogs?"

"A gal like me?"

"A city gal."

Jo took a deep breath. "We do have dogs in the city."

"I heard that," said Mark, as he handed her four cookies. "Give them all one."

As the dogs sat in front of her, she offered each a cookie, but they remained motionless. Jo looked in Mark's direction. "They don't seem to like them."

"They like 'em," he said. "The chocolate is the alpha, try her first."

Jo did, and after the dog accepted the cookie, the others took theirs. "Wow, polite dogs, they didn't snatch or anything. What do I do with the last one?"

"Give it to Charity."

"Charity, you mean like the Red Cross or something?"

Mark smiled. "That's cute," he said. "I meant the dog, Charity." He pointed to each dog. "Yellow—Faith. Black—Hope. And the chocolate is Charity."

Jo handed the cookie to Charity, who gently took it and headed back into the woods, closely followed by the others. "Now where are they going?" asked Jo.

"To my dad."

Jo looked quizzical, recalling the maniac thing. "To your dad, Mr. Newcombe? I don't mean to be rude, but isn't he dead?"

"That, I know. He's buried out back. Charity is taking him a cookie."

Oh, this just gets better and better, she thought. "Your dad is buried here—is that even legal in 2014?"

"The cemetery is appropriately consecrated for family use. It's this way, let's go visit. If the girls are right—"

"The girls?" asked Jo, finding her situation increasingly surreal.

"The dogs. If they're right about you, I think you'll find it interesting."

Mark strode off but he didn't have to shorten his pace. Jo was tall and kept up.

"Jo," he said. "Is that short for Joanne?"

"No such luck. My parents were hippy wannabe's. They traveled the world trying to find themselves, and the meaning of life. They vowed their children's names would be wherever they were conceived. Considering all the places they traveled, I count myself lucky."

"How so?"

"I could've been called Katmandu or Galapagos." She finally saw a genuine smile from him. "As it was, a little too much wine and a night of passion in a VW bus left me with Jericho Palestine Monte Claire-Fitzgibbon."

Mark stopped in his tracks. "Whoa, that's a mouthful. So, I assume Weston is your married name."

"Was, I'm a widow," said Jo, a catch in her throat. It was the first time she'd actually said it aloud, and the hollowness of it proclaimed her loneliness was real.

"I'm sorry," said Mark tenderly. "I didn't mean to pry."

"That's okay," she said. "Chris's accident was years ago. It was he, who first called me Jo. I think he got sick of the political discussions that inevitably followed the Palestine reference."

"I can see where that might get heated. So, I should call you Jo?"

"If I can call you Mark."

"What's good for the goose is good for the gander."

Jo smiled. "That's pretty funny coming from a farmer."

"I wouldn't in any way style myself a farmer. That was my dad's bag. I pitched in when he got sick then took over full time after he died. By profession, I'm a chemist, with a yen to do what your folks did."

"Be a hippy and travel the world?" asked Jo.

"Nothing quite so bohemian. I was thinking more about setting up a laboratory in the amazon rain forest and discovering a cure for cancer."

"I don't mean to sound rude," said Jo. "But isn't that a bit of a cliché?" As soon as the words were spoken a wave of embarrassment flowed over her. Those she worked with were used to her blunt honesty. But she barely knew Mark Newcombe and this wasn't the time for snarky remarks. "Er, sorry that was un…"

"Maybe you're right." Mark gestured left. "This way, up the logging trail."

Jo suddenly realized her jibe might have hurt him. "Well, this has got to be a first," she said, attempting to lighten the mood. "I drive into the middle of nowhere to buy a property from a trio of Labradors and march into the woods with a thwarted apothecary to view a cemetery. If I told anybody about this, they'd think I was crazy."

"Don't worry," said Mark. "This is Maine, we do crazy."

☙❧

As they walked the trail, Mark looked at his watch. He'd been at the house forty minutes and it seemed like a heartbeat. She might be from the city, but Ms. Jo Weston was proving to be way more interesting than any other buyer. He hadn't missed the slight break in her voice, and her hesitation saying the word "widow." But he could also feel her strength and dogged resolve to start anew. Right now, she was in the same place he'd been seventeen years before. And he knew all she needed was time. His empathy with her was unexpected. Moreover, the affinity their joint experience created was an unanticipated bond he found difficult to quantify. He smiled. She was no nonsense, but sensitive. Mark's mind raced. It had been an age since he'd related to a woman on equal terms. His life revolved around his daughter, and of late, his only interaction with another woman was with Dani's math teacher, Mrs. Fisher. Being on the receiving end of an attractive woman's decisiveness and sincerity was a novelty he liked. If he didn't have so much going on with Dani, he wouldn't mind getting to know Jo better.

❧❦❧

When they arrived at the cemetery, Faith, Hope, and Charity were sitting next to a new gravestone. The cookie sat before them untouched. "That is so sweet," said Jo. "Which one of them eats it?"

"I don't know. The romantic in me says none of them."

"Romantic?" giggled Jo.

"Maine farm boy who loves poetry, art, and the metaphysical. Hopeless, right?" Mark paused. "You're pretty blunt, aren't you?"

Jo blushed. "Sorry, I didn't mean to be. I've been on my own too long. Social interaction hasn't been on top of my to-do list."

"You don't say."

"However, in my defense—"

"Ah…the defense," said Mark, grinning. "Enlighten me…" He made a sweeping gesture to give her the floor.

Whoa, this is new, she thought. *Was that gruff exterior just a front? Was he actually flirting with her?* Jo continued. "In my defense—my husband was pretty one-dimensional in the hopeless romantic department. Bunch of flowers on birthdays, that sort of thing. I've never met a guy who actually admitted to the condition."

"Well, that's certainly a shame," he said, looking at her with new eyes. "However, bowing to the realistic, I've been here and seen a couple of cookies—next time they're gone. I'm assuming the locals ate them."

"Locals?" asked Jo.

"Deer, moose, coyote, the occasional bob-cat and bear, we have an assortment."

"Yikes, do I need to worry about that?"

"You really are a city girl, aren't you?"

"Not quite. I grew up on a farm in Ireland. My folks brought me to Boston when I was fifteen."

"So, you have what...five years of exposure to the land?"

"Now who's being blunt?"

"Just saying."

"I can hold my own out here. But you come down to Boston, and I'll laugh my socks off while you attempt to navigate the remnants of the big dig. Now, seriously, do I need to worry?"

"You just need to learn how to use a shotgun," said Mark matter-of-factly. "Unless being an experienced farm girl, you already know."

Just then, she heard his phone buzz.

He pulled it out of his pocket. "Sorry, it's Dani's principal, I have to take this." He moved to the edge of the cemetery. "How many times do I have to address this with her? Should I simply give you a supply of her meds? I know, trust. Okay, let me talk to her. Thank you for letting me know." He pocketed his phone and came back alongside her. "Sorry, family crisis."

"You seem to have a fair number of family crises."

"And you don't," he answered brusquely.

"Actually, no. My life is pretty boring. Me, myself, and I. Oh, and work."

"You don't have kids?"

"My husband and I couldn't," Jo said.

Mark couldn't miss the pain in her voice. "That was insensitive, I apologize."

Jo nodded. "Me too, sorry. I'm not used to—"

"So, where were we?"

"There must be forty stones here. Wow, this one is 1600." Jo glanced around. "They're all Newcombe or Lord. Are these all your relatives?"

He brushed his hand across the top of his dad's stone and nodded. "The Lords are distant cousins on my wife's side." Mark pointed to one of the less weathered stones. "She's over there, next to her mother."

"I'm so sorry," Jo said. "Here I am thinking I'm the only one who had a spouse die young."

A strange light shone from Mark's eyes. "You'll never be the only one. But life has to go on. Especially when there are others to think about."

"At least you have some family to help on the farm."

"There's just my daughter, Dani. Seventeen, going on seventy. Her mom died when she was born, so she's grown up pretty independent. Comes back to bite me every so often."

Jo smiled. "The joys of parenthood."

"Tell me about it," he said.

"It can't be all bad, so many people do it," said Jo, warming to him. "The only thing I have worth thinking about is my career. I'm a freelance jingle writer. But according to my boss, I've lost my mojo since Chris died. Buying this place is my first step to moving on."

"Well, you certainly don't do things half-heartedly. I know you've lived on the land, but that was a long time ago. Are you sure you've really thought it through?"

"Umm. That doesn't sound good. Is this where you politely tell me I don't belong?"

Mark grinned. "Not exactly. I want to give it some thought. From what you've said, I'll assume you're going to make me an offer. I'll let Sandy know by tomorrow. Okay?"

Jo smiled bravely, but she wasn't okay. She could feel

a heavy storm gathering. And it was about to rain on her parade.

Chapter 2

The school bus set Dani Newcombe down at the farm's cattle grid, and, flipping the pedestrian gate latch, she jogged to the house. She was late, as usual. "Hi, Mrs. A," she said to the housekeeper, as she stripped off her school clothes.

"Slow down, Miss Dani. No good comes from a young lady charging about the place. You put those clothes in the hamper, you hear. I'm too old to be chasing after you all day."

"Yes'm," said Dani, bounding to her room.

The elderly Mrs. Ainsworth was as close to a grandmother as Dani had, and she obediently dispatched her clothes to the hamper. Then pulling on jeans, she flipped hangers in her closet for several minutes before deciding which top to wear.

"Miss Tardiness," as Nick often called her, was fully prepared to deal with sarcasm when he arrived in eight minutes and twelve seconds. He, of course, was one of those egghead genius types who didn't need a timepiece to tell him what time of day it was. In fact, Dani was pretty sure he received notification of time via cosmic rays or some such thing. However, quirks notwithstanding, Nick Brewster was not only her truest friend but also a whiz math-buddy. That alone pretty much gave him carte blanche to be as out there as he pleased.

Dani had barely buttoned her blouse when Nick's old truck razzed over the cattle grid and skidded to a halt at the front door. She was counting on him allowing her the usual five minutes grace period. However, a sharp toot from his horn signified that today he was in a hurry. Fussing with her hair, she hurtled downstairs.

After grabbing a couple of Mrs. A's shortbread wedges, Dani pecked the elderly lady on the cheek, scooped up her books, and headed for the truck.

The passenger door was open as she ran forward, and Dani threw her books beside him. She offered him a piece of shortbread.

As Nick wedged the cookie in his teeth and engaged the gears, Dani fell across the bench seat. "Hey, speedy, hold your horses, what's the rush?"

"Zipper," he mumbled mouth full.

"What?"

"Zipper." Nick nodded in the appropriate direction. "I don't want your dad to think I've ravished you on the way over."

Dani zipped her jeans and continued fussing with her hair. "Like that will ever happen."

"You never know."

"I know," said Dani, finishing her cookie.

"I might surprise you one day. Carry you into the woods and install you in a tree house atop the abhorrent duff. Shower you with my essence and the extravagant obsession of my soul. Make you a slave to my love, and a stranger to the light of day."

Dani giggled. "You've been reading those books again—behave."

"Got to do something. I'm not making any headway with a real girl."

"Maybe you simply need to ask the right one."

Nick was silent for a few seconds. "You know it's been you since first grade. One day you'll understand, and then you'll take me seriously."

"Yeah, yeah," said Dani.

"You look really nice today. I like your hair sort of wild and all over the place."

Dani pulled down the visor and primped in the mirror. "It's not supposed to be all over the place. Jeez, whoever said red hair was beautiful. I look like I've been dragged through a hedge backward."

"No you don't. Crazy long curls are romantic and sexy. You're Kathy in Wuthering Heights, or Lady Chatterley just risen from her bed. Orbs newly open to gaze upon the tortured soul of one who yearns."

"Puleez…just refocus, and drive. I swear I'm gonna bar you from reading D. H. Lawrence or whoever is giving you these ideas."

Nick glanced at her and smiled. "You're giving me these ideas."

"Yeah, right. Anyway, what's the big rush today?"

"Your dad had another viewer this afternoon," said Nick. "I'm anxious to see if he sold my house."

"Not your house," said Dani. "Gramps left it to the girls."

"You know what I mean. I've loved it from the minute it was built, and since I've been taking care of it, I'm determined to buy it one day."

"First you have to get through college, find a decent job, and then save a bunch of money."

"Mere technicalities. One day you, me, and a whole bunch of kids are going to live there."

"In that little house? It's barely big enough for you and the girls now. Besides, leave me out of this, I'm going to college in New Zealand. Then I'm going to be a famous vet, doing animal research, and find the cure for all sorts of—"

"Yeah, yeah, we know that already, but first you have to pass calculus. Did you bring your work book?"

"Yes, sir, Mr. Teacher sir, now stop nagging, and drive."

"Did you take your meds?"

"Jeez, since when are you my keeper? You're worse than dad."

"Don't screw around Dani. You're bi-polar—did you take your—"

"God, relax, why don't you? You're not my doctor yet. I took 'em." Dani cursed under her breath. It was his fault. He'd rushed her out of the house. She had forgotten to take them—again.

℮⁄ℑℰ⁄ℑ

When the kids pulled up to the house, the girls mobbed them. Dani dropped to the ground for the inevitable slobber-fest. And as Nick came around the truck, the dogs dived at him. Mark was on the deck, and, upon his whistle, the dogs bolted up the rise to the house.

Dani waved at her dad and turned to Nick. "By his look, I'd say it went well."

"Don't tell me that, he only had to wait a couple of years."

Dani punched him playfully on the arm. "The place will be infested with squirrels by the time you get out of college."

"I'll have you know, I plan to ace my degree and get into med school in—"

"The whole world knows that. Top of every class, grade point average seven. SAT score in the millions, scholarship anywhere in the known universe."

"Sarcasm is the lowest form of wit, smart ass." Nick followed Dani up the deck's stairs. "Hi, Mr. Newcombe. How'd the showing go?"

"Good," said Mark. "Nice gal from down south."

"Damn. So, when do I have to be out?"

"Hold your horses, I haven't sold it yet. You living here is one thing. You grew up here. You worked with my dad, know the seasons, what needs doing, and when. But handing over to a city gal unfamiliar with rural living could be disastrous. I don't think mending the harrow in the middle of the pasture is going to fly with a fifty-dollar manicure."

"Whoa, Dad," said Dani indignantly. "Let's have none of that sexist talk here. Since when have I ever shirked my responsibilities in favor of a manicure?"

"Okay, I yield," said Mark. "But you, young lady, will always be farm first. She lives and works in the city. There is a difference."

"Oh, really—"

"Dani, chill," said Nick. "Your dad has a point."

"Well, if you want my opinion," said Dani, looping her arm through her dad's. "This place belonged to Gramps, and you really don't want to sell it. Why don't you take it off the market and wait a few years until Nick starts earning the big bucks?"

"I might."

"There you go," said Dani, turning to Nick. "Now—how are you at catching squirrels?"

Nick smiled, knowing he may still have a chance to buy the house. "Brilliant, just like everything else. And right now, I have to use that brilliance in your direction." Nick inclined his head toward Dani as he addressed Mark. "'Miss Thang' here ain't gonna pass no math exam without my help. So, let's get on it."

Mark smiled. A bad boy accent was funny coming from Nick the smartest, most levelheaded young man he'd ever known. "Okay, so are you two going to eat here, or should I have Mrs. A put something aside?"

Nick looked at Dani. "Anything from Mrs. A. would be great. However, I'm expected at home. It's mom's night to cook. Gigot a la Moutarde."

Mark smiled. "I believe that's roast lamb with some sort of herb mustard?"

"Yup. Mom's using one of my books and it shouldn't be half-bad if she remembers to turn on the oven. Either way, I can't abandon Dad on mystery meat night. If it's okay, we'll cram for a couple of hours, and I'll have Dani home by seven?"

"Fine by me," Mark said. "I'll see you later."

౭౫౭౫

Driving away, Mark remembered how easy it had been to familiarize Nick with what needed doing about the place. But the youngster had spent a lot of time with his dad. And it was no secret Nick adored the property and one day wanted to own it. Mark smiled. He really was a fantastic kid, who had his heart set on marrying Dani. And providing his determined daughter did what she wanted before settling down, it would probably happen. Now there was a solid reason to hang on to the place. However, being realistic, would anyone in his right mind leave a house empty for the six years it would take Nick to become a doctor.

Mark had a dilemma and knew it. Ms. Jo Weston had impressed him. She might not be country, but she seemed smart and committed to look after the place. Besides, she was funny and easy on the eye. Would it really be any hardship to show her how things worked? Maybe even offer her some muscle support for a while until she got the hang of the land.

On the other hand, what about his own plans for an extensive organic expansion at the farm? And with Dani getting to *that age*, being erratic with her meds, and exploring her boundaries, he needed to keep an eye on her. Something had to give.

Chapter 3

As promised, Nick returned Dani to the farm promptly at seven. "Will I see you tomorrow?" he asked nervously.

"You see me every day, why should tomorrow be different?"

"Because now you know how I feel about you."

"I've always known how you feel about me, we're best friends." Dani leaned through the truck window to peck him on the cheek, and he turned his face to receive her lips. She backed off abruptly and swiped her sleeve across her mouth. "Ew—grown up stuff. Get out of here, I'll see you tomorrow."

❧❧❧

As Dani turned and walked toward the farmhouse, Nick banged his head on his hands tightly gripping the steering wheel. He couldn't understand why he'd attempted such a juvenile move on her. And with a frustrated moan validating his emotional cowardice, he slammed the truck in gear and peeled out of the yard.

❧❧❧

The noise of Nick's truck razzing over the cattle-grid caused Dani to pause in the doorway. She'd heard the sound a million times, but this evening, it reverberated through the air, vacant, hollow, and thick with meaning. She followed his taillights to the farthest range of her vision, and with the yawning chasm of night closing in, she was compelled to think about what just happened. He was always serious, but he had never been so emotionally intense with her. And he'd certainly never turned as she pecked him on the cheek. For several seconds, she stood transfixed, wishing he'd come back and explain why he chose now to do it. But there was no razzing grid, no racing engine, no bouncing headlights, just her whispered question to the heavens.

ের৺

As Dani entered the kitchen, Nick evaporated from her thoughts. "So, Dad," she asked. "I didn't want to ask with Nick there, but what's the new owner like?"

"As I said, I haven't decided to sell yet."

Dani whirled her fingers around her face. "So, what was *the look* all about?"

"What *look*? Where do you get your ideas?"

"Let's review the evidence and confirm the committed guy on display."

Mark shook his head in exasperation.

"Did said prospective owner pass the tests?"

"Yes."

"The girls liked her?"

"Yes."

"She did the cookie thing?"

"Yes."

"You took her to see Gramps?"

"What're you getting at, Dani?"

"Did you, or did you not, take her to see Gramps?"

"Yes."

"And this…" Dani gave him the "quote" fingers. "'Nice gal from down south.' Are you going to ask her on a date?"

Mark remained silent.

"Don't want to discuss it eh," said Dani. "Oh, yeah, you got it bad. You like her. What does she do? Is she pretty?"

Mark smiled at his precocious daughter. "She came to buy the house. How do you leap from that to dating? What even makes you think she's single?"

"I'm your daughter. I know things about you that are a dead giveaway."

"Like what, Miss Smarty Pants?"

"Like you're blushing as we talk about her. She's pretty, and…wait for it…"

Mark swiped a finger over an eyebrow.

"And there it is—the 'tell'—she's available." Dani punched the air triumphantly. "Daughters rule—the tell—tells all!"

"Just quit your nonsense is all."

Dani sat beside her father and put her hand over his. "No, seriously, Dad, this could be huge. You haven't had a girlfriend in ages. Really, you must be pretty desperate by now."

Mark glared at her. "Enough of that."

"No, no, really, hear me out. This could be good. Number one, you won't have to travel far. Number two, you always said you wanted someone who loved the—"

"How about we just eat our dinner and talk about your day."

"Wait, Dad, got to have details, need to know details—blonde, brunette, red head?"

"Enough, Dani. She came to buy the house. Anything else is just your overactive imagination in overdrive. Have you been skipping your meds?"

"Uh? Now that's just wrong. What makes you think every time I show a spark of personality, you assume it's because I'm not taking my meds. I'm very witty and you are absolutely, positively, no fun."

"That's what makes me the dad and you the kid, now eat."

Chapter 4

When her phone rang and the screen showed Berry Realty, Jo's heart skipped a beat. However, when Sandy told her that Mark Newcombe had decided not to sell her the house, it seemed to stop.

"But why?" said Jo, mustering as much composure as her disappointment allowed. "I know he has this cockamamie thing about the dogs choosing an owner. But I got on well with them. Did I really not belong?"

"Actually," said Sandy. "He didn't say that at all."

"Excuse me?"

"With every other person who saw the place and made an offer, he simply said they don't belong. No explanation, no additional information. With you, he came into the office and explained why he couldn't sell to you."

"Couldn't, not wouldn't?" asked Jo.

"Precisely. The bottom line is he thinks you may belong. But he feels a woman alone wouldn't be able to handle all the stuff that goes along with owning a log house on fifteen acres of land."

The hackles on Jo's neck bristled. She might look like a girly girl. She might be pushing forty. But she was no needy wimp. "Oh, really. Well, I'd like to tell Mr. Mark Newcombe exactly where to put his sexist opinions." Jo took a deep breath. "However, I will resist. The mere fact he took time to explain his misbegotten theory means, in my book, that there's hope. Give me his number, I'll call him."

"I'm sorry, it's not ethical for me to do that."

"Sandy, please. He said himself I belong there. Ethics have to be on the backburner today. I desperately need that property. It's everything I've dreamt about to get my life back in order. I'll do whatever it takes to convince him I can handle it. Please, please, give me his number."

There was empty air. Then Jo heard paper flipping.

"I could get into so much trouble for this," said Sandy. "However, I saw your eyes light up when you were there. And dammit, there are thousands of women handling farms alone. Fifteen acres is nothing for a determined soul. Besides, I think you should have it. If anybody asks, you didn't get his number from me. Good luck."

❧❧❧

Mark answered his cell immediately. "Jo, hi. I can't say I'm entirely surprised. How did you get my number?" He was always worried about Dani's health and to ensure teachers or medical personnel could get hold of him, should she have an emotional episode, he had given it to very few people.

Jo's cheeks colored. "Er…I work in advertising. We have all sorts of databases and stuff…"

"Yeah, databases and stuff…killer," Mark teased. *She said she wasn't above a bit of cheating to get what she wanted. And it's clear Ms. Jo Weston has won over at least one local to the dark side.*

"Please, Mr. Newcombe. I know you've made your decision but—"

"It's Mark, we agreed on Mark."

"Okay, Mark. I so want to move to Maine, and your property spoke to me. Could we meet somewhere and let me prove to you that I can look after the place alone."

"Wow, Sandy really did spill the beans. What could you say that might convince me a gal from the city can handle rural life?"

"As I said, I'm not *from* the city. I can milk cows, shear sheep, and handle a tractor with the best of them."

"Oh, really."

"Yes, really. Being a jingle writer wasn't my first career choice. That happened when my folks moved to Boston. I worked on the farm because I always intended to be a veterinarian."

Mark was shocked. It was obvious Jo was comfortable on the property, and her knowing something about the land was an unexpected bonus. However, the revelation that she planned to be a vet completely stunned him.

"Mark, I'm serious about this. Just tell me where and when, and I'll be there. I'll milk your cows, plow your fields—set me a task, and I'll do it."

"You can simply drop everything and come back to Maine?"

"The property is important to me. I'll do whatever it takes."

"Okay. Let's have dinner tomorrow at The Farrington Inn in Cornish."

"Tomorrow? Yikes."

"Is that a problem?" Mark asked, knowing the answer.

"Absolutely not, what time?"

He could hear the grin in her voice.

"Call me when you've settled into the hotel, and I'll come over."

"You can simply drop everything and come to Cornish," Jo quipped.

"Touché. I'll see you tomorrow." Mark grinned, as his

mind became a whirlwind of possibilities. *Whatever Ms. Jo Weston has to say will have to be good. But I know she's going to fight me until she gets what she wants. Ordinarily, I have enough of that nonsense with Dani. However, Ms. Jo Weston is different. She has a way about her that makes her an intriguing woman. And there's absolutely no hardship in having dinner with an attractive, as well as intriguing, woman.*

Chapter 5

As Jo drove north, she couldn't help thinking about the path her life had taken. When she moved into Chris's house, she wouldn't have believed anything could match the serenity of the ebbing and flowing of the ocean against the dock. Then she remembered the lonely times when he was away flying. She'd finish work for the day, sit on the porch with a glass of wine and a box of crackers, and feed the birds. Or watch the seagulls, bold and brassy, cackling and posturing as they squabbled over flotsam washed high by the tide. It became a ritual. A ritual that locked her into a life built around the vagaries of Chris's flying schedule. It was true, she should have gotten out more, made an effort to make her own friends. Because *their* friends were Chris's friends. Airline friends who weren't bothered by working weird hours with odd days off. Airline people with itchy feet and a wanderlust that had them at their happiest when they were some-place else. And after Chris died, those friends like the wind on which they flew, moved on, and her life outside of work became a vacuum.

Jo now knew why moving to Maine was the right thing. Why new beginnings north, meant emotional freedom, and a much-needed return to her roots. How the waterfall and brook on Mark's property evoked the same feelings of inner peace as the waves. And how the silent predators hanging above the pond, clinging to reeds swaying in the water's current, brought her the Zen-like peace she craved. As she closed her eyes, the spectacle of tiny birds skillfully picking insects off the surface meniscus, captivated her. And when she recalled the waterfowl's beachhead trail, running from the pond to the house, she smiled. There was a pond with ducks in Ireland, and she had always wanted one. But living in Salem, Chris worried about the mess. From the long dead hemlock, with its bat-house, past the artesian well overspill, fashioned into a shallow frog-pond, Mark's property was more than she had dreamed of. And her mind was set. The rest of her life was no longer negotiable. The verdant oasis in the forest haunted her. She needed that oasis. And it should be hers alone. Not a space overlaid with someone else's life. She would find a way to make her dream a reality.

Chapter 6

The Farrington Inn was a seventeenth century mansion set in extensive English style gardens, complete with gazebo. Finished in white clapboard with black shutters to every window, its wrap-around porch held rocking chairs to catch the sun at any time of day. A shiny brass plaque beside the front doors said, *Built in 1811 by Jeremiah Farrington*. As Jo strolled into the lobby, the smell of Murphy's Oil Soap and gardenia enveloped her. It was as if she'd stepped back a hundred and fifty years. The reception desk was obviously an addition. But the wood matched beautifully to the sweeping staircase, and, as she pinged the counter bell, an ancient Doc Holliday look-alike popped up from nowhere.

"Yikes," she said stepping back.

He wore black pants and weskit, a pale blue shirt, sleeves neatly restrained by garters, and a cravat secured with a diamond stickpin. And with the piqued features of someone who'd had a hard life, his drooping mustache and mini goatee might have given him a sinister demeanor, had he not smiled. "Howdy do, little lady."

Jo smiled. "I called yesterday—reservation for Weston?"

"Just you?"

Jo nodded. "All on my lone-some."

"Now that's purely sad for such a pretty lady." He was a transplant because his voice was southern honey. "You'll be staying the one night?"

"Yes. I'm looking at property here."

"City gal, eh?"

"Not for long, I hope." Jo handed back the registration card. "I'm expecting someone for dinner this evening. Do I need to reserve a table in the restaurant?"

"Tonight it should be quiet. We have the finest food and views in the county, so on the weekend, it's a zoo and people come from all over," he said. "They start serving at…" He pulled a gold watch from his weskit pocket and shaking it a couple of times, put it to his ear. "Now. I'll have someone take up your bag. You can go right back and get situated or have a cocktail at the bar until your guest arrives."

"Thanks, I only have my overnight bag, and I'd like to wash up first."

"Okeydokey. I put you in room two-oh-seven, follow the signs. If you need anything, call down. I'm Doc. Welcome to The Farrington Inn."

Jo shook her head as she made her way to her room. Who was this Mark Newcombe? The Farrington Inn was totally her style. It was as if he'd read her mind.

᠃᠃᠃

In the restaurant at the rear of the inn, panoramic views of the distant mountains confronted Jo. And it seemed the Inn's gardens stretched for miles before dropping down a hill and running uninterrupted to the peaks. She chose a table easily seen from the door and perused the menu. It was everything Doc promised. The offerings were not pretentious nouvelle cuisine, which she felt didn't fit anywhere other than in the big city. And the wine list was extensive, but not big city expensive. Food was an eclectic mix of American and European standards, and the homemade desserts convinced her to keep her main course light.

Looking around, she counted twelve couples in "The Overlook" and could almost feel the vibes of celebration. Clearly, The Farrington Inn's restaurant was *the* place, for special occasions. Jo mulled over how much of a celebration Mark Newcombe might allow her.

She hadn't had any alcohol since her conversation with Marvin. It had been easy to get into the habit of mindless drinking. It had dulled her pain. However, he'd galvanized her into putting her life into perspective. But now that she was on her way and confident about her direction, she deserved a small celebration. Jo ordered a bottle of Sauvignon Blanc, and when Mark arrived, she planned to order a small Caesar salad followed by herb-roasted chicken. That would leave room for the Inn's specialty dessert. Something called "Nothing Overlooked." A ganache covered, walnut-encrusted, triple-layer chocolate cake, stuffed with fresh strawberries and crème fraiche. She was so deep in thought, she didn't notice Mark approach her table.

"Not exactly The Ritz," he said. "But pretty nice for the back of beyond."

Jo looked up. "Oh, hi, sorry. This menu is great. I could eat one of everything."

"Then let's do it," he said.

"And on whose fork lift would you carry me out of here?"

"I've got a front loader, would that do?" Mark smiled. "Can I sit?"

"No. I changed my mind, I prefer to eat alone."

"Sassy too," said Mark. "How's that wine?"

"Pretty good. Is white okay or do you prefer red?"

"White's fine." He pushed over his glass.

"Thank you for agreeing to let me plead my case."

Mark took a sip of wine. "Good choice. Sandy did warn you about my fixation on having someone who belonged."

"You know that. But it appears I aced the belonging bit. It seemed it was my being a woman alone that bothered you."

Mark's cheeks flushed. "Wow; that must have been some chat."

Ah-ha gotcha, thought Jo, mentally high fiving. "So now you know I'm serious about the property, I've worked on a farm, and I'm not averse to getting my hands dirty."

"Even with the fingernails? Fifty buck manicure if I'm not mistaken."

Jo glanced at her hands. "Well, you are mistaken, Mr. Judgmental. On occasion, I do them—myself. But most times, they're broken and raggedy from rooting in my garden or hauling trash off my dock. Since when does a farmer care about a gal's fingernails?"

"Sorry. It's just something I said to—" His phone vibrated and he glanced at the screen. "Will you excuse me a minute I have to take this call." Mark stepped out of the restaurant and returned looking annoyed. "Sorry, another *emergency*," he re-took his seat.

"Do you need to go?"

"My daughter has problems with what actually constitutes an emergency."

Jo smiled. "We gals can be a handful. But you seem to be handling things pretty well. But I have to say, rather you than me."

"It's not as bad as it seems."

"Well, if you have to leave, I'll understand. Fortunately, you chose the exact hotel I would have so it will be a pleasure simply hanging out here."

"You'd go back south, and come back again if I asked you to?"

"Told you. I want your property, badly."

Mark smiled. "I get that now. So, tell me what it was like for you growing up on the farm. Let's see what we have in common."

ℰↃℰↃ

Jo slipped beneath the fluffy European duvet and fell instantly a sleep. Her dreams were full of her and Mark talking. It was a spiraling kaleidoscope of puzzling images. Her on the farm. The maelstrom of water from the pond to the brook on Mark's property. Clients screaming about her lack of new ideas in her present Job. She knew where she'd been, but she couldn't get to where she needed to go. And Mark, in a judge's gown, sitting behind a giant desk giving her the grilling of her life.

She was coming out of sleep when the phone rang. She looked at the clock. It was 8 am.

"Did I wake you?" asked Mark.

"I was dreaming about our conversation. Are you calling to give me a decision?"

"I'm calling to ask if we can share breakfast. I can be there in thirty-five minutes."

Jo was suddenly wide-awake. "Oh-oh. Face-to-face. Is that a good or bad sign?"

"You won't know until I get there."

ℰↃℰↃ

Jo was sitting on the porch when Mark's beat up track rattled into the parking lot. He saw her, waved, and flashed a smile she hadn't seen before. As he strode toward her, she didn't know whether it was the morning sun or what, but his wavy hair shone like burnished copper. And when he sat opposite her and took off his aviators, his eyes were green, sparkling with a golden light. She hadn't noticed either before.

"I had them set an extra cup. Would you like coffee?" asked Jo.

"By any chance is it that Colombian blend they crow about?"

Jo smiled. "Yes, it is. It seems we have something else in common."

Mark smiled as he added half-and-half. "Remember when you first visited the property, I asked you how the girls reacted?"

"How could I forget? It was all slightly surreal."

"Before he died, my dad made me promise I would only sell the house to someone who would take the dogs. Naturally, I was skeptical and said, what if someone said they like dogs, but actually hated them. He smiled and told me they'd pick the new owner. They'd bark and carry on at first, then invite 'em in."

"That happened, I told you."

"You did."

"So?" Jo's eyes sparkled in excited anticipation.

"I can feel that you really love the place, Jo. And while it was a few years ago, you've convinced me that with a little help you can handle the land. Would you allow me to help you out for a while? And if at any time it gets too much, could I have first refusal about buying the property back?"

Jo beamed. "Yes, and yes."

"Will you take good care of my dad's dogs?"

"If they'll have me."

He smiled his smile again. "Then it's yours." He offered her his hand.

Jo's eyes widened, and her heart pumped fit to burst. "Just like that, on a handshake?" She took his hand.

"More or less. Sandy opens at nine a.m., so I thought we'd have a celebratory cup of Joe, then go over together and sign the papers."

"So, I'll pay what you're asking?"

"If you like."

"That's pretty casual. Are you so rich you don't care?"

Mark smiled. "I might be, but you'll have to get to know me a lot better before I tell you."

Jo wasn't sure what sort of a whirlwind she was caught up in, but her happiness made her giddy. "And will I?"

"Will you what?"

"Get to know you better," she said.

"I think that's a given. There are tons of things I need to show you to make sure your new house and property don't get swallowed up by the forest. Are you up for a sharp learning curve?"

"I am." All Jo could do was smile. She had the property of her dreams, and an intriguing man was holding her hand. Both felt good. Really good.

Chapter 7

When Jo swung by the house on her way back to Salem, she wasn't surprised the girls greeted her. And after stepping from her SUV, dispensing their favorite cookies, which she'd purchased in Cornish, they disappeared into the woods. Jo proceeded up the rise to the house, where a young man was waiting.

"I see we're both prepared," he said, brandishing a tape measure. "Hi, I'm Nick, and I assume you're Ms. Weston?"

"Right."

"Mr. Newcombe said you'd be coming by to take measurements for furniture."

"I hope I'm not imposing?"

"Not at all."

"Thank you for doing such a lovely job on the property."

"It was my pleasure," said Nick. "I had hoped to buy it one day."

"Aren't you off to Harvard?"

"Yeah, this place was part of my dream. But I can understand Mr. Newcombe not wanting to leave it empty." Nick pushed open the door. "Let me be the first to welcome you to your new home."

"Thank you, Nick. That's very thoughtful."

ᥱᴐᥱᴐ

While the young caretaker helped Jo take measurements, he imparted a wealth of information on how to run
the house. They'd reached the office when Mark unexpectedly appeared. Jo's stomach fluttered and her cheeks
flushed scarlet.

"Hi, team," he casually said. "Well Ms. Weston, I
hope Nick has started you on that sharp learning curve we
talked about?"

"He has," said Jo. "Although there is so much to learn,
I may have to call my office and take a mental health
day."

"The joys of working for the man," said Mark. "My
mental health day would require an actual breakdown. I
swung by to see of anyone was up for a late lunch, early
dinner, break from measuring?"

"Sorry, Mr. Newcombe, I'm booked," answered Nick.
"And now you're here, could I ask you to finish up with
Ms. Weston. Dani isn't the only struggling math student.
I have to be in Kezar Falls in thirty-five minutes."

"Gosh," said Jo. "I'm so sorry. I've been rambling on
monopolizing your time. I'm done, really."

"Okay, Nick, you shoot off. But what say you, Ms.
Weston, do you have time for lunch before heading back
south?"

"Thank you, Mr. Newcombe," said Jo, retracting the
tape measure.

As Nick headed out, Mark moved in close to Jo. "I'm
more than happy to finish up with you." He didn't exactly
know how, but she brought out something in him that
hadn't been there in a very long time. It was a lightness
of spirit. An unspoken permission to be exactly who he
wanted to be. And he instinctively knew that whatever
that might be, she was somehow okay with it.

Jo grinned. "Umm, I'm not sure what to make of that. But thank you for your discretion with Nick. I'm not sure I want the neighborhood thinking I'm playing fast and loose with their most eligible bachelor."

"Rest assured your reputation is safe with me. However, once we 'do lunch,' tongues are bound to wag."

"Oh, well, it is what it is. Besides, I'm famished. I was so excited to do this, all I had for breakfast was coffee. Before we go, can I just measure the cellar for a washer/dryer?"

"Don't you like the ones that are there?"

"Sure, but they aren't on the list of what comes with the house."

"I assumed a washer/dryer, like the fridge, was a given. You can have them if you like. Dad bought them just before he died."

"Thank you, how much can I give you for them?"

"Nothing, how about we call them a house-warming gift."

"Are you sure? Couldn't your daughter use them? Nick was saying she's thinking of setting up an apartment using the tack room in the barn."

Mark looked surprised. "Well, that's a new one. She's been running an impromptu veterinary clinic out of the tack room since she was seven. And while it can be easily converted into an apartment, I rather doubt Miss Dani will be doing any laundry."

"Right," said Jo. "I recall she doesn't even know where the detergent is. I'm surprised that at seventeen she doesn't do more around the house."

"Oh, boy. Where have you been for the past few years? Every time I broach the subject, I get attitude that, quite frankly, I can do without."

"So, as well as farming, you're responsible for housekeeping and catering?"

"Not on your life," said Mark. "My beloved Polly takes care of all that."

Jo's face dropped. "Oh, I didn't think you were—is she your significant other?"

"How diplomatic. I suppose she is, all seventy-odd years of her. Didn't I mention Polly Ainsworth? She's Mrs. A. to most everybody, and our housekeeper extraordinaire. She comes in every day, save Sunday, from eight to five. She's more like family than a housekeeper. Runs the house with military precision and cooks like Julia Child."

Jo breathed a secret sigh of relief.

"Hang on, though. Why would you think I'd have a significant other? Didn't we shake on you buying the house and when you implied you'd like to get to know me better, I didn't say, sorry I'm taken."

Jo's pout was unmistakable. "It wouldn't be the first time, a man, you know…"

"Are you speaking from personal experience?"

"No. But infidelity is not unheard of."

Mark smiled. "Not my style."

"I'm delighted to hear that. And I'm more than delighted to hear you and Dani have a strong female around, teenage girls can get a bit—*difficult*."

"Tell me about it," said Mark. "Care to clue in this confused father."

"Best you not know too much about our secret society. I always think it's easier to roll with the punches than agonize over what might never happen. Who knows, maybe Dani will be the exception to the maturing diva rule. Now, where are we going for lunch?"

"It's a surprise, I'll show you a little of the local area, then we'll head north."

"Okay, lead on, I'm all yours."

Mark smiled, wondering if she had any idea of the importance of what she just said.

Chapter 8

When Jo arrived back at her house in Salem, her message light was blinking. She dropped her overnight bag in the kitchen, kicked off her shoes, and hit the play button.

"Jeep, it's me." It was Marvin, Jo's boss at Bean Town Musicality. "Your assignment for Kate's Krispy Kandy Korn is due in two days, call me with your progress."

Well, Marvin dear heart, she thought, *it's done and brilliant, so be prepared to eat crow.*

"You have won an all-expense paid cruise for two to the Bahamas; all you have to do is call—"

Yeah, right, delete.

"Hi, Jo, this is Mark—Newcombe that is—in case you know two. Thank you for letting me play tour guide and not getting bored with my jokes. I had a wonderful time, could I see you again? To go out with that is—hauling stuff around the property is a given. Sorry I missed you. I'll call again unless you want to call me—you have the number. Er, unless you're really busy, I know you have a deadline. Did you mean it when you said I could come and see you in Salem, or were you just being polite? If it's not doable, I'll understand. I know you have to work. Dang I already said that. Am I rambling or what? Do you want me to call you with updates on the house and the girls? Okay enough, I'm done—call me?"

Jo was surprised how much his voice affected her, and she smiled. *You adorable creature. Yes, I absolutely want to see you again, and I will call you.*

"Congratulations, Captain and Mrs. Weston, you have been selected to—"

The words hit Jo like a poleaxe and flooded her with guilt. She'd just mentally allied herself to Mark in Chris's house. What was she thinking? "Moronic telemarketer," she screamed, slapping the delete button. "At least have the decency to get your facts right."

As Jo walked into the living room, where so many memories lingered, sadness threatened to overwhelm her. In the past, she might have reached for a bottle of wine, but the thought of Mark bolstered her. She smiled. Who was this extraordinarily perceptive man, and how did she deserve to know him, let alone contemplate dating him. Marvin was right. She had been wallowing. Whatever demons haunted her, drowning herself in grief, instead of getting on with life was not the answer. Chris had been dead four years. It was futile to live her life on what might have been, second-guessing questions to which she would never have an answer. Anything she could have said or done was in the past. She was stronger now, resolute about a new direction, and starting over. She pulled Mark's number from her purse. He might not know it, but he'd given her a direction, and she was committed to putting the demons of her past behind her.

Chapter 9

It was a week later during one of their frequent calls, that Mark told Jo he was headed to Boston. A friend of Nick's parents had offered him use of a garden apartment in Mission Hill, providing the youngster kept a watch on the house while they were abroad. Mark would drop off Nick and Dani at the apartment and while they spent some time checking out the medical school and Boston, he'd stop in and see Jo in Salem.

Chapter 10

When Mark appeared at Jo's front door, he was more handsome than she remembered. His hair shone like copper in the midday sun, and his deep green eyes fixed on hers with an intensity she found disturbing. "Hi," she said, as if seeing him for the first time.

"Hi, yourself," he said quietly. "Did you forget I was coming?"

"No, no—sorry. I—er—please come on in."

As Mark stepped forward, his hand brushed her arm. "Is this a bad time, you seem a little nervous to have me in your house."

"Actually, this was Chris's house."

"Oh?" Mark asked.

Jo's cheeks flushed. "Er, we talked about getting a place that was 'ours,' but we never seemed to find anything he liked as well. I moved in after we got married."

"So, my being here must be difficult for you."

"I had no idea it would be feel so strange." Jo smiled thinly. "But I have to move on, right?"

"If you're uncomfortable, I can leave. I'll tie up with them now, instead of picking up Dani later."

"Let them hang out together. I'm being stupid."

Mark took Jo's hand. "You know, been there, done that, got the tee-shirt. If you want to talk about it, I'm here for you."

"Thank you," said Jo with a genuine smile. "I sometimes forget there are others who've lost their spouse."

"You didn't lose him, Jo, he died. Losing him implies you may find him again."

"You're very straightforward about death."

"One of the ways I found to deal," said Mark, feeling the sorrow he caused between them. "Sorry if it sounded blunt. I'm not big on euphemisms."

"You're right, I should say it like it is. However, it can be difficult, especially when I see that."

Mark turned to where she was pointing. "The scarf?"

She nodded.

"Did you just hang it there?"

"No, it must have been there all along. For security purposes, I had to return all Chris's uniforms to the airline, but clearly, I missed that. I don't usually stand in the middle of the living room looking into the hall so I never noticed it before." The navy wool scarf emblazoned which the brightly colored Transcontinental Airlines logo shrieked at her. Guilt struck like a thunderbolt, and she retreated into the living room. "I'm sorry," she whispered. "Am I a bad person for inviting you here?"

Mark was beside her and gently laid a hand in the small of her back. "Am I the first man you've had here since Chris died?"

Jo nodded as tears welled.

"Well, let's take care of one thing right now. You're not any sort of bad person. The hardest part about grief is getting through a series of firsts. Dang, I remember the first time I went to the dentist after my wife died. I sat in the car and blubbered like a baby."

"Because you had to see the dentist?"

Mark ushered her toward an armchair. "Here sit down, its confession time." He sat opposite. "You know how far out in the boonies we live, and the nearest decent dentist is in Portland. Dee and I always went to our appointments together and we made an event of it. We did some shopping, had a nice dinner, and stayed overnight at The Regency. The first time I went alone, I drove straight there and lost it in the dentist's parking lot."

"You've never said your wife's name before."

"Really?"

"That's the first time," said Jo.

"There you go then. All this time, I've held it in and now…"

"Another first."

"Seems crazy after all these years," said Mark. "They sneak up when you least expect them."

Jo smiled. "Yeah I see that. Thank you for sharing with me. Was Dee short for something?"

"Delores—and like Dani, she hated it. Neither of them quite forgave great-great-grandmother."

"Delores is not so bad in this Jericho Palestine's scheme of things. I remember the first time I told Chris—him calling me Jo really was a blessing."

Mark took her hand. "Some firsts are not hard to deal with. And believe me, as time goes on, the tough ones get less. I do realize how hard my being here is. So seriously, do you want me to leave?"

"No. I promised myself inviting you here was part of my new beginning. I will simply cross it off my list of firsts."

Mark smiled, knowing that whatever anyone said, only she could move beyond her grief to emerge stronger at the other side. "There you go. So now it's your turn confession-wise."

"Seriously?"

"Talking does help."

It had been a long time since Jo had felt so in tune with anyone, and she really wanted to know Mark better. "Okay. You're going to hate me for this. But after Chris died, I started drinking. It deadened the pain. It was bad until my boss Marvin told me to get my act together or else."

"Don't feel bad," said Mark. "A lot of us went through that. After Dee died, I didn't see sober for a week. Then something happened and like a light bulb going on, I saw through the darkness and was able to get it together."

"What happened?"

"Dani. They kept her in the hospital because of her traumatic birth. And being on the wrong side of sober, I didn't go to see her. My brother and his wife brought her home. Then after a week, they shoved her into my arms and said 'We're going back to Arizona.'"

"And they just left? What if you'd continued drinking?"

Mark smiled. "Mrs. A was around as back up. But they knew me well. As soon as I saw how small and needy Dani was, what could I do? I realized I was a father. I had responsibilities. And my life started to make sense again."

"Well, I don't have anything near as important to shake me up."

"What about family?" asked Mark.

"Here, I have none. We don't seem to procreate very well, and what's left of mine, returned to Ireland ten years ago."

"So, you were pretty much alone through the whole grieving process."

Jo's eyes clouded. "Still am."

"Well, I, for one, can't profess to be an expert on anyone else's light bulb moment," said Mark quietly. "But buying my dad's property certainly seems like one to me. And as he's buried there, I'll be around quite often. Being alone might be a thing of the past for you."

"Thank you, Mark," said Jo sincerely. "You know I do feel a lot better. And you'll be the first to know when *my* life starts to make sense again. You're very easy to talk to."

"Can I have that in writing for the next time Dani and I have a discussion about something?"

Jo smiled. "It's the least I can do."

"Now, why don't you put that scarf in a drawer, or it'll slap you in the face every time you walk by?"

"You're right. The drawer it is."

"And then I don't mean to be bossy," said Mark. "But how about some coffee? Mrs. A. sent you a tin of her award-winning shortbread. I'll go get it from the truck." He headed for the door. "By the way, I brought the truck to schlep a bunch of Nick's boxes. I'm assuming you've started packing your small stuff. I can take back anything you don't want to entrust to the movers."

"Are you always this thoughtful?"

Mark smiled. "I try."

"That's good to know. But there may not be any movers."

"Oh?"

"Go get the cookies while I put the coffee on. Then I'd like your opinion on something."

⌘

"You are so right about this shortbread," said Jo, taking a second. "Mrs. Ainsworth should go into business."

"She kind of is. Every fete, bake-sale, and church social she sells them. And at the founder's ball, she sets up a stand in the parking lot and cleans up."

"You're joking."

Mark made scout fingers at his temple. "Na-ah. You'll see. All Parsonsfield residents get an invite to the ball. But you have to be among a select few who get there in time to buy her baked goods."

"Village living. I like it."

"So, what did you want my opinion on?"

"I don't quite know how word gets around but it does. Anyway, a local real estate agent has a client who will pay me eighty-five thousand dollars above my asking price for this place."

"Good grief; did they discover gold under here?"

"I thought it sounded too good to be true."

"Hold on a second, I was joking. Did the agent say why his client was willing to pay so much?"

"He wants me to leave behind all the furniture and object d'art. Everything but my personal stuff. Apparently, it's all," Jo made "quote" fingers. "An integral part of the house's charm."

Mark glanced around. "I can see that. You have some beautiful and probably valuable antiques."

"If all this stuff is that valuable, shouldn't I hold onto it?"

"Yes and no," said Mark. "Possessions for possessing's sake seems a bit pointless to me. But walking away from your home with nothing but money is a pretty drastic let go of your past. Is that something you can do?"

"I'm not sure. As I said, this was Chris's house. The antiques and art were here when I arrived. It's all *his*."

"Actually, it's yours now."

"There you go again, pragmatist to the last. I know the legality of it all. I simply can't get my head around anything being mine."

Mark reached across and put a hand on her knee. "That will probably come in time. But if these things don't give you what you want emotionally, why keep them?"

Jo realized that despite talking to a grief counselor, she had never really spoken to anyone who actually shared her experience. It hadn't been easy dealing with her darkness without family to bolster her. But Mark totally understood where she was coming from, and he had morphed into her rock without even realizing it.

"I said I'm up for a new home, in a new state, with a completely fresh start," said Jo. "But I wouldn't have so much as a foot locker."

"If I can offer anything, it's to say that a log home has a completely different feel from an airline captain's house. When you measured up, you said a lot of your stuff wouldn't be appropriate for the smaller space, and the style probably wouldn't look right. Naturally, you have to make the final decision. But if it were me, I'd want furniture more fitting to a log house."

"You're right," said Jo. "However, if I'm going to be working from home rebuilding my career, I'm not sure I can spare the time to shop for 'cabin' stuff. And I don't relish sitting on the floor after a hard day's work."

"So, come stay at the farmhouse until you get situated."

"That's really nice of you Mark, but I couldn't impose."

"What impose, I would love having you about the place."

Jo smiled. "That's what I mean."

"Oh, I see, you don't trust me to be a gentleman."

"Maybe I wouldn't want you to be a gentleman."

"That's my gal," said Mark, grinning. "Given the right incentive, you bounce right back. Living with me wouldn't be an imposition at all."

"Is that right, Mr. Been there, done that?" said Jo, coldly.

"I'm so sorry. I didn't mean to imply…"

"Good grief, relax," said Jo, stifling a laugh. "I'm teasing. You really are a very good person, Mark, and I appreciate your being here for me. Sharing your space is a lovely gesture. However, I'm not sure Mrs. Ainsworth would approve of us co-habiting without benefit of clergy."

"Yikes, co-habiting. Hadn't even considered what the village would make of that. So, the solution is easy. Keep whatever furniture is in the cabin. I certainly don't need it, and you'd save me a bunch of time and effort moving it out."

"I couldn't, your dad's stuff is beautiful. Someone would pay a bundle for it."

"Do you like it?"

"Of course. It's perfect for the house."

"Then it's yours."

"Come on, Mark, you already gave me the washer and dryer as a housewarming gift. I have to pay you for everything else."

"Deal." He held out his hand.

"Duh…how much?"

"Thirty-nine."

"Thirty-nine hundred, thousand, what?"

"Dates," Mark said smiling. "I was thirty-nine when we met, so I figure it's an auspicious number. You owe me thirty-nine dates."

"You're kidding right?"

"I am not. And I want dinner, sister. Can you cook? No matter, The Lakeside Grille does a decent steak. I will accept a lunch. Breakfast would be acceptable." He leered at her theatrically. "And if an overnight is involved, we can discuss the upgrade in a mutually agreeable manner."

Jo giggled. "You're a nut-case, you know that? It sounds like you've been keeping this plan under your hat to reel it out at just the right moment."

Mark bit his lip. "Guilty as charged."

Jo loved his candor, his humor, and the effortless way he made her laugh. In truth, she was warming to him more quickly than she had imagined. "I agree to your terms. And I will take my mountains of money and squander it on the most lavish dates you have ever experienced."

"I was hoping you'd say that." Mark took Jo's hand and brought it to his lips. "I don't know what's happening, Jo, but I really love being around you. You make me smile. You make me feel twenty again. And though I might be teasing now, I hope we can see a lot more of each other when you move to the cabin."

❧❧❧

The heavens opened on the day of Jo's move. The tide ran right up the seawall and pounded against the concrete boundary, calling to mind the many nor'easters she'd endured. And as she watched the breaking waves, it was as if the elements had contrived to bid her goodbye. She smiled and focused on the cabin and the building strength of her friendship with Mark. This chapter in her life was over, and without regret, she was consigning The Witch City to memory.

Chapter 11

Mark was waiting as Jo pulled into the log house's turnaround. Warmth spread through him as he watched her greet the girls and hand them cookies. And when her wave accompanied a beaming smile, his heart skipped a beat. They had been communicating regularly, and there was no mistaking their growing comfort with each other. However, as he walked toward her, with feelings not evident for a very long time, he realized it was her presence he needed.

It took minutes to offload her small stash of possessions, and by one-thirty, they were sitting on lawn chairs, feet on the deck seats looking out over the property. He set down a plate of Mrs. Ainsworth's canapés and handed her a celebratory glass of champagne. "To the new owner, and my dad, who knew exactly how to get the right person to buy his house."

Jo hoisted her glass. "Your dad," she said. "This was very nice of Mrs. A," added Jo, popping a smoked salmon bite into her mouth. "Please thank her for me."

"You can do it yourself. She's invited you and a couple of others to a welcome dinner tomorrow night."

"Wow, I didn't expect to be part of the social scene so soon."

"Is it a problem?"

"No, I just hope I have a dress that's not too badly wrinkled."

"Come as you are," said Mark. "We're not big city formal."

"Most certainly not. An invitation to someone's house for dinner requires a modicum of civility. I will dig out something appropriate."

Mark smiled. From their first meeting, she had been feisty with her own opinions. And he wasn't surprised he was beginning to really like Jo. "Does that mean I have to wear a suit?"

"Do you have a suit?"

"Sure, Uncle Bernard from Down East left one to me in his will."

"You're kidding."

"He wore it once to a wedding in 1966, and the photos show he cut quite a figure. Seems a shame to waste it."

"OMG, this I gotta see."

"And so you shall," said Mark, grinning. "You want another glass of bubbly? I don't get to break it out too often, and I'm warming to it. Sort of goes with the whole babbling brook scenario."

"You're right, it does. I'd forgotten how relaxing that sound is. And with the birds and all this greenery, it feels like I'm in paradise."

"My dad thought that too. He described this place as an island in the forest."

"That's a perfect description." Jo pointed to the pool with its elaborately tethered cover. "But what's with that blight on the landscape? It looks like a trampoline."

"I'll have you know that's top of the line. The advertising bumph says an elephant could walk on that thing, and it wouldn't give way."

"Get many pachyderms in these parts?"

"Jessie Watkins has a hog pretty near qualifies."

Jo laughed aloud. "Remind me to ask him over some time. Pig on a trampoline, that's gotta be worth a photo."

Mark cast a glance in Jo's direction, and her relaxed demeanor confirmed she was most definitely the owner he and his dad had talked about.

"When do I open the pool?" asked Jo.

"Dad did it in April, soon as the snow melted, said he liked to see the water rippling."

"Your dad sounds like a real character, do you take after him?"

"Better ask Dani, though she'll probably say no. She adored her grandfather." Mark smiled. "I'm guessing, in part, because he gave her everything she wanted and then some. I'm a little more...shall we say?...conservative."

"You mean stuffy, serious, straight-la—"

"Whoa, hold on there, I thought we were friends."

"We are, that's why I can tease you, 'cos you know I don't mean it."

Mark frowned. "Do you say a lot of things you don't mean?"

"Depends."

"On what?"

Jo raised an eyebrow. "On whether, you tick me off or not. Why so serious all of a sudden?"

"Sorry, it's the old man oozing out of me." Mark paused, awaiting Jo's comeback. When she didn't bite, he wanted to test the boundaries of their friendship. "Guess I've been alone too long."

"And whose fault is that, old man?"

"Hey, I get enough nagging about my personal life from Dani. I have high standards is all."

"I'll remember that."

"You won't have to," he mumbled.

"Uh?"

Mark took a distracting swallow of champagne. "The

Pool Shed in Buxton will come by and show you how to get the pool cover off. Their number should be in the little black book."

"Why are you changing the subject? What do you mean by 'you won't have to,' and what book?"

"Cos I can—cos you don't—and 'cos it's something I felt you needed."

"Cute, farm boy. Now what's in this book?"

"Anybody and everybody you might need to help you out of a crisis."

"You included?"

"I'm a given…"

Jo reached over and affectionately patted his thigh. "You really are very sweet." She felt his muscle tense, and thinking she'd gone too far, withdrew her hand. "Thank you, I'll take all the help I can get."

"Then you're in luck. More help will arrive soon, Dani is coming over. And as she used it most, the fate of the pool will probably be her first question. Why did you remove your hand, it felt good?"

"She can use the pool whenever she wants."

"The hand?"

Jo pushed a lock of hair behind her ear. "Er, I forgot where I was for a minute. Thought you were—er—it doesn't matter—sorry."

"Don't ever be sorry for affection, it's never misplaced. Does my being 'very sweet' make you nervous?"

"Of course not. I didn't want to make *you* uncomfortable."

"You could never do that. But let it be known, apart from the routine maintenance laid down in my little black book, I come with strings."

"Uh-oh—strings. Not sure I'm ready for those, or your little black book."

Mark saw her cheeks flush. "I like that I can make you

blush. Clearly, access to my little black book is not something you expected." It amused him she cared enough about him to be embarrassed. "About now, it would be interesting to know what's going on in your head."

"Nothing is going on in my head," Jo said. "Apart from having gotten into a conversation running on two entirely different levels, how do I get myself out?"

"So," Mark said, smiling. "I will help you out. What I meant is—I need feeding and watering 'cos I'm a working stiff. When I'm not on the land, I'm eating, or sleeping. They're the strings you'll have to deal with."

Jo inclined her head. "Thank you for the clarification. Forewarned is forearmed. And talking about feeding and watering. While the canapés were delicious, I was so excited about finally getting here I didn't eat breakfast. I'm still ravenous."

"Ah-ah," said Mark, a mischievous look in his eyes. "Now I get to acquaint you with the first lesson on life in the boonies. Limerick has a general store with all the basics. However, we don't have a sub shop. Neither can you pop down to the local Micky D's or Burger King for breakfast."

"Darn it, now what do we do?"

"You're welcome to share what I have," said Mark smugly.

"You have real food?"

"Told you, I'm a working stiff. I have to take my grub with me. I'll break it out in the middle of whatever field I'm working. You're welcome to share, as long as you're not looking for anything fancy."

"Bring it on, Old Macdonald, I could eat a horse."

Mark raised an eyebrow. "Best not say that in these parts."

"Right, sorry, force of habit."

Mark went to his truck and pulled out a cooler the size

of a shipping trunk. He hauled it onto the deck and placed it at Jo's feet. "Madam's brunch, courtesy of Mrs. Ainsworth's House of Epicurean Delights. She had a feeling you'd skip breakfast."

"Wow," Jo said, laughing aloud. "Did she put an entire side of beef in there?"

"Don't know, let's open it."

The cooler was full of the most delectable things—pâté, baked Brie, crackers, crudités, fruit, small finger sandwiches, savory and sweet pastries, and another bottle of champagne with orange juice buried in ice.

"This all looks pretty good," said Mark casually.

"My God, who was she expecting to feed, a presidential welcoming committee?"

"Mrs. A has a knack for turning the mundane into something special."

"This is amazing." Jo rooted through the cooler. "These are all my favorite things. How could she possibly know? Keep this up, and you'll never get rid of me."

"Maybe that's the plan," said Mark quietly.

He and Jo had developed a warm friendship on the phone and always flirted. However, now he was in front of her, saying things face-to-face, it felt very different. Different and surprisingly perfect.

ఌఞఒ

They sat for hours, enjoying each other's company, learning more about their respective lives, family history, loves and hates, and aspirations for the future. The more he talked, the more comfortable she became, and Jo had the distinct feeling he was somebody very special. "Mark?"

"Yo."

"I thought you said you were a working stiff, how

come you've been lazing about here for four hours?"

"I am working," he said.

"At what?"

"Community relations."

She smiled. "Good one. What's the real deal?"

"In a nutshell, I have a bunch of guys who help on the farm, and as I had such an important new-comer to entertain, I swapped a Sunday off."

"You have Sunday off, thought you were a farmer?"

"Monday to Saturday only. Sunday I'm strictly head cook and bottle washer as Mrs. A deserts me. Thought I told you that."

"Right, you did. So, you sacrificed your one day off to be with me?"

"Sort of."

"What do you mean sort of?"

"Now there's the beautiful thing. Being the boss, I'll pay out some overtime, and still get my Sunday off."

She cuffed him playfully, and he rubbed his arm in mock distress. And when she settled back into her chair to soak up the sun, Jo realized she'd never felt so in tune with anybody. She seemed to have natural affinity with Mark, who was nothing like her husband. Mark was funnier, more considerate, and loved the land and all it offered as much as she did. And though she'd been with Chris several years, when she likened the men, one to the other, Mark was the more attractive. With his long ankle-crossed legs stretching out before him, and his tanned, muscled arms lying casual on his belly, he felt so right beside her. And she simply enjoyed the sight of him. From his aviator sunglasses that shielded mesmerizing green eyes, as well as his emotions to his no-nonsense demeanor that she felt certain hid a vibrant and exciting man. Mark Newcombe appeared to be everything she had dreamed of in a man.

Whether she would ever have the guts to find out was an emotional dilemma that riddled her with guilt.

Jo frowned as she berated herself for being emotionally weak. Her marriage had been, for the most part, lonely and empty. So, why did it bother her that she might have found someone who'd help her move on? She'd spent years coming to terms with simply existing in the same space as Chris. So why was her little head voice questioning whether she was entitled to find happiness? Or was she simply realizing that she'd already given her heart, to the wrong man and couldn't handle making the same mistake again. Jo took a sip of champagne, hoping Mark couldn't detect the turmoil he was inadvertently putting her through.

As she glanced in Mark's direction, there was no mistaking she couldn't think entirely rationally while he was so tantalizingly close. However, before she could straighten out the emotions that were causing her confusion and soul-searching, a clip clopping distracted her.

Shifting in her chair, Jo saw a young woman on a piebald horse riding up the drive. She came to a halt at the house's path, amid a maelstrom of dogs. Shooing them away, she threw her right leg over the horse's neck, and slid to the ground. And after patting the black and white rump, prompting the horse to trot off into the meadow to graze, she roughhoused with the dogs before striding up the path. This had to be Dani.

Standing about five-feet-ten, tall for any girl, she had the same red hair as her father; except where his was wavy, hers was a cascade of Renaissance curls halfway down her back. And as she drew closer, Jo could see the skin she thought was alabaster-like was made perfect by a dotting of pale freckles. They gave her the sort of wholesome girl-next-door beauty any modeling agency would kill for. And while Jo had grown up on the tall side of willowy and attractive, this young woman was strikingly beautiful. She would certainly give Mark ulcers in a year or two.

The young woman's easy stride carried her quickly up the stairs and onto the deck. And with the same devastating smile as her father, she extended her hand. "Hi, Ms. Weston, I'm Dani. Pleased to meet you." She turned to Mark. "You were right, Dad."

Jo raised an eyebrow. "Right about what?"

Dani chuckled. "He said you were tall, like me, very attractive, ditto, and extremely elegant—I have some work to do on that."

Jo blushed. "Well, thank you, although I think your dad was just being polite."

"Not my dad," said Dani, bending to peck her father on the cheek. "Honest Abe here— calls a spade a spade."

Mark shook his head. "Okay, ladies, now you're getting sassy. Next, it'll be girl talk and swapping dating tips. And fun as it would be to stick around and take notes, I'm beating a hasty retreat. I have livestock to check on. Here, Dani, take this chaise. It has a great view of the pond." He gave up his seat. "Now, behave, missy, I'll see you later." He turned to Jo and ran a hand down her arm. "Thank you for letting me hang out, I'll call you later."

As something indescribable flowed through Jo's body, she shivered. And when Mark descended the steps, she was left feeling that life had been sucked from where she stood. He whistled as he climbed into his truck, and half the dog pack leapt into the back. Then, with a wave, and a boy-next-door smile she would remember forever, his old Ford rattled off down the drive. As she watched him disappear, a small piece of her went with him.

"Can I have a glass of champagne?" asked Dani, her confidence and poise far exceeding her years.

"Does your dad let you drink?" asked Jo, returning abruptly to reality.

"No…"

"So, what makes you think I will?"

Dani comically pouted.

"Go on, just a sip though."

Dani picked up her father's glass and drank what remained. "It tickles."

"I know. Isn't it fun," said Jo, finishing her glass. "So I have Faith, Hope, and Charity, what are your dogs called?"

"Pansy, Posy, and Poppy."

"That's a lot of Ps."

"We're farmers," said Dani. "It goes with the territory."

Jo smiled. "Nice. You know you have the same sense of humor as your dad."

"Really? I invariably get told I'm being a precocious bossy bazinka. Dad tells me we have something in common."

"Wanting to be a veterinarian?" asked Jo.

"I was thinking more about ditching our given names. Jeez, who in the world would want to be a Dolores? On the other hand, I think Jericho Palestine is way cool. I'd like to be named after a place. Something exotic like India or China. Sadly, I got my monster moniker in an ongoing curse from an ancient grandmother."

"Maybe you look alike, and your mom thought it would be a nice tribute."

"My mom never knew her. She was a Dolores too. They died. Grandma died having my mom and my mom died having me. We don't seem to do childbirth very well."

"How sad. So, you and your dad have always been alone."

"Pretty much. He's had a girlfriend here and there, though don't tell him I know. He thinks I'm too young to understand that stuff. They were awful. Thought because he has money, he'd buy them things. I even heard one of them ask him for a new car. But he doesn't spend money on anybody—except me."

"That's a good thing," said Jo.

"He still won't let me have a cell phone."

"Maybe there's good reason. A lot of kids waste their lives gabbing on those things."

"That's exactly what Dad said. But all the kids at school have one."

"Why would you want to be like everyone else?' asked Jo. "It's good to be different. I don't have one because I hate following trends and doing what other people do."

"Is that why you're here? Dad said your husband died—what did he do?"

"It's sort of why I'm here," said Joe. "I wanted to put all the bad stuff in my life behind me. My husband was killed in a crash, he was a pilot."

"Whoa—an airplane crash?"

"No, a crew bus."

"Bummer, who'd have guessed that would happen."

"Not me, that's for sure. But enough about me, it's in the past. Your dad mentioned your wanting to be veterinarian. Sadly, my folks moved from the farm into the city and forced me in a different direction. But here you have plenty of opportunity to practice animal husbandry in preparation for college."

"Dad does let me do stuff with the animals. So, what did you end up doing?"

"I'm a writer."

"Novels and stuff?"

"Only stuff. I'm in advertising—commercials, jingles that sort of thing."

"On TV?"

"Yup. Remember Toothgoop?"

"So shiny bright," Dani reenacted the commercial. "Mom will see you at night. That is soooo cool. You must be rich then."

"Why would my being rich make a difference?" asked Jo.

"It wouldn't to someone like Dad. But if you marry him, I'll get more stuff."

"Hold on there," said a shocked Jo. "I barely know him. How do you jump to marriage?"

"Dad's gonna need someone to keep him company when I go to college in New Zealand," said Dani, matter-of-factly. "Plus, Mrs. A isn't getting any younger, and he'll be a basket case by himself. You're not going with anyone, right?"

"As a matter of fact, no. Are you always this direct with strangers?"

"Sorry. Dad says it goes along with being bi-polar and not taking my meds."

Jo frowned. "Why wouldn't you take your meds?"

"It's not on purpose," said Dani petulantly. "It's just a pain in the butt and…well, other things get in the way sometimes. I catch up when I can."

"Umm, I don't know much about bipolar disorder, but I know you're going to have to work on that."

"Wow. Look at you, already watching my back. You are so supposed to be here." Dani reached to add more champagne to Mark's glass.

"Na-ah, missy." Jo set aside the bottle. "What do you mean I'm supposed to be here?"

"Apart from nagging me like a mom, you passed the tests."

"Tests?"

"The girls, the cookies, the cemetery. Plus, Dad is different around you. You make him feel good, I can tell, I'm an expert."

"Well, I feel good around him too," Jo admitted.

"Ah-ha—told you so."

"Don't you dare repeat that. It's strictly between us gals."

"I won't say anything. Seriously, can I have some more champagne?"

"No."

"Aw come on, you're supposed to be on my side."

"There are no sides," said Jo firmly. "You're too young, and I'm sure whatever meds you take, they don't mix with alcohol."

"You're so straight-laced—exactly like Dad."

"'Fraid so."

Dani smiled. "But I like you anyway."

"Well, thank you, Miss Dani," said Jo. "Now, did you just come over to say hello, or do you want to clue me in on exactly what I get with this house."

⌀⌀⌀

Jo spent the rest of the afternoon enjoying Dani's girl-talk and learning just how much Mark had left to maintain the cabin and the property. Several times Dani mentioned using the pool, and as she so enjoyed the youngster's humor and positive spirit, Jo decided to open it immediately. As they hung clothes, Dani asked why Jo had left the excitement of the big city to come to "the boonies." And she was pleasantly surprised she could talk to Dani about her former life without getting upset.

By six-thirty, the sun had started to fade. Dani seemed to be comfortable remaining with Jo. But after being reminded that riding a horse after dark was more than a little suicidal, the youngster agreed it was best she get going. As Jo waved goodbye, an odd thought washed over her. *This must be what it's like to have a daughter.*

Chapter 12

As the piebald's clopping faded, dusk fell and the country's nighttime order closed in. Jo turned back to the house with the smell of pine and night scented stock heavy in her nostrils. A chill breeze swept over her, as she realized she was truly alone for the first time since her husband died. Moreover, the disappearing sun accompanied a sharp drop in temperature. And it was quiet. Much quieter than she imagined. Way quieter than it had ever been in Salem. There, something was always moving. A bus, car, or ambulance, even an airplane overhead. And Jo shuddered. As much as she had craved it, about now, being alone with the peace and solitude of the natural order, was overrated. She clapped her hands, to summon the girls, the hollow sharpness echoing about the trees. But for several seconds, nothing stirred. When the dogs emerged from the undergrowth, Jo breathed a sigh of relief.

After their customary tick check, Jo let the girls into the house and set out their dinner. As usual, they politely ate from their own bowl, and Jo couldn't help wondering what an amazing man Mark's father must have been to foster such civilized behavior in a pack of dogs. And as she watched them, she realized she'd been too wrapped up in her conversations with Mark and Dani to eat much.

As she retrieved a selection of Mrs. A's tidbits from the cooler, her mind flashed back to the last time she was single...

೧೨೮೨

She'd just graduated college. It was her first day in Boston and although she had an apartment and a job lined up, she felt somewhat lost. The efficiency was miniscule with hand-me-down furniture. And an electric toaster oven ensured take-out, leftovers, and toast would be her primary means of sustenance. Like tonight, she survived her first evening on the contents of a food package her aunt had given her. However, then it was ham and cheese sandwiches, with a bottle of sparkling cider. It was a strangely exhilarating déjà vu moment to go through the same, albeit up-market, meal for a second time.

೧೨೮೨

With the full setting of the sun, Maine's evening chill set in. Jo looked out the window, noting how the sharp drop in temperature caused moisture to form on the trees. However, despite retaining some warmth from being so near the forest, Mark had told her it would be another month before the night warmed enough to do without heat.

As a damp eeriness descended on the house, Jo put a match to the potbelly stove Mark had set for her. Within minutes, the girls jostled for position in front of the fire's throaty roar, and warmth permeated the space. Nevertheless, Jo couldn't shake the cold of loneliness.

When the phone rang, she nearly jumped out of her skin. A glance at the clock told her exactly who it was. "Hi, I'm so glad you called," she said.

"I said I would. Is everything okay? You sound a bit odd."

His voice was so comforting, and her tears began to well. "I'm okay-ish. Just feeling a bit displaced."

"You were a huge hit with Dani. She said you let her drink and that you feel good around me. Is that right?"

"I'm so sorry, Mark. I had no idea she was taking meds. It won't happen again."

"I don't care about the champagne. I know you wouldn't let her take more than a sip. You sure you're all right?"

"Yeah, now I have someone to talk to, I'm good."

"Someone? You mean me. Dani said you feel good around me."

"That was supposed to be a 'girls only' secret."

"Then it's true," he said, more casually than he felt. "It's nice to feel needed. So, first night in the backwoods, what're you doing?"

"Trying to stay warm. Attempting to adjust to the quiet. Coming to terms with being cut off from everything. It's a bit scary."

"Whoa, where did that come from? There's TV, radio, cassettes the whole Blockbuster experience. Didn't Dani give you the grand tour?"

"She did. But it seems rude to go through drawers. It's your dad's stuff."

"No, it's not, I bartered for dates, remember. You are such a goose. And be warned—you welch on the deal, I know a couple of guys with more muscle than brains who can pay you a visit."

"I won't," Jo whispered, her voice thick with emotion.

"Hey, what's going on?" asked a concerned Mark. "You're supposed to give me one of those snappy comebacks. You are most definitely not okay."

Jo was overcome with the enormity of being in the

middle of nowhere with nothing familiar around her. "I'm sorry," she whispered. "I don't mean to be such a wuss." Tears rolled down her face. "It's all…I'm not sure. It's so quiet and painfully dark and there's so much I don't—"

"I'm coming over," said Mark.

"No really," she sniffed. "I'll be okay once I—"

"I'll be there in ten minutes, tops."

Jo pulled herself together as best she could. Then wrapped a throw around her shoulders and went out to wait for him. The deck lights had popped on as soon as she stepped beneath the motion detector. Nevertheless, she could feel the claustrophobic silence, and overwhelming impenetrability, of rural Maine closing in. The girls had followed her out, and sensing her fear, clung to her legs.

Having them close bolstered her. But what she really needed was Mark's shoulder.

As she paced, it seemed she'd been outside longer than ten minutes. Her anxiety began to rebuild, and she decided to wait in the house. However, as she reached down to usher the girls in, she saw headlights turning onto the drive.

Her relief was palpable as she walked around the house to the garage side of the deck.

As soon as Mark pulled to a halt, the girls took off. The automatic light over the garage door had lit, and she could see he was smiling. She counted his strides as he came toward her and, when he met her at the top of the deck stairs, she fell into his arms.

"I'm so sorry to drag you out," she whimpered. "You must think I'm a complete idiot."

"I'm the idiot for thinking you could simply dispose of all your things without caring. We'll call the guy tomorrow and see if we can buy your stuff back."

"No, I love what's in this house. It's just…I…" She coughed and wiped away a tear. "I'm sorry, I'm such a wuss."

Mark took her face in his hands. "Look at me, Jo."

She tried to turn away.

"Look at me."

She turned her face to his.

"There's no need to be afraid, it can be—"

A startled gasp caught in Jo's throat as the timed auto lights left them in the pitch dark.

Mark held her tightly to him. "I've got you, there's nothing to be afraid of."

"Can we go inside?" she mumbled through tears.

"Sure. But we have to deal with this, otherwise you'll be on the next bus back to Massachusetts." He whistled for the dogs who appeared from somewhere in the dark. Then he put his arm around her and led her forward. The lights popped back on. "All you have to do is walk to the sensor side of the house."

Once they were inside, Jo felt safe enough to separate from him. "I'm so sorry, Mark. Really, I didn't mean to drag you over here. But I'm so glad you came."

Mark smiled. "Part and parcel of the little black book's ownership."

"Be serious, Mark. That was for emergencies and help with things I can't handle."

"Seems to me, whatever is going on with you right now qualifies."

"Whatever is going on is that I've been a townie too long. Even at night, there's sporadic traffic or the residual hum of the streetlights. I don't remember Ireland being so black and mind-numbingly quiet. It's like being dead."

"Well, that's certainly not a notion I want to leave with you. Why don't you come stay with me for a few days, ease into country life gently?"

Jo smiled thinly. "We addressed this a few days ago. I still think it's too soon to be moving in together—"

"There you go, humor back. The offer stands, so, are we bunking at my place or yours?"

"Excuse me? 'We' and 'bunking' should not be in the same sentence." She gave him "the look."

Mark pouted theatrically. "Still too soon?"

Jo's mind was doing mental cartwheels. Alone, she had been so afraid. But now he was here it was if nothing but having him near mattered. She felt safe and protected and didn't want to share him with anyone. "I know I owe you for the furniture and all," she said, with a deadpan look. "But you badgering me for something more than friendship is awkward. Don't you think you're presuming a bit much?"

Mark immediately backed away. "Jo, I'm so sorry. I didn't mean to offend. You're right—we hardly know each other. But I feel like I've known you for a hundred years. Please, don't be upset with me."

Jo laughed aloud and cuffed him playfully. "Gotcha— you should have seen your face. I'm not upset with you. But we have to deal with this, otherwise you'll be on the next truck back to the farmhouse."

"Funny, lady, real funny."

"So, Farmer Fix-it, it's odd how you can take me from terror to sarcasm in a heartbeat. But, seriously, how *are* we going to deal with *this*?" Jo nodded her head toward the outside.

"Well, first, I have to say. You are so cute in your PJs with the ponytail. What are you eighteen?"

She bobbed a curtsy. "Thank you, kind sir, I love you already."

Stepping forward, Mark wrapped his arms around her. "Do you? Because I haven't met anyone like you in such

a long time. I want to behave, but you make it very difficult."

"Is that right?" said Jo coyly.

"You've affected me like no-one else ever has. I'm
truly sorry if my clumsy advances spook you. But I'm
woefully out of touch with what's expected these days. If
I do anything wrong, I want you to tell me so I can fix it."

"You've been a perfect gentleman, why would you
think you did anything wrong?" Her arms were around
him too and she unconsciously ran her hands down his
spine.

"That feels so good." His voice turned husky. "But I
don't think you should do that thing with your hands unless you're prepared for the consequences."

Jo released her hold and stepped back. "Now I'm sorry. I haven't really hugged a man in a while."

Marks eyes shone as they fixed on hers. "You'll get
used to it you know."

"The lack of hugging, being prepared for the consequences, what?"

"For now, I was thinking more about what you call
'the silence.'"

"What about the being alone, with no hugging?" she
asked.

Mark smiled. "Truthfully, I don't think you ever get
used to that. But let's take it one step at a time. First, the
silence. Grab those seat cushions and follow me."

"Where are we going?"

"To sit outside and get used to it. Although I think you
might be surprised." Mark pulled several blankets from
the drawers of the armoire. When they stepped outside,
the auto lights popped on. He took the seat cushions from
Jo and dropped them next to the log wall. "Let's get cozy."

As Jo sat close to him and he pulled the blankets over

them, she focused on his eyes. Their mesmerizing depths transmitted his innermost feelings, and when he smiled, his warmth and sincerity caused an unexpected pounding in her heart. Lost in the moment, she was compelled to peck him on the lips. Her intense need so confused her, she pulled back. "I shouldn't have done that." Her voice was a sultry rasp, exposing deeply suppressed feelings.

He pulled her back to him. "Yes, you should. I want you to do it whenever you like."

"I'm sorry. It was impulsive and leading you on isn't fair."

"So, you're never going to kiss me again? I'm a big boy. I think I can handle a kiss or two without tearing your clothes off—however, you can rip my clothes off anytime." He smiled.

"Do you have any idea how devastating your smile is?"

"Of course. I practice forty minutes a day in front of the mirror."

"Fool!" As Jo playfully cuffed him on the shoulder, the auto-lights went off. "Dang, there's that dark again."

"But I'm here, so relax."

"Mark?" she whispered.

"Yo."

"Thank you for being here."

"You're welcome. Now, enough of the mushy stuff, I have some friends I'd like you to meet. The moon, the stars, and the heavens are going to be your friends too. Look up."

"Oh my God—how—beautiful!" Even though she lived by the ocean and thought she had a spectacular view of the night sky, the glare from street lamps and civilization still obscured. Here, the heavens were without dilution, ablaze with a billion points of light. "It's breathtaking. I've never seen so many stars. And they're so bright, it seems like you could reach out and touch them."

"That's what will eventually give you comfort," said Mark. "Just remember, no matter where you are, no matter how far from the ones you love, when you look up, you're seeing the same thing. And, if you whisper something down here, waves up there will carry your thoughts and love to your special someone. 'Over time, like shooting stars we fall, love endures, leaving traces behind. And whatever journeys we may take, you'll never be far from my mind.'"

"A poet as well as hopeless romantic —you never cease to amaze."

"Can't take credit for the poem. It's from Emiline Pete Lord, 1865 to 1882. Great, great, great something or other. She died at seventeen and is out back with the others."

"Is it comforting to have such history surrounding you?" Jo asked.

"Actually, it is. Some might think it creepy to have relatives buried in the garden. But it's really not. There's a sort of permanence and purpose for my being here."

Jo's hand accidently brushed against his, and she could feel the hairs bristle. "Mark?"

He fought hard not to react to her touch. "Don't you love the universe?" he whispered. "Makes you realize what specks we are."

"Mark?" she repeated.

"Yes."

"You were right. There *is* a connection between us. Like you, I've felt it from the beginning. Do you like me the way I think you do?"

"Yes."

"Did you bring me out here to impress me with the universe, or get closer?"

"Yes."

Jo hesitated, wondering whether the question in her

mind would be premature. But she felt so at ease, so right, and so in tune with Mark, her heart needed to know the answer. "Do you want to make love to me?"

Mark paused for several long seconds, as if his answer might damage the feelings between them. "Yes."

"Not saying much are you."

"I can't. If you only knew how hard it is for me to stay on my side of these cushions. I've wanted you from the minute I saw you. You're so different from the women I've met since Dee died. I can't even think straight when you're not around. But I've said enough, and about now you probably think I'm spinning a line."

Jo smiled. "Are you?"

"No line. If it was, I could have picked up my check from the realtor's office, gone home, and forgotten about you. But I couldn't do it. I've thought about you every minute since we met."

"Isn't that a little impetuous. I'm a stranger, you barely know me."

"Everyone was a stranger once. Besides, I can't help it," said Mark. "I have no control. It's like I've been waiting years to find you. Now you're here, I have to let you know. Besides, look me in the eyes and tell me you haven't felt the same way."

Jo laughed. "It's pitch black, I can't even see your eyes."

"Don't be pedantic, you know what I mean."

"Okay, I won't lie to you. I do like you, a lot. But it's still too soon after Chris. I have so many conflicting emotions, so many unanswered questions. I'm not ready."

"I know, I can feel that. But I'm patient. I can wait."

"Do you want to?"

"No—but I will."

Jo replied in a tone a lot more matter-of-fact than she felt. "So, it's settled then. When I'm ready, you'll be the first to know."

Mark squeezed her hand. "Promise?"

"I promise—whoa what's that?" She pointed west.

"A shooting star—make a wish."

"Only if you make one, too."

"I already did," said Mark, pulling up her hand to brush it against his lips.

Chapter 13

For several weeks, the excitement had been building for the graduating students of William Pete Lord High. Now, with the county's most anticipated party barely an hour away, Dani Newcombe stepped carefully into a full-length emerald green dress. Mrs. Ainsworth deftly dealt with the myriad of baby buttons, hardly believing her charge was not only celebrating her eighteenth birthday, but also that she'd needed little persuading to wear something other than the jeans and boy-shirts she usually wore. After the dress, small yellow roses were pinned in Dani's waist-length titian hair, and in another once-in-a-blue-moon event, she slipped on heels.

As she twirled in front of the mirror, even Dani was shocked by her appearance. The green dress perfectly matched her eyes, and with the rosebuds setting off the color and texture of her hair, she had never felt so mature. Straightening her skirt, the almost six-foot-tall teenager took her first tentative steps forward, and although it took a couple of lengths of the upstairs landing to acclimate herself to the shoes, she made her way downstairs.

Mark and Jo had already been primed on what to expect from the birthday girl. Nevertheless, they were taken back when she floated regally into the kitchen.

"Sweetie, you look absolutely gorgeous," gushed Mark. "I can hardly believe you're my daughter."

Dani blushed. "You have to say that, Dad, it's my birthday."

"Nope, this is different, I've never seen anyone so breathtaking." He kissed her on both cheeks.

"Hopefully you were also as enthusiastic about Jo's dress," said Dani with a beaming smile. "It's fabulous."

Jo bobbed a small curtsey, acknowledging Dani's thoughtfulness. "Why thank you, Miss Newcombe, as a matter of fact, he did. However, your dad is right. You win the prize. Emerald green is perfect on you."

Dani graciously accepted the compliment but she couldn't resist touching Jo's dress. The pale apricot, heavily embroidered silk organza slipped through her fingers. "This fabric is so beautiful, where did you get it?"

"Paris."

"No way," said Dani, gushing. "Is it from a famous designer?"

"I wish, but no. It's from a young up-and-comer called Merisel LaFor. She supplied the clothes for a perfume commercial my company was making. Like you, I couldn't help admiring the fabric, and, as she wanted to introduce her clothing line into America, she gave it to me."

"Gave, as in free?"

Jo smiled. "I used to attend a lot of film premiers and receptions. I also promised to wear it to swanky parties—like this one, to get her name out there." Jo adjusted a lock of Dani's hair that her father's embrace had dislodged. "There, almost perfect."

"Almost?" asked Dani.

"One more thing is needed." Jo pulled a necklace from her evening purse.

"OM triple G," said Dani. "Who's wearing that?"

"You, if you want."

"If I want? Why would I not?" Dani nervously ran her fingers over the necklace. "Holy crap—"

"Dani!" snapped Mark.

"Sorry, that just came out. Jewelry isn't usually my thing, but this is soooo awesome."

The necklace was a single row of diamonds set in gold, with a diamond and emerald pendant. "My grandfather bought it for my grandmother fifty years ago. I've worn it a couple of times, but with that green dress and your red hair, it couldn't be more perfect." Jo handed the necklace to Mark. "I think you should do the honors."

Mark carefully clasped it around Dani's neck as Dani stood in front of the hall mirror. "There. As Jo said, perfect."

For several seconds Dani stood and stared. And as she touched the pendent with perfectly manicured fingernails, her face was aglow with excitement. She turned to the adults. "I feel so sophisticated I could spit."

Mark laughed aloud. Despite grown-up clothes, hair, and make-up, the elegant beauty before him was still Dani.

Upon hearing the familiar razzing of the cattle grid, he stepped to the window. "Well, ladies, it's five o'clock, and if I'm not mistaken, your carriage waits." Mark linked arms with his beauties and steered them toward the door.

Mrs. Ainsworth had already opened it, revealing a large white limousine.

Dani unhooked herself from her father and kissed the elderly housekeeper on the cheek. "Thank you so very much, Mrs. A. I couldn't have done it without you."

The old lady pulled a lace-embroidered hankie from her apron pocket and dabbed proud tears from her eyes.

"Off you go, Miss Dani, have a lovely time. I'll expect to hear all about it in the morning."

ᘒᘖᘒ

The drive to The Farrington Inn in Cornish took forty minutes and by the time they arrived, most of the graduating class was already there. When Dani saw her school pals congregating on the veranda, she left the adults, and glided model-like toward them. The gaggle of teens disintegrated into fits of giggles. They all looked beautiful in their party best. Nevertheless, the statuesque Dani outshone them all.

Mark turned to Jo. "Do you think they'll be all right out here? It's getting chilly."

"Of course," said Jo. "They're teenagers. They have enough inner fire to light up Broadway. Now come on, old man, let's find you a chair so you can worry in comfort."

ᘒᘖᘒ

Imagining Jo might be a little nervous being thrown into the village's lion den, Mark took her hand. "Okay, let's do this."

"Umm that's new," she said playfully. "For your benefit or mine?"

Mark smiled. "Yours, of course. I bet there's already some gossip about the attractive single gal from down south. Let's give them something talk about."

Jo squeezed his hand. "You are so out of the loop."

"Excuse me?" asked Mark innocently.

As they entered the ballroom, packed with anyone who was anyone in the county, several women nodded as Mark and Jo walked by.

"Wasn't that the predatory Sally Thompson in pink?" asked Jo. "Ginny at the post office told me she had quite the thing for you until I appeared on the scene."

"What? She said no such thing."

"Oh, yes, she did," Jo teased. "And, I have it on the same unquestionable authority that Beth Robelard—" Jo nodded in that particular lady's direction. "—has had her cap set on you since grade school."

"Hang on," said Mark, pulling Jo to a halt. "You're supposed to be the subject of the evening, not me."

"Yeah, right. Keep moving, Casanova." Jo floated to the rear of the ballroom, nodding and smiling as if she were royalty. But a little voice in her head was chuckling. She liked stirring things up, and from the grip Mark had on her hand, it appeared he was as anxious as she was amused. "You must know whoever you brought to this shindig would be the supporting act. Most of these single ladies are here to see you."

"And where exactly did you and Ginny at the post office get that from?"

"Coffee Klatch at Bess Lord's on Wednesdays. Ellie Barker at the mercantile, and Patty Parsons feed exchange at Metcalfs. It's good, need to know, info, right?"

"And you believe everything the Parsonsfield grapevine tells you?"

Jo smirked. "Naturally. And while we're on the subject, let's address the Peters twins. What's with you and them?"

Mark tightened his grip on her hand. "You gonna quit, missy, or do I march you home right now."

Jo laughed. The small show of irritation was an endearing characteristic she'd never seen before. She leaned in and pecked him on the cheek. "I'll quit, as long as you remember who you were waiting for."

"Do you remember everything I say?"

Jo smiled. "Pretty much."

Mark had been hoping for a major move forward in their relationship. And while they had been on several of his bartered "dates," her accompanying him to the ball, where everyone could see them together, was a huge step. He smiled wide and repositioned his hand intimately on the bare skin at the small of her back.

⌁⌁⌁

Before long, it was clear that Jo was actually drawing as much attention as Mark. And while he simply introduced her as the new owner of the log house, his ever-present grip on her hand, or an arm about her waist, hinted to everyone that something more was going on. It had been some time since anyone had seen the handsome gentleman farmer with a woman, and the locals were having a field day speculating on the true nature of his relationship with the "gal from far away."

⌁⌁⌁

On the other side of the room, Dani mingled with her crowd. They didn't care in the least about her father's companion. The girls were interested in the fact that Jo had entrusted Dani with a diamond and emerald necklace, which looked like it was worth several thousand dollars. And the guys cared not for the piece as a necklace. They speculated on how easy it might be to barter it for a halfway decent car.

As Dani floated from one group to another, she didn't immediately notice the young man who'd arrived later than the rest. It was Nick Brewster, and in his weeks away at Harvard, he'd matured into a stunning-looking young man.

When one of Dani's friends told her to turn around, she saw him and rushed forward. And despite the peril of running in four-inch heels, she threw herself at him in an undiluted display of affection.

Clasping Nick's hand, Dani led him to Mark and Jo's table. "Dad, look who finally arrived," said Dani breathlessly. "Now graduation and my birthday are perfect."

"Hi, Mr. Newcombe, Ms. Weston, sorry I'm late," said Nick. "I had a bit of trouble with the tie." He fiddled with the perfectly tied bow. "Mom had to bail me out."

"Isn't he handsome, Dad?" said Dani. "So grown up I can hardly stand it."

Mark smiled and extended his hand. His daughter's obvious display of affection concerned him somewhat. However, seeing Dani so happy in the care of a young man he trusted quickly dispelled his worries. "Nice to see you again, Nick, glad you could make it. I know it means a lot to the birthday girl. Are you here for the weekend?"

"Actually, I have 'til Tuesday. I'm being given credit for tutoring some of the kids at Middletown High in Standish."

"Are you finding it difficult to work and take classes?"

"Dad," whined Dani. "No work talk, we're here to have fun."

"I better get her dancing," said Nick. "Will you excuse us?"

Mark recognized Nick's resigned smile. Now he wasn't the only male wrapped around the finger of the exquisite Dani. And as Nick lead her onto the dance floor, she looked back and smiled. It was the smile every father dreaded. As the youngsters disappeared into the crowd, Mark brought Jo's hand to his heart. "I think my baby is about to fly the coop."

Jo smiled. "You do have that look on your face."

"What look?"

"The one which says you're about to become the number two man in your daughter's life."

"That obvious, eh?"

"Seen it before," she said. "On my dad." Jo patted their clasped hands. "You knew it would come."

"I anticipated having another ten or fifteen years. Doesn't seeing the intensity of their infatuation make you feel ancient?"

Jo grinned. "Oh, I think they might be working on something deeper and more long-lasting than infatuation. But look on the bright side."

"There's a bright side?"

"He'll be graduating Harvard, and she'll be graduating veterinary college. You'll have your own doctor and vet right there on the farm. Multi-species healing—one stop cures all."

"Trust you to put a positive spin on it. You really think they'll stay on the farm?"

"Not a chance," said Jo patting Mark's arm. "They're going to live their own lives. It's just gonna be you and me, old man."

"Damn. I could've used a break on my veterinary bills, and my arthritis kills me in the winter." Mark took her hand and brushed the knuckles against his lips. "However, if it's going to be you and me, maybe I can negotiate a cut rate with Doc Wilson and put up with a bit of pain now and again."

She moved close to whisper in his ear. "Maybe by that time, I can think of something to make you feel better."

"Oh, I know you can." Mark grinned, wondering if she knew exactly how much her show of intimacy pleased him. However, he'd agreed to let her dictate the pace of their relationship, so he took a deep breath and pecked her on the nose. "Come on, let's dance before I get any ideas."

Jo had no doubt about Mark's feelings toward her.
And as she melted into his embrace, she could feel the
strength of his body against hers. Nothing had ever felt so
right, and she beamed as they joined the others on the
dance floor.

∞∞∞

The birthday girl and her handsome Harvard man also
fit perfectly together. She was as tall as he was and Nick
held her close. "You're stunning, Dani, I can't believe
you're so grown up."

"You look pretty sharp too. I didn't know you had a
suit, let alone a tux."

"Hospital functions. Mom gets these bees in her bon-
net, and Dad and I get dragged along."

Dani laughed, she liked Nick's mom, Dr. Emily. "Bet
you missed her while you were at school?"

"I only missed you."

"Duh."

"I'm serious, Dani. I miss you so much and I'm terrified you'll forget me now that I'm in Boston."

"Why would I forget you? You're my best bud."

"I don't want that anymore."

Dani frowned. "Cos you're away at college, you don't
want to be my friend?"

"I don't want to be your best bud anymore."

Shock shadowed Dani's eyes as she pushed him away.

Nick held firmly onto her hand. "Wait. That didn't
sound right." He'd missed his best friend and wanted to
get her alone. But seeing her looking every inch the elegant young woman made him a little nervous. "We need
to talk. Let's go outside."

Once outside, Dani moved to a darkened corner of the
patio. "Spit it out, Nick, what's happening here? Are you

dumping me, on my birthday, before we've even had a proper date?"

"Of course not. Why would you think that? You know I've always loved you—do love you—will always love you."

"So, what's with all the weirdness?"

"I don't want to go back to Boston. I can't bear not seeing you every day, talking to you, knowing you're there."

"I won't be here much longer. I'm not passing up my opportunity to go to college."

"I don't expect you to," said Nick. "I want to come with you. You know how smart I am. I can get into a college anywhere."

"Are you crazy? You can't beat a Harvard education and on a scholarship. It's your passport to the world. You know I adore you, and something more will happen for us one day. But we agreed. College first, then we'll think about—"

Nick lunged at Dani, catching her lip with his teeth.

"Jeez, Nick, what the—do you intend to bite me into submission?"

"I'm sorry, I couldn't wait. I've wanted to kiss you so many times."

"Then why didn't you?"

"You'd make fun, push me away, and say eeheuw. Let's face it. I've always been the nerdy guy who helped you with math."

"Why would you think that?"

"Look in the mirror lately, Dani? You're drop-dead gorgeous."

"Duh," said Dani, shaking her head. "Look in the mirror lately, Nick? You're drop-dead gorgeous too."

Nick blushed. "There you go, making fun of me."

"I'm doing no such thing. I've liked you forever. You've always been my closest friend."

"But do you really like me?"

"I just said that. I've liked you since we were kids, what is wrong with you?"

"Not like kids, Dani. I mean, really, like me." He took her hand and brushed it across his crotch. "Like this."

Dani pulled her hand from his. "Yes," she whispered.

"A little…or…a lot?" When she didn't immediately answer, he chucked her under the chin. "Dani, please. I couldn't handle knowing you're with someone else while I'm in Boston."

"Why would I be with anyone else? It's been you and me together since first grade. It's always been you and me. Everybody knows that."

"I don't know."

"What's gotten into you, Nick? What happened to Mr. Shy Guy, who would rather die than talk about romance?"

"He grew up. Being alone in Boston made me realize what I really wanted from life. What's more, if I didn't go out and get it, I might miss the opportunity."

"You're thinking of sacrificing a career in medicine to be with me?"

"Yes, it will be worth it."

She pulled away from him. "No, it won't, it's dumb. I'm not sacrificing my career to be with anybody. I'm going to be a veterinarian and then I'll think about the love stuff. And I have to tell you. I wouldn't be happy with anyone stupid enough to give up a golden opportunity to end up schlepping feed in Metcalf's."

"So, it's that simple?" asked Nick. "You get your ticket and off you go. You give no thought to my feelings because you don't really care about what I want at all."

"That's idiotic and you know it. Come here." Dani's fingers entwined his, and she kissed him softly. "I care for you more than you know. However, I'll care for you a lot more when you have achieved your dream of becoming a doctor. I never, ever, want either of us to say 'if it hadn't been for you, I could've been a—'"

Nick's arms encircled Dani, his body pressing hard and obvious against her. And when he kissed her deeply, she moaned softly. Waves of pleasure coursed between them as passion ignited on more levels than was prudent for so public a place. He pulled back. "Do you really love me?"

Dani looked into his eyes, a mesmerizing shade of blue, and someone much more exciting had replaced the boy she'd seen to this point. "Yes," she whispered. She kissed him again, moved her hand down his back, and felt his body react. However, she knew what was inevitable, when two people care deeply about each other, and broke away. "Nick, we have to stop. This isn't the right place."

"Tell me where," he whispered. "I will follow you to the ends of the earth if I have to. Just don't turn me away."

"I'm not. This is what I want, but sex is a huge step."

"It's natural when two people love each other. We'll get married."

"I'm barely eighteen," said Dani.

"Not in your head."

"It's too confusing," she said quietly. "I've thought about us being together. But we have to—"

"Love each other every second of every minute of every day of—"

She put a hand over his mouth. "I get it."

"I've waited so long, imagining what you would do and how it would feel when I really kissed you."

"And how did it feel?" she asked.

"Heavenly, Dani, heavenly. I desperately need there to be an 'us.' I want to taste your skin, feel your body next to mine." His voice turned husky. "I want to make love to you, until you beg me to stop."

Dani frowned. "Nick, I'm sorry. This is way too intense to deal with right now. I think we should go inside. People will wonder what happened to us."

"I don't care. I want life to be just the two of us."

"Maybe. But if we don't get back inside, Dad and half the town are going to be out here, and the life you want will be over."

"There you go, pushing me away again. Now there'll be awkwardness. You'll hate me for making a pass, and I've lost my best friend."

"What a load," said Dani sharply. "You'll never lose me as a friend. And when have you ever known me change my mind when I've set my heart on something?"

"This is different," said Nick. "We're not talking about simply changing minds."

"So, what are you talking about?"

"I want to give you my heart and soul. I want to share my body as well as my mind. I need to be sure you want that too."

"You know I do. But having quickie sex at a party won't confirm that. All I can say for now is, you and I feel right. But I'm not altogether adjusted to the new, assertive you. You were always so laid back. So best friend, big brother. Suddenly you're so…mature. It's confusing."

"You said that already. But I haven't changed at all. I've always felt this way. I was simply too afraid to show you. Now I'm not." As he kissed her long and hard, he ran his hands over her body.

Dani moaned as she felt a deeply satisfying stirring. Despite any reservations she might have had, her body wanted him too. Surrendering to his embrace, Dani knew her inhibitions were about to evaporate. She'd heard stories from her friends about giving themselves in the heat of the moment and regretting it later. And even though she was sure of her feelings for Nick, she wanted to wait a while. She pulled sharply back.

Nick was shocked. "Did I do something wrong?"

"No. I'm scared by it, is all. I need some time to get my head together."

Nick smiled. "You know I can't refuse you anything. It's going to be a pain, but you're right. Whatever I want, it has to feel right for both of us." He brushed a lock of hair from her face. "Are we good?"

Dani nodded.

"For real?"

She pecked him on the lips. "One hundred percent."

Nick put his arm around her. "Then I guess we better get back to the party."

༄༅༄

While the pair was inseparable that evening, on the odd occasion Dani danced with someone else, she could feel Nick's eyes on her. An exquisite warmth of belonging flowed over her. And at eleven fifty-five, with the band wrapping up and people filtering home, she and Nick approached Mark's table.

"Okay, ask," she said to Nick.

"Mr. Newcombe," said Nick. "Would it be okay if I drove Dani home?"

Mark raised an eyebrow. "Straight home?"

Jo was amused to note the possessive way Dani and Nick clung to each other.

Whatever was happening between them, it was clear their relationship had taken on a new dimension. And as she watched old Father Newcombe re-surface, she put a hand to her mouth to keep from laughing.

"Yes, sir," said Nick. "I have to tutor tomorrow, and I'm already way past my bed-time."

"Okay," said Mark. "Off you go then. We'll be right behind you."

As the youngsters left, Jo leaned in to Mark. "You re-alize they may make a small detour. Are you ready for that?" she whispered.

"I'll give them twenty extra minutes."

"That seems more than enough time to—"

Mark frowned. "Don't go there, Jo, this isn't funny. I'm having an anxiety attack here."

Jo put a hand on Mark's arm. "It's all about trust, old man. Those two have been alone a thousand times, and now you're playing the heavy father. You know Nick wouldn't do anything untoward."

"Since when were you a horny young man with enough testosterone to light up a town?"

Jo suppressed a giggle. "Is that the voice of experience speaking?"

Mark gave her "the look."

"I think they'll be just fine," said Jo. "Come on, I have to get some goodies for my lunch tomorrow before they clear away."

"How can you be so cavalier about my child?"

"Because she's not. She's eighteen now and using your own analogy—probably going on eighty."

"Dang," said Mark, taking her hand. "What is it with you and the memory?"

෴

When the limo passed Nick's truck parked in the post office lot, Jo couldn't miss Mark's tightened grip on her hand. "He kept to his word," she teased. "This is on the way home—ergo, no detour."

"Not funny, lady."

"Oh, come on, they're young, they want to neck." Jo giggled uncontrollably when she saw how uncomfortable Mark was with the concept.

"So, Miss Know-it-all, how long do I give them? Do I wait up…what? I've never been in this position before."

"Well, it's only five minutes to the farm, so I figure another ten minutes should do it."

"Do it?"

"I can guarantee at least one of them saw this huge white beast swooping past. If it was Nick, he should be about scared witless at his point. If it was Dani, she'll be eager to get home and stay in your good books."

"Why would she do that? Aren't kids meant to be rebellious?"

"Correct, father dear," said Jo. "But yours is also very smart. Tonight, she'll come home on time. Next time, she'll tweak the deadline a bit. The time after, she'll stretch you to an hour, and before you realize, you'll trust her to be out all night."

Mark appeared horrified. "Doing God knows what?"

"Oh, yeah, God will know exactly what," Jo teased.

"Aghh—is that what you think?"

"It's what I know," said Jo. "Did it myself. Fathers are such prudes." She smiled as fidgeting and constant attention to his watch accompanied Mark's discomfort. "Mark, relax, they're good kids. They know what they want in life, and they're responsible and focused. Be thankful you know where they are, and with whom they spend their time." Jo squeezed his hand reassuringly, lifted it to her lips, and kissed his knuckles. "This can't be that much of a surprise for you."

Before Mark could say anything, their limo razzed over the cattle-grid and pulled up to the farmhouse.

"I feel weird coming here first," he said. "Isn't the man supposed to escort his lady home, let nature take its course, and sated with love and affection, stagger back to his lonely garret."

"Normally, yes, but tonight we're playing a special game of 'who da boss?' Assuming one of them saw the limo heading this way, they'll know you didn't drop me off first. And, as Dani knows I don't overnight here, she'll have Nick scooting right along."

"You're pretty confident."

"You better believe it. If for one moment, they thought you were at my place for a nightcap, hanky-panky, whatever, it'd be a different story."

"Why did you never adopt kids? You'd make a terrific parent."

Jo smiled. "Wasn't meant to be."

"Well, I have enough ignorance to ensure you will henceforth be called upon to advise me on parenting the woman-child."

Jo pecked him on the cheek. "My pleasure. Now get out, I want to go home."

"I need to know something."

"Yes."

Mark whispered in her ear. "When do I get the hanky-panky, whatever part?"

"Umm, let me think about that." Jo kissed him passionately. "That's on account."

Mark smiled. "Oh, lady, you do not play fair."

"All's fair in love and war." She giggled, opening the door. "Now get out of the car." She pushed him from the limo. "Goodnight, Mr. Newcombe, it was a delightful party. Driver, Maplecrest Rise, please."

෴

Mark shook his head and smiled as he watched the ghostly vehicle sweep down the drive. And almost immediately, Nick's car razzed over the grid, approaching the yard. *Dammit,* he said to himself, *she's not only an incredible kisser, she's right.*

When Nick pulled up, he leapt around to Dani's side of the truck. The pair looked sheepish as they strolled arm-in-arm to the porch.

"Good timing, you two," said Mark. "I was just about to send a search party."

Dani pouted. "But we came straight here, Dad."

"Right," said Mark, opening the farmhouse door.

The Ps and girls spilled out, briefly stopped to check whether the elegantly dressed people on the porch were their humans, and continued about their nightly task. Dani and Nick watched the pack disappear into the night.

"You've got ten minutes, young man," said Mark. "Then I'm coming back out."

"Yes, Mr. Newcombe, I'll just say a quick goodnight."

The pair took up a position on the porch's loveseat.

"Your dad is real mad at me," said Nick nervously. "Who takes over an hour to come from Cornish?"

"Stop worrying. He knew we stopped at the post office."

"You're kidding. Do you think he saw me kissing you?"

"I'm sure he did—chill. If he didn't approve, you wouldn't be sitting here right now."

"Oh, God, I better get out of here while I'm winning."

"He said ten minutes." A dog emerged from the darkness and settled next to Dani. "See a chaperone. When the others arrive, our ten minutes are up, and I'm outta here."

"So, you really think your dad is okay with us being alone?"

"Nick, for goodness sake, we've been alone together since we were six."

"But it's different now."

"You're worried because he saw you kiss me?"

"No," said Nick. "I'm worried because he was once a nineteen-year-old guy. He'll know where I'm coming from, and that I'm hopelessly in love with you."

"You said you've always loved me."

Nick lowered his voice. "But I needed you to be old enough to do something about it."

"That sounds awfully cold-blooded. Are you sure you've thought this sex thing through?"

"Shush, not so loud. Your dad might be listening."

"Nope, he's not that way. However, the rest of the canine clan is here, so our ten minutes are up. I have to go in."

"Will I see you tomorrow?" asked Nick.

"Of course."

"Do you love me?"

"Of course," said Dani, pecking him on the lips. "Now get going before Dad does come out. A ticked off Newcombe is a force to be reckoned with."

Nick smiled. "I'll remember that."

Chapter 14

Daybreak trees hung fat, like green velvet dowa-gers dripping with diamond dew, and Jo sipped coffee blanketed in an Adirondack chair. It had taken weeks to get used to the pace, and peace, of her Maine oasis. But now, bundled up against the early morn-ing damp, she sat hypnotized by the flawless melody of the dawn chorus. She'd always been an early riser, and today she woke with her senses in tune with nature's message. Hearing the music that came from rushing wa-ter as it echoed over the falls to tumble across the pebbled streambed. And almost tasting the frigid wood silence of night giving way to the warming pinesap day. But her paradise, though found, was fleeting. Soon, the heat would force her inside. With no difficulty listing a dozen reasons for remaining in place, she tilted her face to the fast warming air. She was comfortable blissfully ruminat-ing on nothing. However, indolent reflection was a luxury she couldn't afford. Today she had a deadline to meet.

Jo rose, bent by the whim of the less than ergonomi-cally sound Adirondack chair, and stretched a kink from her back. Then she dumped the dregs of her coffee onto the plants below the deck. Over the past month, the wiz-ened clumps of nothing recognizable had burst forth into the airy delicacy of purple astilbe. And as she glanced at the profusion of vividly colored blooms filling her personal piece of paradise, she couldn't help smiling about the turn her life had also taken. A very special someone and his daughter, had brought her more tangible contentment than she'd known in years.

⁊⁊

After spending the morning putting together her latest presentation of jingles, Jo broke for lunch. Her thoughts again drifted to Mark and Dani. She was acutely aware how Mark made her feel, and Dani filled a particularly empty place in her heart. It had been easy to set aside work for a few minutes each day, to hear about the youngster's angst-filled adventures. And as Mark's land surrounded hers, his pop-ins for lunch, or a chat, had become an integral part of her day. However, when a second glance at the clock told her it was twelve-thirty, she'd neither heard from nor seen, either Newcombe. She wasn't a worrier by nature, but farming could be a dangerous business. She called the farmhouse. However, even the attentive Mrs. Ainsworth was conspicuously absent.

Jo tried to settle back into work, but it proved impossible. And she decided to hold off on lunch until one-thirty then get in her car and drive over to the farm.

Pacing back and forth, Jo attempted to distract herself by running ditties through her mind. Then she wandered onto the deck for the twentieth time. While it was comforting to find the familiar sight of the girls chasing each other around the pasture, a beat-up truck chugging up the drive would have been better. Then, for no reason she could see, the dogs stopped their game, sniffed the air, and charged off down the road.

Seconds later, a crazed pack of cavorting canines reappeared. Pansy, Posy, and Poppy, were not allowed to roam free, and she breathed a sigh of relief. Mark or Dani must be somewhere close.

She heard, before she saw, either Newcombe. Two horses were approaching, and as they turned onto her drive, it was Mark riding his buckskin, leading Patches, Dani's piebald mare. When he reached the end of the garden path, he jumped down, and strode toward a smiling Jo.

"Where've you been," she said, pecking him on the cheek. "I left a message at the house."

"Ah—so you do miss me when I'm not around," he teased.

"I was simply deciding whether to go ahead and have lunch without you."

He planted an affectionate kiss on her forehead. "Liar."

She blushed. "So, what kept you?"

"Got caught up with the land assessor. I have to re-assign some of your boundary markers. Unless you fancy going out and doing it yourself, I figured I'd add this to the conditions of your purchase agreement. So, you busy? Want to take a break and come along?"

"Weren't boundaries established when I bought the house?"

"They were. But I gave you more land than was on the original deed. Now I have to check the guys fixed the markers."

Jo raised an eyebrow.

"Don't look so surprised. It's all legal. I recorded it and paid the taxes. Farmers are good guys. We share our bounty."

"Stop playing the fool. Why would you do that?"

"Cos I intend to evict you on a technicality, and claim back my birthright."

"You, sir, are also a liar."

Mark pulled her into his embrace. "I love it when you fight back."

"Stay focused, mister, how do you know I can ride?"

"Dani told me. Come on, the pack know an adventure is in the offing."

"What about lunch and my deadline?"

Mark patted a bag slung behind him. "Mrs. A made some sandwiches. And in the big scheme of things, the other isn't important. Come on—step outside your self-imposed box. You can still multi-task. The horses know where they're going, so we can discuss the universe, practice your ditties, and eat, all from the comfort of a pair of fine equine armchairs."

Jo smiled. "Not exactly what my mother would call digestively conducive, but what the hay. Let me put on some boots, get some water, and I'm all yours."

He hauled her back into his embrace. "All mine—are you really?"

"Do you want me to ride or not?"

He flashed her an "are you kidding me" look and kissed her hard. "I want you to ride very badly."

Jo was absolutely clear what chain of events she'd set in motion and pushed him away. "Down, Romeo—the four-legged animals are also getting restless."

Jo ducked into the house, pulled on boots, and grabbed water, a hat, and sunglasses. And after Mark boosted her onto the mare, they set off toward the woods.

"This is going to take about four hours," he said. "Are you up for that?"

"Today should be fine. Ask me again tomorrow, when every bone in my body is screaming uncle."

"Well, Ms. Weston, we are so going to have to get you over that, because you and I are going to be doing a good deal of riding in the future."

"Oh, really," she said, with a hand comically clutching at her heart. "Be still this pounding heart."

Mark shook his head and swung onto the buckskin. "Thought we'd check your piece of the pie first then circle around back to the farm house."

"Back to the farm, you got something special planned?"

"Not me, Dani. She decided she wanted to make dinner. We've decided you're family now, so you get to be a guinea pig too."

"You mean she's actually cooking?"

"Yup."

"Has she done it before?"

"Nope. But she seems to be doing quite a few things she hasn't done before."

Jo didn't comment but guessed from Mark's tone that he had suspicions about the change in his daughter's demeanor. "Okay, farm-boy. I'm game for most anything today, let's move out."

∽∾∽

The pair ate their sandwiches as the horses sauntered along. And at every opportunity, Mark told Jo the name of each tree, plant, and creepy-crawly they encountered. Moreover, as they traversed the woodland trails, he showed her sun-streaked glades, where lady's slipper and trillium secretly bloomed. Led her around low-lying watery areas harboring swamp candles and fallen trees covered in velvet lichen. And introduced her to an open dell showing off vibrant banks of day lilies and blue flag. Then, he pointed to a stand of trees.

"The trees with red 'Ns' mark the property line."

"So, everything this side is mine?" asked Jo.

"Right. This is one of the bits I re-assigned. I wanted

you to have all the pretty stuff we just saw."

"Well, thank you, kind sir. I had no idea a seemingly impenetrable forest could be so magical."

"You ain't seen nuthin' yet. Can you jump?"

"Jump?" asked Jo.

"We have some gullies and streams to cross and, when Dani is on Patty Patches there, she launches over everything less than six feet."

"Yikes, I guess those riding lessons came in useful after all. I just hope she doesn't take off and leave me flat on my back."

"Don't worry about that, I have a bunch of less traumatizing ways to get you flat on your back."

"Is that so, Mr. Confident," said Jo, smiling. "Lead on, I'll manage."

"Okay, let's go. Shout if I'm going too fast."

❦❦❦

Winding around areas too thick to penetrate, Mark led her across a pasture, over a brook, and onto a wide logging trail, with ditches either side. They cantered along for several minutes until no more red Ns marked trees. Then, jogging left over a ditch, they joined a logging trail with trees marked with red on both sides. The pair hurtled along, until Mark slowed to a trot and cut through the forest.

When they came upon another open pasture, Mark pulled to a halt and smiled. "You're still with me."

"God, I haven't had this much fun since I was a kid. How often do you do this?"

"Every week from spring to fall. Winter, some trails are impassible or only accessible with the snowmobile. Then I get mechanized."

"Well, I'm hooked," said Jo, pulling alongside the

buckskin. "Can I come with you every week?"

"That's my girl." Mark leaned across, took her hand. and kissed the knuckles. "Now you know why I went to such unconventional lengths to find the right caretaker for this property."

"I'm glad you did, thank you."

"Come on, we have a lot more to see."

ℰↃℰↃ

They kept to the trails for some time, until Mark pulled up abruptly and dismounted. He whistled, and the dogs gathered around him. "Stay here, girls, sit, all of you, sit."

"What's up?" asked Jo.

He gave her his horse's reins. "Stay here with the dogs. Something doesn't look right over there." He came back carrying a metal trap.

"Oh my God," said a shocked Jo. "Is that a bear trap?"

"It is. The bounty on them is enormous. If I find out whose putting these down, I'll shoot the bastard."

"You went into the forest alone? Aren't you afraid the bear might be around?"

"I've only seen one. They're rare this far south and the truth about them is rarer. Generally, they sleep during the day, and if you leave them alone, they'll not bother you. Besides, I have the girls and there are enough of them to be intimidating to all but the largest black bear."

"But you left them with me."

"If I'd needed them, they'd come."

"So, what do you do with the trap?"

"Take it home to destroy it. Then log the discovery with the bureau." He rammed the trap into his backpack. "Poaching is bad at any time, but on my land, it's death to whoever I find doing it."

"We're miles from anywhere, and I'm completely turned around. How do you even know if we're on our land?"

Mark smiled. "The markers. Outbound from the forest are like that." He pointed. "Going into the woods, over there. When we get back, I'll teach you the code."

"I had no idea country life would be so complicated. What if I'm out for a walk, get lost, and can't see any markers?"

Mark put his hand on her knee. "How often do you intend to head out into the forest without me?"

Jo pouted. "I might—one day."

"Well, Ms. Townie, you don't need to worry. As long as the girls are with you, tell them to go home, and they'll lead you right there."

"God, who knew? I thought I could simply walk in a big circle and end up at the cabin."

"You might get lucky. But these forests are criss-crossed with hundreds of miles of firebreaks and logging trails. You could end up on a long, cold walk, along with moose, deer, bear, and coyotes."

"Coyotes—you're joking right?"

The look on his face said he wasn't.

"Then I'm making damn sure I never go anywhere without you," said Jo.

Mark took the buckskin's reins from her and smiled. "That's a plan I'll sign on for. But just in case, promise me that at the very least you'll always take the girls, plus a couple of other gadgets I'll give you."

"Not a gun, I hope."

"We'll start with an air horn and a Taser," he said seriously.

"Maybe I'll simply wait for you."

Mark reached for her hand and kissed her fingertips. "Okay, deal. Let's keep going."

They moved on until they got to a narrow pathway.

"Watch your head along here," he shouted back. "Low branches."

As the trees thinned to nothing, they emerged from the forest, and the horizon exploded into a blinding swath of yellow.

"Wow," said Jo, shielding her eyes from the glare. "What is this?"

"Mustard." Mark headed the buckskin through the wafting yellow on a direct line to a stand of trees. The piebald mare followed without encouragement.

Snorting and yellow-flecked, the horses plodded through the pollen-packed brassica. Tiny jewel-hued birds seized the opportunity, created by the horses' advance, to steal the loosened seed. And as the temperature soared, at least twenty degrees higher than the forest, Jo felt like a Bedouin traversing the rolling dunes of a surreal desert.

In the center of yellow sat an oasis of green. And from the blazing sun, they moved into the coolness created by maples and pine surrounding a body of water. From Jo's vantage point, she saw they were at the end of a lake covering a substantial number of acres.

"Let's dismount here," said Mark. "The horses can roam."

"Are we going to walk home?"

"They won't go far. We're surrounded by trees."

The horses were apparently familiar with their surroundings. They moved directly to the lake's-edge and splashed their hooves playfully in the water then plunged their noses into the cooling shallows. Jo saw their snuffling had blown pollen from their nostrils.

As she looked around, she noted that the drooping tendrils of the weeping willows placed about filtered the harshness of the sun. And they provided safe haven for families of ornamental and native waterfowl. Moreover, the area, as far as she could see, had been set up to accommodate its human visitors with benches and tables. The grass, cut with park-like precision ran down to the water's edge. And at intervals, posts held life-preserver-rings, back-up for swimmers' brave enough to tackle the lake's frigid-looking water. A well-established duck-house sat next to a large boathouse at which a rowboat was tied, and a nearby tree was hung with a multi-person swing. A barbecue pit was evident between water and trees, and to Jo's left, a small wild area was left untended. The frenetic abundance of birds and dragonflies made it clear someone intended for all God's creatures to enjoy the mustard field oasis.

"Do you like it?" Mark said, arms encircling her waist.

"I love it—where are we?"

"Nana Randall's Pond."

"It's huge, shouldn't it be a lake?"

"Not in Maine. Remember our trip to Sebago, that's a lake. You only saw the Naples end by Brady Pond. But next time, we'll take a ride on the paddle boat, you'll see the difference in size."

"Well, I don't care, this is fantastic. Do you own it, or is it for everybody?"

"These days, pretty much anybody who finds it can use it. But when I was a kid, my great grandmother made sure it was strictly for the Lord's and the Newcombe's."

Jo raised an eyebrow. "A tad elitist don't you think?"

"Don't blame me, it was Nana's idea. She said she wanted a picnic spot for the family to enjoy, without being bothered by 'them from away'—that'd be you."

Jo laughed. "When you put it like that, I can't say I'd want all the visiting hoi polloi raining on my parade either. Do you come here a lot?"

"As a kid, I did. And a little bit before Dani was born.

But mostly I come now to maintain it, and make sure the ducks are getting enough food. It has bazillions of memories, which can only be shared with someone special. One day I'll bring you here at sunset, it'll blow your socks off."

"I must be special then."

Mark turned her to face him. "More than you know." He kissed her tenderly. "A lot more."

In an ocean of yellow beside an enchanted lake, Jo began to truly understand the intensity of his feelings. And she couldn't ignore the desire in his eyes, a deeper, more intense green, than she'd ever seen. It was a little disturbing and once again, the confusion demons that plagued her raced to the forefront of her mind. She was becoming intensely attracted to Mark. Was she ready to admit it and commit to him?

"I bet you say that to every woman you bring here," she quipped, attempting to lighten the mood and sort out what was in her mind.

"Oh yeah, there's been oodles of 'em," he whispered, running his fingers down her cheek.

Feeling the sensuous touch of his hand on her skin, Jo shivered. "You know, we should have had our sandwiches here, brought a bottle of wine, and made a real picnic?"

"Ah-ha, great minds think alike." He led her to one of the benches. "I have a surprise, watch and learn." Mark located a piece of string tied to the bench leg, and reeling it slowly in, fished a bottle of wine from the water.

"You have got to be kidding," said Jo. "Don't tell me you have glasses down there too?"

"Wait, I'll be right back." Stepping into the boathouse, Mark reappeared with blankets and cushions. He fashioned them into an island, then went back and returned with a picnic basket. "Voila, madam, your wish is my command."

Jo opened the basket to find it contained another selection of Mrs. Ainsworth's delectable nibbles, and two glasses. She beamed and kissed his cheek. "Very clever, darling, but you forgot one thing."

"Like what?" he asked.

"Cork screw."

Mark smiled. "O, thou of little faith." With a flourish, he produced a Swiss Army knife from a belt holster, and after an extensive search, isolated the bottle opener.

She giggled. "You are so…"

"Romantic—yes, I've been told. Handsome, debonair, ditto, ditto…"

"I was going to say organized. You've thought of everything."

Mark's theatrical salaam accompanied a beaming smile. "Did you mean it?"

"Excuse me?"

He took her hand. "Just then. You called me darling."

Jo flushed. "I did?"

"You most certainly did."

"You really are something," Jo whispered. "You said you'd wait until I made the next move and I haven't. You could have any woman in four counties, why on earth do you put up with me?"

He handed her a glass of wine. "Because."

"An excellent reason. I never thought of that." She took a sip of the perfectly chilled Chardonnay. "Seriously, Mark, what if I couldn't ride with you today?"

"I still had to check the markers. I'd have simply left the food here for the bear. He'd have had a field day. This is a good bottle of wine."

"You'd have left him some wine?"

He shot her a "gotcha" face and kissed her.

ల/ఎ౬/ఎ

Their oasis picnic was blissfully peaceful, save the occasional quacking tirade between the local ducks, and "them from away." Doves cooed contentedly as they pecked at the scattered crumbs on the ground or danced in dizzying circles as they flirted shamelessly with their mates. And as the hypnotic warmth of the sun filtered through the waterside trees, the wine and Mark's presence made Jo feel like they were the only people alive. She couldn't stop her mind drifting, and she became aware of the country's distinct hum. In the city, it had been traffic, streetlights, air conditioners, sirens, and other abominations. Here, it was bird song, buzzing insects, and the occasional splash as a waterfowl dived to pluck an unsuspecting minnow from its watery playground. Coots hooted mournfully, and as she opened her eyes to make sure she wasn't dreaming, two huge herons, wings outstretched, glided across her line of sight to land on the topmost branches of a distant tree. Jo had found a peace she never imagined possible, and it was all due to the delightful man whose hand lay casually on hers. She had never felt more secure with anyone, not even her husband.

"Can we stay frozen in this moment forever?" she asked, squeezing Mark's hand.

"Nope."

"Why not?"

"Can't."

"Why?" she whined.

"Need to do stuff."

"Ignore it," said Jo matter-of-factly. "What could be more important than the perfection of this day?"

"This." Raising himself up, he positioned his arm on the other side of her body, and lowering gently onto her, kissed her passionately. It was several seconds before he backed off. "Have you any idea how much I care for you."

She smiled. "I think that about makes it clear."

"What about you?"

"Yes, I care for me too," she teased.

"You're exasperating, you know that? Be serious."

"Maybe you won't like what I have to say."

He stared at her earnestly.

"It's been hard, Mark. You've been so patient, and I think I'm finally beginning to get my head together."

"So that's a yes, no, what?"

"That's a—you are the most special person in my life and I cannot imagine how I would have gotten through several sorts of personal hell without you."

"I'm reading 'good' in there. However, it sounds like there's a 'but'?"

"Isn't there always?" she asked.

"So, I'm right in thinking you're not entirely leading me on. You care for me…" He held his thumb and forefinger about half an inch apart. "A little."

Jo reached up and widened his fingers as far as they would go.

Smiling, he leaned down, and brushed her lips with his. "I'll take that—for now." As they lay side-by-side, he clasped her hand tightly. It was several minutes of silence before he spoke again, "Jo?"

"Umm."

"Do you think Dani and Nick have had sex?"

She practically choked as she jerked bolt upright. "Whoa, where did that come from?"

"Haven't you noticed a change in them? They're somehow, more mature."

"Er, yes, I noticed something. But they aren't children anymore, it happens."

"So, do you think they are?" he pressed.

"Would it bother you?"

"Yes...no...maybe...damn, this is tough! They've been together since first grade. So, what do you think...are they?"

"Maybe-ish."

"Has she said anything to you?"

"No," answered Jo honestly.

"So how would you even have a suspicion?"

"Women are intuitive," said Jo. "We know certain things."

"Would you say something to me if you did know?"

"Probably not. Sometimes it's best a father doesn't know certain things."

"That's sexist!"

"That's life!" said Jo. "Don't worry, she's a sensible young woman, and God knows he's the most mature kid I've ever met. If they're having sex, they'll finish college before getting all marriage and kids on you. Feel better now?"

"Uh...no. I expected they'd get together one day. But for a father, thinking his daughter is intimate, and knowing for sure, are galaxies apart. In the back of my mind, I was imagining they'd be like thirty or something."

"This is 2014, Mark, kids are maturing much earlier. Dani tells me at least two of the girls in her class have already had abortions."

"Aghh, and that's supposed to help?" Mark gasped. "I definitely didn't want to hear that."

"See, fathers shouldn't know certain stuff. It's too...disrupting."

"So, what do I do?"

"I'm not a parent, why would I know any better than you?"

"Because I'm just a dumb guy and have no idea how

to approach a teenage girl on that subject. You're the only person I trust to tell me it like it is, not what you think I want to hear. Besides, you're a woman. 'Aren't you intuitive, don't you know certain things?'"

"Ouch, touché farm boy." She pinched his arm. "Why are you worrying? This is not a summer fling. They're committed to each other. If you move beyond the sex thing, you can see how adorable they are together. He's a wonderful kid from a good family. He's focused, hardworking, and he worships Dani. Can't you see how he melts every time she's near?"

"That's what bothers me—the melting thing."

"You're just an old fuddy-duddy."

"She's almost all I've got Jo."

"Almost?"

He lifted her hand, and brushed his lips across her knuckles, "You know what I mean."

"Trust her, Mark. She could've tied up with some slack-ass loser with no prospects who'd keep her barefoot and pregnant, living on your dime for the rest of their lives."

"I suppose so."

"So, what else is bothering you?"

"I'm that transparent, eh?"

"I'm a woman, we're intuit—"

"Yeah I know, intuitive, you know certain things." He laughed. "It's weird, my daughter is having sex, and I'm not."

"We don't know about Dani and Nick for sure. And the other is entirely my fault."

"It's not anybody's fault. It just worries me that I can't convey how much I love you."

"What?" she asked quietly.

"Love you—I love you."

"When did this happen?"

He looked at his watch. "Four months, eight days, four hours, and seventeen minutes ago."

"You've only known me four months!"

"See my point, I'm hopelessly lost." Mark caressed her leg and, leaning over, kissed her tenderly. "I'm clearly not saying or doing enough to convince you of my feelings. If you knew, it would release whatever is blocking you from loving me."

She put a hand either side of his face. "Who says I don't love you?"

He smiled. "Then why aren't we…"

"Sleeping together?"

Mark smiled. "There is that."

"I don't know either. I know what I feel for you. I know where I want to go with you. My head and my heart are in some crazy vicious circle, and when I figure out how to break it, I'll set your toes on fire."

"That sounds like fun," he said, brushing his lips to hers.

"Really, Mark, you could be with anyone," she whispered. "Why on earth are you letting me torture you like this?"

"Told you, I love you. Now, stop."

There was something uncharacteristic in Mark's order to "stop" that caused a fluttering in Jo's belly. And when he held her, exerting a sensual gentle control, a fire ignited deep within her soul. His kiss was dizzying and erotic, and she melted into his arms. And when his hands ran lightly over her body, it took her breath away. But—

When they broke apart, Mark gazed deep into her eyes. "I will wait as long as it takes because I can feel you love me," he whispered. "You simply don't love me enough to let go of Chris…yet." He backed off and stood up. "And though I'm giving you space and time, we really have to leave right now, before I ravish you."

Jo giggled. "Ravish me? Right here, out in the open?"

"Now who's a fuddy-duddy? I want you everywhere and anywhere," he said. "Do you have any idea how hard it is for me to keep my hands off you?"

"Do you think I'm leading you on?"

"Yes!"

"And you don't mind?"

"I mind. I also remember how I felt after my wife died. Conflicting emotions, anger, and pain from such depths I thought I'd go mad. Guilt about what I did, or didn't, do. What I should or shouldn't have said. Stuff I could never explain to anyone—but you. You're going through everything I did. Good thing is, you don't have to go through it alone. I'm here for you, Jo, unconditionally. Talk to me. I'll be there whenever, wherever you want." He reached out and hauled her to her feet. "There is an end to the pain. But I know very well it can't be forced. It just has to happen. And one day, when you want me like I want you, I'll know. Until then, I'm here for you."

"Promise?"

"I promise, assuming when the time comes, you'll want me."

"Of course, I'll want you. Who else will plow my field for free or buy my seeds wholesale."

He pecked her on the cheek. "Monster—let's pack up, and get home."

His "monster" rang comfortable in her ears. It sounded right, and when Jo thought about what her life might be without Mark in it, the cold emptiness of dread swept over her. As a stray tear slid down her cheek, she desperately wanted to stay in his arms until she understood what feelings caused such conflict in her. But had she any right to treat him as a rock and sounding board for the angst she harbored? No matter how many scenarios her mind created, she kept returning to the same thought. Mark was more sensitive and caring than any man she'd ever known. And he had become a definable necessity in her life.

As Jo watched him put the last of the picnic things away, she called the dogs. All six gathered at the horses, and on that perfect day, in a perfect scenario, Jo had no doubt the person responsible for her peace and happiness was but fifty feet away from her. She might not be able to sort out her heart versus her head in this instant, but one day soon, it wouldn't be that way.

Chapter 15

It was approaching dark when Mark dropped off Jo at the cabin. And the emptiness she had lately felt when he left her, morphed into something more intense. From deep inside, her longing for him was palpable. She watched him leave and almost picked up the phone to ask him to come back. However, if she did, there could be no more excuses. No more, I'll-let-you-know-when-I'm-readys. No more ifs, ands, or buts. He'd made it clear she was playing with his emotions, and it wasn't something he liked. So, if she asked him to stay over, there could only be one outcome. She paced, hoping movement would clear her head. It did not. Her mind was in turmoil, telling her the mere fact she was conflicted meant her vicious circle of guilt and regret was not yet broken. She was not ready to give him the sign he awaited. She was not mentally ready to commit to him wholeheartedly. Nevertheless, her heart ached. It told her something entirely different.

With a blanket draped around her shoulders, and a mug of hot chocolate by her side, Jo settled on her favorite deck chaise. And as she reclined, her field of vision altered. Facing the intensity of another navy sky resplendent with its myriad points of light, she felt as if she were floating in space. She simply lay there, smiling.

It seemed a lifetime since Mark had introduced her to the stars, and she wondered if right now, he might also be looking up at them. He'd been so right about the purity and tangibility of the Maine night. It wasn't silent, frightening, or empty as she first thought. It was full, robust, and brimming with expectation. Mark had helped her tune in to its nuances. Now, she could embrace the night's diversity, and from it, gain solace and strength.

An owl hooted above the roiling of the waterfall, and she recognized sounds of the forest's denizens, foraging in the undergrowth, just yards from where she lay. She smiled again, and closing her eyes, felt the forest's pulse. The brook babbled hypnotic as it tumbled over rocks, causing her mind to wander to places she'd previously denied. She had no doubt that the solitude and serenity of Maine was bringing her peace. And as she surrendered to the light of truth, feelings hidden deep by years of rejection emerged. While her soul soared, free and enlightened, her mind flooded with clarity. And Jo finally understood why she couldn't commit to Mark. Neither she, nor he was to blame. It was her unspoken and unresolved animosity for her late husband.

She'd known Chris in high school. They dated a couple of times, but when further education forced them along different paths, they drifted apart. They met again after college, on his first flight as a qualified airline pilot. They began seeing each other, and on a crazy layover in Vegas, they married. With him being a pilot, away a good deal of the time, and she traveling extensively in her job, they fell into a singularly distant version of domestic bliss.

As Jo continued to analyze her former life, she entirely understood that sporadic liaisons operating within the confines of his flight roster, and her business trips, left no room for personal development. They were married twelve years. However, each time they got together, in crew hotels from Miami to Marrakesh, it seemed they were on a date. Their torrid couplings were exciting and heart pounding. Also, stressful and frustrating. Once, in a rare moment of sanity, she'd attempted to set down roots by starting a family. Then she remembered the years of agony trying to get pregnant. Chris somehow thought if he simply kept at it, she would miraculously conceive. And when she suggested that a deeper more meaningful relationship might ease her anxiety, his mocking conde-scension became grating. He wouldn't even discuss adop-tion, saying men were weird about taking on another guy's kid. Besides, she wasn't "trying." He never, for one moment, considered his attitude made her feel worse and contributed to the pressure her doctor said was the con-ception killer. Moreover, his refusal to accept responsibil-ity for anything beyond his job, defined their marriage. On reflection, she should have had the guts to move on. But even a quickie marriage vow in Vegas was serious to her. And Chris was a good provider, and faithful. In his profession, she had to be grateful for that. No couple had everything. So, she existed in her bubble of perceived comfort and endured their version of marriage while hav-ing less and less in common with her husband.

Jo unconsciously shifted in her seat and reached for her chocolate. It was cold. Much like her memories of the past. Was she now, at thirty-nine, attempting to equate the shallowness of that life with the possibility of a lov-ing, nurturing relationship with Mark? How stupid and how sad. There was no comparison between what the two men offered her. So why was she agonizing? What value was there in attempting to recapture lost years and return to a time of innocence? What good was there in attempt-ing to negate the previous years? Did she somehow want to imagine herself a callow teenager tormenting about the glamor of the star quarterback, versus the steadfastness of the president of the chess club? It was folly. As a tear of regret, realization, relief…she wasn't sure what…rolled down her cheek. Jo knew she couldn't recapture anything she had lost during those years. Nor did she truthfully want to. The past belonged to youth, in its soft dewy days when everything was fresh and new. When nothing tarnished dreams and ideals, because one was protected from life. Protected until the instant of innocence's abandonment. That irretrievable instant, when life and the mantle of maturity, inexorably overshadowed. A mantle she willingly threw off. That allowed her to go forward with certain knowledge. Knowledge to be celebrated not brushed aside.

As she drew comfort from the night, Jo couldn't help making one of her mental lists. She wasn't entirely surprised to find her dead husband's "cons" were many. And thinking back as generously as she was able, she couldn't help adding his predictability. At first, it came off as endearing. A man who always had a plan. But in retrospect, she was never really happy joining him at crew hotels on the company dime. And the "no getting on an airplane on my day off" rule meant they rarely ventured from home for more than a night. Naturally, being a pilot predisposed him toward caution and the orderly management of things. But he never did anything wild or the least bit spontaneous.

Then she recalled her time with Mark at Nana Randall's pond. They had a mutual love for the land and chemistry a-plenty. To date, he might have expressed his feelings in a restrained and gentlemanly way. But underneath his patient and considerate exterior, Jo knew something mildly dangerous and indescribably passionate simmered. It radiated from him when he walked toward her. Oozed from him when they sat close. And filled the room with possibilities during the quiet moments they shared. As she scratched *yes, yes, yes* to Mark's list in her mind memo, she blushed.

In the end, there appeared to be no competition in the what-is-best-for-Jo challenge. And as she sat under the stars, stars that now fascinated rather than un-nerved her, she made a decision. The infinite cosmos had proved to be the great clarifier. Mark's quiet understanding and un-erring devotion had won her over. She could only think of a future with him in it.

With the night air chill in her nostrils, body warmed by blankets of wool and long-awaited reason, Jo fully embraced her understanding. Youthful naiveté and vir-ginal wonder was known but once in each of our lives. However, it could thenceforth be found, and appreciated, in another form. She had used the excuse of grief to keep an extraordinary man at arm's length. Not because she was afraid of loving him. But because she was looking to regain something impossible. Now, for her sanity, and the love of a wonderful man, she must divest herself of self-pity. She must say goodbye to youthful expectations and unreasonable aspirations and reach for genuine happi-ness.

Whatever benchmark her mind needed to establish a relationship, craving the excitement of a stolen moment in places unknown, versus sharing secrets and the electri-fying brush of a hand in a room full of people, she had to accept she was no longer a naive innocent. Too much had gone before. She was a different person. A person in her own right. And only someone who would let her be her-self, and live life on joint understandings, would be worth her time.

As she thought of Mark, she finally realized his atti-tude and emotional strength were something he worked at. They weren't merely the fleeting thrill of a sexual romp on layovers. They weren't colored by the angst of waiting to discuss issues on a mutually engineered day off. They were devotion, inner strength, and stability. And the more she listened to the dictates of her heart, the more she wanted Mark.

A chill ran through Jo now. And it wasn't simply the night closing in. It was the cold hard voice of reason. Reason she couldn't fault. And though she may never know how the seemingly endless void of sorrow brought her to so perfect a place, how years of emptiness had been so exquisitely replaced by the fullness of her island in the forest, she didn't have to understand the way the cosmos worked. She'd leave that to Mark. All she knew was that, with the girls by her side, and the man she was learning to love but a phone call away, she'd never be alone again. And she couldn't help whispering to the stars.

"Wherever you are, Mark Newcombe, hear this. I could relive four lifetimes and never encounter anyone who loves me as much as you do. And I promise, in the not too distant future, you and I will get together, and I will make your toes curl."

Chapter 16

Mark watched the Ps run across the yard for their nightly forage. It was deathly quiet save their snuffling, and as he switched off the porch light, the night enveloped him. It was pitch black as he looked up at the heavens, which gave him pause and brought him peace. There, the lights were on, allowing him to appreciate that despite his seeming importance locally, he was a speck in the cosmic scheme of things. A speck who knew that someone special, not light years away, was destined to be with him. She simply didn't know it yet.

To get his mind off Jo, Mark mentally identified this or that star system. However, though he'd stood right in this same spot beneath the heavens a thousand times, to-night it all seemed more tangible. And there was a frisson in the air. An indescribable something positive he hadn't felt before. Could Jo be looking up at the stars too? Might she be making up her mind about them being a couple?

He swiped a finger across his eyebrow. Jo had his senses reeling. She made him feel like a schoolboy fanta-sizing over the prom queen—even though he'd been the nerdy chemistry kid who hadn't a hope with any of the popular girls. The ones who wouldn't be seen dead with anyone less than the captain of the football team. Was that anticipation of possibilities, supposed to disappear with time? In his world, it did not. But so much had happened since, he barely recognized himself. He'd dealt with his family being scattered. Had loved, and lost, a wife. Had taken on responsibilities he never imagined after his father's death. And Dani—Dani had brought him closer to knowing how to handle a flighty, petulant female. Would that he knew all this back then.

Now he was in love with the sassy, independent Jo, who'd persuaded him that life would be easier if he quit sweating Dani's small stuff. And, in truth, she'd been right. Some of his angst at raising a daughter alone had equalized. Then there was the joy. It came easier. Even riding the fences was a pleasant adventure with Jo along.

As he thought of riding fences, their afternoon at the pond burst into his mind. Without doubt, he'd declared himself too soon. He'd intruded on the way she was dealing with her grief. But it was something he could barely control. He'd not been able to get himself fully together since they met. She seemed to realize that and let him down lightly as she put him on hold. And while he fully understood, where she was coming from, being so near yet so far from her wasn't ideal. Despite that, they made time to be together most every day, and enjoyed a more empathetic relationship than many people who did share their bodies. He'd never deny it was difficult. No man as in love as he would be content with a celibate lifestyle. But he'd promised to give her whatever time and space she needed to get her head together. And without doubt, he would.

As the Ps milled around his feet, Mark knew this night's time for reflection was over. "Come on you, varmints," he said, opening the farmhouse door. 'Tomorrow is another day." He smiled. Love really was a matter of timing.

Chapter 17

Nick spent every waking moment of his long weekend from Harvard with Dani. And when Tuesday loomed, and he picked her up, his mood was sullen. His focus on study was almost impossible because he could barely think of anything but the possibility of making love to her. Every time he saw a photograph of a vibrant young woman, it morphed into her face. TV commercials of happy families living their life, forced his mind into a place almost too much to bear. And whenever he saw anyone kiss, embrace or share affection, his frustration stabbed like a knife to his heart. He was a med student, knew about testosterone and male urges. But his were agony. And the thought of returning to college and leaving Dani at the mercy of other guys, filled his soul with indescribable pain.

"Nick, you gotta stop this moody stuff," said Dani. "I thought we straightened this out. You can't get all iffy every time you go back to Harvard. It's decided. You will return to Boston. You will become a doctor. And you will stop fixating on my going off with someone else."

"It's hard."

"If it was easy, anyone could do it."

"Stop making fun of me. Besides, since when did you become so committed to school?"

"Mr. Tanner's top ten careers round-up," Dani said playfully. "Seems being a doctor is one hot career choice. All the girls are seeing dollar signs around you. And, get this. There's more than one Dr. Nick fan who's taking up nursing so she can join you in surgery."

"Shut up, Dani. I'm not in the mood for your bullshit."

"Excuse me? I do not bullshit."

"Absolutely, you do."

"On what planet?"

"Just forget it. I'm a nerd. Have always been, will always be. The only girl I've ever wanted to be with is you. I'm gonna end up alone in a Winnebago parked at the clinic."

"With cats and a mangy parrot."

"See, bullshit—it's so you."

Dani pulled a notebook from her backpack. "I knew you'd go off on some sort of dipstick rant, so I took names. One—Babette Newman. I know you luuuuv her."

"She, kissed, me," Nick protested. "It was all a misunderstanding."

Dani smiled and patted his thigh. "Yeah, like I believe that."

As her touch fired feelings Nick desperately held back, he pulled up at the farmhouse. "No really, Dani, I would never—"

"Sheesh, I know. Lighten up, I'm teasing. I will continue. Two—Sally Squires, already signed up for LPN training. Three, four—Susan Martin and Carol Fleming, both RN wannabes. And five—Joel Anders, nurse anesthetist. I rest my case."

"Joel Anders is a total jock with hands like a gorilla. How in hell is he going to delicately handle being a nurse anesthetist?"

"Seems pretty determined to try. Anyway, your appearance at the prom won you a boat-load of devotees."

"And are you?"

"Am I what?"

"A devotee."

"Hopelessly," she answered matter-of-factly.

Nick tried to kiss her but she held him back.

"Wait," said Dani. "I've been talking to my friends—"

"About us?"

"No, about them—about their experience with…you know. Did you know two of the girls in my class have been date raped? They said they didn't know what happened until it was all over. They think certain someone's slipped 'em something."

"My God, who would do that?" asked a shocked Nick.

"Couldn't get that out of 'em."

"Do their parents know?"

"You kidding—they were too scared of their fathers."

"That's awful, I feel so bad about what I said now."

"What you said?" asked Dani.

"At the prom. About making love to you. I'm so sorry. I didn't mean to pressure you. It's just that I love you so much I can't think straight."

Dani didn't have any doubts about his feelings. She could feel the vibrations of his love across a room. And when she told him at the prom, she wasn't ready for such a huge step in their relationship, his attitude toward her never changed.

He was still attentive, loyal, and steadfast. Dani smiled. She was looking for that. Particularly when certain of her friends had not been so lucky with their first sexual experience. Now, she truly realized how special Nick was.

"Do you have something?" she whispered.

Nick looked at her quizzically. "Something—you mean a condom?"

"Yes."

"I do."

She raised an eyebrow. "You're pretty sure of your-self."

"Not really, it's a guy thing. I've carried it around for years."

"Is it still good?"

"As long as it's sealed."

"Do you know how to use it?"

Nick smiled thinly. "That's a guy thing too—I know."

"Come with me." Dani led him across the farmyard to the tack room, and when she opened the door, the rich smell of leather and saddle soap enveloped them. "This is where the guys sleep when we're waiting for the animals to birth."

"You want to do it here?" whispered Nick.

Dani nodded. "It's really clean. Mrs. A sees to that."

"Do you think we should? What if someone comes looking for us?"

"Isn't the chance of discovery part of the fun?"

"Good grief, Dani, don't be an idiot. I, for one, am not exactly thrilled with the possibility of ticking off your dad. He'd probably kill me."

"He's at Jo's. He's always at Jo's these days. God, they must be at it like rabbits."

"Dang, that's cold."

"Oh, really," said Dani, turning to leave. "So, we'll wait."

Nick caught her hand, pulled her back toward him, and locked his mouth on hers. It was several seconds before they broke apart. "I can't wait, Dani—I've dreamt about this moment so many times. Lock the door."

❧❧❧

As Nick kissed her deep, he began to unbutton her blouse.

"Just get the top ones," she whispered. "I'll pull it over my head."

The action of her reaching up and removing the blouse accentuated her figure and sent undulating waves of longing throughout his body. And when she stood in her bra and panties, as perfect as any model he'd ever lusted after, she took his breath away. "Take off the rest," he whispered.

Dani removed the expensive lingerie she'd received for Christmas. Fully aware the effect her body was having on her handsome lover, she reveled in her power over him. "So, what now—do I dance or something?"

"No, you stay still for a minute." His finger traced a line from her neck, between her breasts to her abdomen, and the involuntarily quivering of her body beneath the line he'd drawn fascinated him. He'd never imagined her skin could be so delicate, or her body so perfect. He reached back to pull her forward, and her butt fit perfectly into the open expanse of his hands. And when his lips contacted with her breasts, the exquisite swirling of his tongue on her nipples, caused an uncontrollable shivering throughout her body. "Are you cold?" he whispered.

"Nervous," she said.

His voice was thick with controlled passion. "We don't have to do this if you don't want to."

Dani traced lines across his eyebrows and kissed his forehead. "I want to. I just can't stop shivering."

"I'll warm you up." Nick stripped in seconds and pulled her onto the bed, letting her take the spot nearest the wall. As she lay beside him, he caressed her body. "You're so much softer than I thought."

"And you're not," she said, squirming to a more comfortable position. "Is that thing going to fit in me?"

"Dani, are we doing the right thing? I had no idea you'd be so frightened."

"Nervous is not frightened. I've seen animals, I know what happens."

"We're not animals."

"I know that, they don't do this—"

Dani kissed him with an intensity that took his breath away, but he drew back. "I want you so much, Dani, but here doesn't seem right. Seriously, what if your dad walks in on us?"

"We're naked. Whatever happens, if he comes in now, it will be assumed. Besides, door's locked, and I told you, he's with Jo. We should be good until midnight."

"Midnight? That's hours off. I'm crazy about you, but I'm not sure anybody could last that—"

"Stop talking, Nick. This is what you've waited for, now make love to me."

He eased himself gently on top of her. "Am I too heavy?"

"No," she whispered. "It feels good. Like you fit. Is this bed going to hold both of us?"

Nick smiled. "We'll soon find out…"

ʚৎ৩ৎ৩

Dani was surprised how gentle he was, and when his hand roamed across her skin finding all manner of pleasure spots, she squirmed with delight. She'd seen videos, so she wasn't completely ignorant of what was about to happen, and was thankful he didn't rush her. She moaned softly as his hand moved down to explore her deep within. And when his fingers slipped in and out with gentle thrusts, she matched his actions.

She instinctively knew how to move. But when it seemed his hand would dissolve into her, he removed it.

"Don't stop," she whispered. "It feels so good."

"Condom needs to go on," he said breathlessly.

Dani watched as Nick carefully unrolled the Trojan about himself and gasped as he dropped into position between her legs. He seemed enormous against her belly, but as she squirmed to understand the corded feel of him, he remained outside her. As she let his erection flow up and down against her belly, she didn't entirely understand why her actions were so pleasing him. She matched his rhythm as he moved back and forth on top of her. But the delicate friction, while enjoyable, wasn't enough for her. She needed to experience everything. "Put it in now," she whispered, running her hands either side of his hips.

"Feel it first, Dani, I don't want to surprise you." His voice was thick with desire.

She gently took hold of his length. "Oh God…it's big. Will it hurt?"

"You ride horses. I don't think so." Nick locked his mouth on hers and reaching down gently guided his penis inside her.

Dani felt an infinitesimal pinch, followed by the most delightful sensations she'd ever imagined. She had no concept of his hardness, just silk upon silk. Liquid friction. The mellow ebbing and flowing of undulating warmth, like waves in the ocean. And when he encouraged her to move with his rhythm, an ecstatic welling of something deep inside made her dizzy. His driving power seemed to reach the depths of her soul. All she wanted was the exquisite sensation of him deep in the pit of her belly. And when his teeth brushed against her nipple, she thought she'd pass out. The hard soft, hot cold, light and dark connected to pull sensations from somewhere impossibly deep. And she fed off his rhythm, enveloped in such deep, inexpressible satisfaction she bit down on his shoulder. And when she arched into his path, exposing her inner depths, he moved faster and deeper. She moaned softly, hovering on the edge of reason.

ℰ∕ᴆℰ∕ᴆ

The silken smoothness of the abyss he was exploring, defied Nick's expectations. She was matching his thrusts, pulling down on him. And the power of her muscle contractions shocked his system. He wanted to be inside her forever. And when she moaned softly, urging him on, he wanted to drown in the torrid pool of indefinable pleasure in which he was swimming. As Nick thrust deep inside her, a perfect fit, he hadn't realized years of wanting her would bring him so quickly to the edge. But when he attempted to slow the surge coursing through his abdomen, she moved to compensate. It so heightened his sensitivity he screamed her name. With years of repressed emotion flooding his hypersensitive body, he'd miscalculated his ability to hold back. And when he felt Dani's pelvic muscles drag hard on him, he was lost. He plunged deeper and faster than he imagined he could and growled deep in his throat. Then the explosion of a rolling climax racked his body, and he collapsed atop her.

"Don't stop," said a shocked Dani.

"Don't move," he begged, the exquisite pain of orgasm replacing his sublime pleasure. Then as he felt a slackening of the glorious tension in her abdomen, he withdrew from her.

"Why did you do that?" she asked, reaching for him.

"No, no, no, don't, not yet, too sensitive."

"But it felt so good— do it again."

"It's not that easy. I need some time."

"How much time?" she snapped.

"I'm sorry, Dani, I was too quick. I love you so much and wanted you so desperately, when I was inside you, I couldn't hold back. Next time, I promise, I'll—there will be a next time, won't there?"

"Yes—yes—yes. Kiss me."

Her hunger was clear, but Nick knew what she needed. Teasing her with his tongue and lips, he moved his fingers down her body. She pushed against his circling penetrating fingers, and when her breath came in sharp gasps, he brought her to the coursing undulations of an orgasm. And, though his eagerness for her had lasted only a few minutes, when she took hold of him again, he was aroused.

"Come inside again," she urged.

"Dani, stop. You know I want you more than I could ever explain, but we can't."

"I want you to."

"I used the only condom. It would be too risky."

"Don't care," she said petulantly. "You want me, I want you—it's worth the risk." Her hand circled about him, pulling down. "You can't stop now. I want to come when you're inside. Like you did. It felt so good. Come on—do it again—"

"Dani! Dani, stop! It's hard enough for me to stay sane around you. There's tomorrow. I'll get condoms—a case of condoms. We have to stop."

"You don't love me, or you'd do what I want." The hand she raised to slap him was deflected. "I hate you. Anyone else would—"

"I'm not anyone else—neither are you. Where is this coming from?"

"I've spoken to friends," Dani snapped. "They say their guys just do it, again and again. Like right after one another."

"Is that how you want me to treat you? Like an object. Just someone to fuck?"

Dani giggled. "Fuck? When did you ever say 'fuck'?"

"Quit swearing. I was making a point. We have plans remember?"

"Oh, so now, 'we' have plans. I guess that means Mr. College got what he wanted so it's back to Harvard. You are so selfish, I hate you."

"I'm not selfish at all, Dani. You will never know how hard it is for me to stop now. But we aren't just anybody. Think about what we want, our future. You want to get pregnant and risk all that?"

"So now you're all Mr. Mature. Well, it stinks. Just get off me."

"Oh, no, missy, you listen to me. I can make love to you, will make love to you, every minute I can when I get condoms, but not tonight." He caressed her cheek tenderly. "You don't really hate me, do you?"

"Yes, I really do."

He kissed her eyes. "Now?"

"Yes, I do."

He kissed her nose. "How about now?"

"Yes."

When he ran his tongue delicately over her lips and kissed her, she smiled. "No—I love you desperately, hopelessly, insanely, and I want you to make love to me every day until I die."

"That's a pretty big challenge."

Her eyes twinkled mischievously as she placed her hand on the subsided object of her affections. "I have every confidence in your abilities."

"Dani, no fair."

She smiled. "Just testing."

"You know I'm right," Nick said softly. "We have plenty of time."

"Before you go back to Harvard?"

He smiled indulgently and pecked her on the lips. "I would like us to stay here until I go back to Harvard, but we can't. Seriously, you know I'm right. Come on, get dressed before we get into trouble."

☙❧

As they headed to the house, Nick encircled her with his arm and asked the question that up until now, she'd never taken seriously. "Dani, this is serious so don't blow me off. Will you marry me?"

"Like now?"

"I said don't fool around. Not about this. Will you marry me?"

"Have you ever doubted it?"

"Every time I leave you alone," Nick whispered.

"That doesn't show much faith in me."

"You're beautiful, smart, and funny. And from the little display, back there…well, you're pretty easy to get along with. Plus, it seems you're really into what we just did. Given a hint of encouragement, guys will be all over you."

"Why would I do that? I love you. I've always loved you."

"Soooo, you finally admit it," said Nick smugly. "You will marry The Brew-ster. I am irresistible."

"Not at this moment! Besides, shouldn't you get permission from my dad?"

"Already did."

"When?" Dani asked.

"We were bailing hay out on the east pasture, you were wearing a red sweater with sparkly things on. You went back to the house to get lunch, at which time—"

"Are you serious? That was years ago—you were twelve."

"And your point?"

"Shouldn't you sort of update your resume or something?"

"Nope. He said it was okay then, and dammit, I'm holding him to it."

"He's six-four, Nick. Probably bench presses three hundred pounds."

"Right...yes. Farmer, muscles, lifting stuff all day. The need for caution and an update seems entirely appropriate. I will approach him...soon."

"Ah-ha! Now, tell me again. What's irresistible about a wuss?"

Nick pulled Dani into his arms. "If you could only see what's in my head, you'd know I'm the most committed guy you'll ever meet. I promise at the drop of a hat, without a second's notice, on peril of death, for ever and ever amen, to always be there for you."

"Yes," said Dani.

"Yes what?"

"Yes, Nickolas Christopher Brewster, I will marry you. Good grief—with that many clichés, what's a girl to do?"

His smile said it all, and with an ache in the pit of his stomach, which only she could satisfy, he kissed her goodnight.

ᶜ⁄ᵟᶜ⁄ᵟ

Dani ran upstairs to watch him go, and after his truck disappeared into the distant trees, she caught sight of herself in the cheval mirror. Did she look different now, had her experience permanently etched joy into her face? Was the flushed color of her cheeks as perfect as it looked? Would the blush stay forever as reminder of her experience? Stripping off her clothes, Dani threw everything into the hamper, and jumped into the shower. Adjusting the head, she closed her eyes as the pulsing jet set her body tingling with a new sensitivity. But even the warm rivulets of water streaming sensuously over her, could not produce the divine sensations of his fingers on her skin. How would she cope with waiting until he made love to her again?

Afterward, sitting in bed, head a whirlwind of dreams coming true, she could still feel the satisfying hardness of him inside her. She knew that some of her friends had been horribly treated after they had sex with someone they thought cared for them. But she knew without a doubt that the man she had chosen would love her for eternity. She spent a few minutes writing in her diary and closed with the words. *I love Nickolas Brewster and have positively no doubt he loves me.* Then she practiced her signature. Dani Brewster. Dani Brewster. Dani Brewster.

Chapter 18

Jo was in her office overlooking the pool. A warm breeze flowed through the open window carrying the sound of moving water and a faint smell of chlorine. When she lived by the ocean, it was breaking waves and the sea's briny fragrance. Back then, waves were a comforting companion. They bolstered her spirit during lonely days and nights as she waited for her husband to return from this or that trip to points exotic. Now, a man-made water feature set in her forest oasis gave her the same feeling. But she was rarely alone as Dani and her friends had become poolside fixtures.

The two women had become firm friends, and as Jo watched the teens interact, it seemed there was an even more pronounced maturity about Dani. Jo's instinct told her she and Nick's relationship had taken on a new dimension during his last visit. And that dimension was probably sex. It was abundantly clear the pair were besotted with each other, so it was but a matter of time. However, Jo decided to say nothing to Mark. He probably had his own suspicions, after all his daughter was, by his own admission eighteen, going on eighty.

Dani really was a good kid, the sort anyone would be proud of. She worked hard at school and on the farm. Knew who she wanted to be, and how to get where she wanted to go. Of course, there had been a couple of over-heated teenage dramas. But Jo chalked up the amped emotion and defiant irrationality more to Dani's bi-polar disorder than being a teen. For the most part, the young woman's confidence and curiosity led to teenage exuberance and normal boundary pushing. She'd been there herself. Had given her own father the grey hair he'd rather not have. Dani was simply finding herself. Naturally, she'd given Mark a heads up on one or two things. But she'd leave him to get his head around Dani and Nick and sex, in his own time.

As for she and Mark, he never let a day pass without talking to her. It felt good knowing he was there. And as Jo let her mind meander, it was easy to imagine being part of his family. He had said it was up to her. He had declared himself and it was now up to her to set the pace of their relationship. That had been so smart, and she couldn't help smiling. Mark read her like a book. He so got her. Who she was. What she wanted from life. And who she needed to be. She loved that about him. And she so appreciated that their relationship had become a loving partnership. They still hadn't slept together, because of her conflicted emotions about grief and guilt and moving on. But they enjoyed a more empathetic relationship than many people who did share their bodies. His patience with her seemed limitless and she had no doubt his sensitivity was drawing them closer. Moreover, unlike Chris, whose job was the be all and end all of their existence together, Mark had no trouble making time for her. He was a phone call away. Moreover, Mark had proven his devotion time and time again, something Chris's insular, aloof personality had not allowed him to do.

And as she took stock, there it was, front and center on her desk. One of her lists. She'd been making them since she was a kid. Weighing the pros and cons of everything from rock bands to sneakers. In fact, the only time she didn't make one was when she and Chris ran off and got married. And look what angst that brought her. Nevertheless, still making them was childish. Sort of. And setting stock in them was surely crazy. Maybe. No matter. They were part of who she was, and in order to reconcile the final raw piece of her emotional pie, the little voice in her head, had to be satisfied. She had to get to work and opened the drawer to put it away. She hesitated, questioning just how foolish she was being. No kind of list would convince her head of something that wasn't in her heart. And she wondered if Mark would be amused. He had said her quirkiness fascinated him, and God knows lists were up there on her list of "my quirky things."

Settling back in her chair, she couldn't help going over it one last time. It started with "Attitude."

Thinking back as generously as she was able, Jo couldn't help hating Chris's predictability. At first, it came off as endearing. But in retrospect, she was never really happy with the Friday night ritual dinner at "our special place." Or the no-getting-on-an-airplane-on-my-day-off rule. And while she noted that being a pilot made him naturally predisposed toward caution and the orderly management of things, Chris never did anything wild or the least bit spontaneous. She had scribbled the Maine towns of Naples, Egypt, Peru, Mexico, and China in Mark's column, and right away, he had the advantage.

Moving down, "Parenting" caught her eye.

Like her husband, Mark appeared to be the perfect father figure. They both had a column filled with steady job, good provider, no excesses of alcohol, smoking, or gambling. Initially, they both looked good on paper. The sort of guy who should marry and surround himself with kids. Kids she couldn't have. And as she remembered the agony of the years trying to get pregnant. How Chris blamed her. How he wouldn't even discuss adopting. And her heart led her to the word Dani in Mark's column. They had spoken about her efforts, and she knew her barrenness wasn't a problem for him. After all, he had a child. A child who at some point would be a mom and fill any void in Jo's heart. Half way down the alphabet and without even trying, Mark had the clear advantage.

Jo smiled as she arrived at the final item—sex. Chris had been perfunctory, businesslike, and predictable. As his profession required him to be. But Mark as a lover? Her smile widened. She only had clues. The warm, fuzzy, feel-good kind. Was that enough? She surmised yes, because she felt that underneath his kind, considerate exterior something indescribably passionate simmered. It radiated from him when he walked toward her. Oozed from him when they sat thigh to thigh on the deck. And filled the room during the quiet moments they shared. Despite no experience to back up her theory, Mark still had the advantage.

A tear slipped from Jo's eye and her hand shook as a revelation of change washed over her. She was at the end of her list and there appeared to be no competition in the, who-is-best-for-me-challenge. And as she swiped a tear from her eye, she finally accepted that memories of her dead husband had been an illusion. She had been at best hopefully sentimental. She had stayed too long in a place that was convenient and comfortable. She had sacrificed true love to be with someone who simply shared her space. She had set aside the truth for an illusion of her own making. With Mark, she felt his underlying passion. She experienced the frisson when their fingers touched accidentally. Felt her heart pound at unexpectedly seeing him across a room. Now she knew what was missing in her life and she never realized it until now.

Mark's patient devotion had won her over. There need

be no more what ifs. No more give me times. No more I need to get my head togethers. It was all there in black and white. And as she dropped the list into the shredder, and watched it ribbon, any threads of guilt she had harbored went with it. She had exorcised the demons in her head and would now only listen to her heart.

Chapter 19

It seemed like an eternity, but with her heart and mind finally in a joint place, Jo planned something special to show Mark how much she cared. However, a call from Marvin at Bean Town Musicality put a damper on that.

He "suggested" she steal away from her rural retreat and venture down to Boston. Apparently, Maine had rekindled her "quirky essence," and sponsors who had distanced themselves from her were demanding her attention. As always when she had a crisis of conscience, she called Mark.

"You know, I really dread going," she said. "It's flattering to be in demand again, but the timing is pitiful. The drive in is horrendous. I'll have to leave the girls unattended. And…what if I have to stay over, who'll feed them?"

Mark smiled. "Sounds to me like a bunch of hooey. If you ask me, you're making excuses to appease that little inner demon."

"Well, no one is asking you, Mr. Sarcasm."

"Didn't you just call me to discuss going down?"

"Damn, you always win. Yes, I did."

"Then what's really going on? You sound different."

"How so?"

"I don't know," Mark said, testing the water. "Like you're resigned to something?"

"I simply don't want you to be second fiddle to a job, like I was."

"That's new. I know you owe Marvin a certain loyalty for sticking by you. But come on, what's really happening?"

"I was planning something."

"Oh, really. And this something is so important it can't wait a few hours?"

"Maybe it can't."

"I thought you always said work would come first."

"That was before," said Jo smugly.

"Before what?"

"Before it's none of your beeswax, that's what."

"It's me right? I'm irresistible," said Mark, affecting a comically sexy voice. "You're planning a fabulous dinner to thank me for Nana's pond. I knew that would clinch it and put me on top of your must have list."

"You don't know dip," Jo fired back.

"Okay, so I'll drive you down. We can book into a swanky hotel, and I'll cash in one of those dinner dates you still owe me. And as you well know, Dani will be perfectly able to look after the girls."

"You'll be alone all day while I'm in meetings. What will you do?"

"Now you're reaching."

"What about the house?"

"Sweetie, this is Maine," said Mark. "No-one is going to come in and trash the house. Besides, as Dani will probably want to put in her time by the pool she might as well stay over. I really don't see any problem."

"Know-it-all."

Mark laughed aloud. "And don't you forget it."

అుఎు

Seven a.m. saw Jo and Dani sharing breakfast on the deck. Dani was in pajamas, fluffy bunny slippers, her hair a riot of unpinned copper curls. "Dad should be here in a few minutes. Are you two staying over in Boston?"

"What did your dad say?"

"He said it was up to you."

"Then it's probably a no," said Jo. "This is my sanctuary now. A day in the city is plenty. I hate the thought of spending time away from here."

"Why?" said Dani, sitting cross-legged on her seat. "I can't wait to finish with school, start up my veterinary practice, and get a job in a zoo somewhere exotic."

"So, no cats and dogs for you?"

"I'll always have dogs and probably horses. But I want to treat tigers and elephants, whales and alligators. I want to be Doctors Without Borders, for animals. I have big plans."

"Of that I have no doubt," said Jo. "But there's a lot to be said for peace and tranquility."

"Yeah…boring…boring…and boring."

Jo laughed. "My office is on Boylston Street, which is not far from Nick's place. Shall I drop in and say hi for you?"

"I'd rather you brought him home."

"I bet you would. How's it going with you two?"

"Good," said Dani coyly.

"Just good?"

"When he's here, better than good," said Dani. "He's…well, he's awesome. When he's not here, I can hardly bear it."

"Thought he was only your math partner," said Jo, more obvious than she intended.

Dani gave Jo "the look."

"Oops, didn't mean to pry, guess there's more, huh?"

"We have...what do you oldsters call it? an understanding."

"Hey, less of the oldsters, missy," said Jo. "But I take the point. Mind my own business. I will say, however, that your dad thinks he's terrific, so you've won half the battle."

"What about you?"

"I like him too."

"Not Nick silly. What about you and Dad, do you have an understanding?"

"You better ask him."

Dani smirked. "I did."

"You're kidding, you did not! What did he say?"

"Ah-ha! Now that's the tone of a woman without an understanding. He likes you more than I can say. But I get the feeling he's bothered about something. As you'll have a couple hundred miles drive, and all day in Boston, I guess you'll work that out."

"I'll be working," said Jo matter-of-factly.

"So, you'll be totally silent all the way there and all the way back."

"Pretty mature for your age, aren't you?"

Dani smiled her approval at what she understood was a compliment.

"So, do I say anything to Nick or what?"

"Can you take him a note?" asked Dani.

"Sure."

"But you absolutely cannot read it or show it to Dad."

"Dani, please, I wouldn't dream of it. Now be quick, he'll be here any minute."

"Do you have any of those note-card thingys?"

"Red box, top drawer of the bureau—be quick."

As Dani scribbled her card, Jo threw a mountain of paperwork in the back of her SUV.

Mark was in the driver's seat when Dani came out. "Hi, pumpkin," he said. "Might have known we'd be waiting for something from you."

Jo took the envelope and teasingly held it up to the light. "Umm, now I wonder what this is?"

"You promised," whispered Dani.

"It's safe with me," said Jo. "Now, remember two things. Medication and sunscreen."

Yes, Mommy Dearest," Dani said, realizing she hadn't, in fact, taken her meds. Then, with a wave and a blown kiss, she watched the car disappear from sight.

Chapter 20

With the late morning sun warming, and blinding ripples on the pool beckoning, Dani settled on a chaise. She'd washed the breakfast dishes, made her bed, and refilled the cooler. Now, with the girls peacefully bedded down on a large blanket beside her, she put on a headset and closed her eyes. The music had her floating on a cloud of erotic anticipation as she recalled the exquisite things Nick did to her body.

With heads low and flat, ears picking up the faintest sound, the dog's hackles rose. And when a vehicle turned onto the drive, they silently rose to their feet. Charity moved forward first and took a half step off the blanket with her paw hovering. A measured growl rumbled in her throat and Faith and Hope came alongside.

When the truck pulled to a halt in front of the garage, all three took off down the path barking furiously.

Shocked into action by the unexpected commotion, Dani sat up. She turned toward the barking, but as she didn't recognize the truck, she decided to let the girls scare off whoever had invaded her deeply passionate dream space. She laid her head back on the chaise and returned to the erotic ministrations of her favorite doctor-to-be. She slapped at the dogs when she felt them jostling beside her.

"Get down, you silly girls," she said, pushing them away.

The dogs continued to growl menacingly, and an unexpected coolness overshadowed her.

"Howdy, miss," he said.

"Whoa!" snapped Dani. "Where the hell did you come from?"

"My truck."

"Jeez, really? I know that. Who are you?"

"Name's Chase, come to see Ms. Weston—she home?"

Dani wrapped her pareo about her body. "No...er...she'll be back soon. What do you want?"

"Donaldson Brothers said she wants some logs cut. Swung by on the off chance, I could get started."

"Well, I don't know anything about that. She never mentioned it."

"Well, I'm sure Snappy Donaldson spoke to her."

"As I said, she never mentioned it. You better come back another time."

"Dang, that's a crock. Don't have the wherewithal to be coming and going for nuthin'. Could I maybe just get started?"

The dogs growled hard when Chase took a step forward.

"Girls, sit down and shush," Dani said. "Sorry about that, they're very protective."

"I can see that. No sweat, I know when I'm beaten." His voice was rough-hewn, oozing testosterone. "See, miss, it's like this. I came a ways. You say she'll be back soon. Could I wait?"

Dani blushed, caught in a lie. The girls remained in a defensive position between her and the stranger. However, as Dani swung her legs off the chaise to assume a more dignified position, she kicked a can of soda, which catapulted into him. "Oh, God, I'm so sorry."

"Don't apologize, no hardship being attacked by a beautiful woman. You Ms. Weston's gal?"

"No, I'm house-sitting for her. Look, you should probably go and come back tomorrow. I can't help you."

"Oh, sugar, you can help me plenty," Chase said. He eyed her body appreciatively as he ran a tanned hand over his chin. "I got a chainsaw that's in need of some hard work."

The suggestiveness wasn't lost on Dani. But she was warming to the handsome twenty-something's playfulness. "Really? Do you want to leave your number and I'll give it to her?"

"Don't have no phone. Prefer to do things face-to-face, if you know what I mean."

"I understand innuendo," Dani said. "Do you always talk so suggestively to strangers?"

"Only if they look like you."

"Sheesh," Dani said, unconvinced. Jo and her dad had said call them if there was an emergency. Chase whatever his name was, wasn't it. "I'm really not sure what time she'll be home. Seriously, could you come back tomorrow?"

"Yeah, I could. But it's a ways home. Mind if I sit a while. Maybe bum a drink from that cooler?"

"Sure. Where are my manners? Girls, move back. Lie down." The dogs moved to a position behind her.

"They's good dogs, got names?" asked Chase.

"Faith, Hope, and Charity."

"Cute. And you?"

"Dani."

"Well, Miss Dani, pleasure to meet you." He held out a hand.

Dani was flattered someone his age found her worthy

of flirting. And she felt a fluttering of something familiar when she took his well-worked hand. "Did the Donaldson's really send you?"

"Nah," said Chase casually. "Heard 'em talking at Metcalf's. If I go through them, they take twenty percent. Thought I'd get a jump on them, came over on the off-chance."

"Very enterprising. Aren't you afraid to tick them off," asked Dani. "Word gets around you're jumping the gun, nobody will hire you."

Chase smiled. "They will. I'm the best gyppo around."

He was sitting on a chaise alongside Dani, and when he turned to face her, out of the sun's glare, he was movie star good-looking. His eyes were coal black and mysterious, he had the long dark hair of a rock-star, and his skin was tanned. Dani blushed as she realized she was thinking his looks promised an exotic, and possibly dangerous, personality.

"Modesty is clearly not what you're best at."

Chase Markum had seen that look before, and a youngster like Miss Dani wasn't worldly enough to hide such introspection from a man like him. She looked good, with that flaming hair and perfect skin. And while her mind might tell her one thing, experience told him that with a little encouragement her body would take off in an entirely different direction. He smiled warmly. He was imagining how those long legs would feel wrapped around him, and how loudly she'd beg for more when he gave her his special kind of personal attention. "So, you don't think she'll be back today?"

"She was planning to. Could be around five or maybe seven or eight-ish. I think it depends on her meeting."

Chase ran a hand through his hair. "Umm. Time is money, and that's a bunch. Could get in a couple of trees by that time. I best push off. Sittin' here jawin' ain't gonna make my truck payment. Will you tell her I stopped by, and I'll swing back tomorrow."

"Sure, no problem." As Dani watched him leave, T-shirt barely restraining a perfectly muscled body, she couldn't help focusing on his lean toned thighs and a butt that fit jeans in all the right places. She mouthed a "wow."

Sinking back on her chaise, Dani took a deep calming breath. The rock-star woodsman had rattled her sensibility, and as she listened to the sound of his retreating boots, she closed her eyes. As she absorbed the sun's warmth, she drifted into sleep amid images of Nick making love to her. However, his lithe, blond, elegance was fractured by flashes of a darkly compelling more muscular figure. It was Chase Markum.

ℯↄℯↄ

Dani heard footsteps beneath her consciousness, and the rumbling in the dogs throats returned—

"Excuse me again, miss," said Chase.

"Whoa," said Dani, once again bolt upright. "You scared the bejeezus out of me, I thought you'd gone."

"Nope, still here. It's a real long drive home. Could I change my mind, wait a while, see if she comes back? Maybe have that drink."

"Sure. What would you like?"

"Got beer?"

"Not real beer. I don't drink," she lifted the cooler lid. "There's root beer."

He pulled a face.

"Or Pepsi?"

"That's a pussy drink," he said, casting his eyes over her body.

She laughed. "Then it's all down to OJ."

"Hold that thought," he said. "I'll be right back."

Chase went to his truck and flipping the lid off a box on the passenger side floor, he removed a bottle of vodka. Then prying away a corner of the material at the base of the seat, he removed a small plastic bag containing several tiny white pills.

He might not be getting a job today. But these babies would ensure this would still be a good day for him.

Returning poolside, he poured a large measure of vodka into a plastic cup and topped it off with orange juice.

Dani smiled. "Is that good?"

"Wanna try it?"

Her nose wrinkled and she giggled. "I'm really not supposed to…"

"It's mostly juice, how bad can it be?"

"Okay. The rule is one sip. I can handle that." Dani took a sip. "You're right, it's juice." Then she took several slugs, emptying the cup. "Umm, really good juice. I like it."

"Screwdriver," Chase said.

"Excuse me?"

"That's what it's called, a screwdriver, want some more?"

"Sure, OJ is OJ."

He poured a larger measure of vodka, and as he added juice, palmed two of the tiny pills into her cup. "You live here?"

"Told you I'm house-sitting. Not too swift are you? But Jo does let me come over to use the pool whenever I want."

"I can see that," he said. "You have a great…tan."

His delay on the last word left Dani in no doubt what he really wanted to say. She ignored the implication and continued sipping her screwdriver.

"This is a great piece of property, what does sumthin like this cost?"

"She paid my dad a hundred and fifty thousand."

He whistled. "Damn, she must be loaded. What's she like, maybe she needs a friend?"

Dani giggled. "Not sure you're the type of friend she needs."

"I'd make a great friend."

"How so?"

"Know how to make a woman feel like a woman." His eyes darkened as he ran his icy drink cup over her thigh.

Delicious shivers ran from the top of her spine to her belly, and the hair on Dani's body bristled. "I'm sure you do, but for now, that's uncomfortably cold."

Chase removed the cup, but not his hypnotic glare. "Drink up, there's plenty more where that came from."

"Thank you. I think I will."

As Dani lay back focusing on her surroundings, the world seemed brighter, more sharply defined. Things she hadn't noticed before stood out. Colors she thought common, screamed with a new vibrancy, demanding her attention. The trees danced in the breeze, pendulous and heavy with the essence of pine, bending to lend their fragrance to her skin. And the rushing brook, flowing swift across rocks and pebbles full with a crescendo of discordant notes, sang a Koto serenade to the sun. Birds, in pairs, brightly colored, and exotic, warbled a melodic spring symphony, celebrating life, love, and new beginnings.

Dani had never felt so blissfully alive, emphatically energized, and ready to take on the world. Despite what she'd heard about alcohol clouding the mind, hers was crystal clear. And her body tingled. She felt spectacular. The day had taken on a new dimension, and she reveled in the freedom it gave her.

"I need to move." The voice she heard was hers. But its quality was different, more mature, and worldly. "I'm going in."

"Good idea," said Chase.

She watched as he removed cowboy boots, black leather, inset with orange and blue snakeskin and silver toecaps. He aligned them neatly beneath the chaise.

"You're soooo tidy," Dani giggled.

"Cost me three hundred bucks, nice ain't they?" He unbuckled his belt.

"You got swim shorts?" Dani asked.

"Don't need 'em," he said, revealing he did not have any underwear.

Dani dived into the water, moving away from him with long easy strokes. If the water was cold, she certainly couldn't feel it. And as she tumbled into a backstroke, she caught a glimpse of him naked. Planting her feet on the treated aggregate below, she half rose from the water. She watched him raise his arms and run long artistic fingers through hair shining blue-black in the sun. She gasped at the bronzed, perfectly muscled creature before her. She'd had little experience. But his body, clearly defined by the action, stirred something lustful deep inside her belly. Pushing water behind her, she backed against the pool wall. And as the cocoon of water flowed viscous in her body's wake, she studied him. Her heart pounded when he made no attempt to hide his manhood and it was impressive. She had been nervous about accepting Nick inside her. But this was a real man. The sort of man reserved for movies. The sort of man who made you beg for mercy. The sort of man she had dreamed about.

As he walked around the pool, Dani smiled nervously. The unfettered sight of the most intriguing part of his anatomy had awakened a reckless demon in her. And knowing her body would require several energetic laps in the pool to quell the interest raised by so extravagant a promise, she prepared to push off from the wall. Before she could move, he dived in. He emerged, inches from her face, swept his saturated hair aside, and brushed his body against hers.

Electrifying pulses radiated between them, and before Dani could move aside, he planted a kiss on her mouth. It was a fitting prelude to everything she'd read about. But with a languid blink of her eyes, she pushed him away.

Chase knew exactly what effect the pill-laced Screwdriver and his body were having on Dani, and he pinned her into the pool's corner. "This isn't fair," he whispered, melding into her.

"What isn't fair?" she said, breathing shallow.

"I'm naked—you have a suit on."

She smiled. "And it stays on."

Considering he'd given her two pills, Dani was more alert than he would have thought. But she was in better shape, and taller than any of the girls he'd previously tackled. He resorted to charm.

Smiling disarmingly, Chase brushed her cheek with his knuckles. "Come on, don't be cruel," he pleaded. "I can't see anything, we're in the water."

"It stays on." Dani ducked under his arm and with graceful strokes headed for the deep end.

He followed her, equally comfortable in the water, matching her speed. When they paused for breath, he approached her again. "You're pretty fast, done any racing?"

"County all-around champion, State, freestyle and backstroke."

"Right on," he said. "You're good—wanna race me?"

"Sure, if you don't mind getting your butt kicked." Dani set off down the pool with him close behind. And when she returned to the deep end, she waited for him to catch up.

"That wasn't fair…you got a head start…we need to do this proper."

"Okay. Get out," said Dani. "We'll do a racing start."

When Chase climbed from the pool, glistening water deeply defining his musculature, Dani's focus was on his lower mid-section.

"Like what you see?" he asked.

Despite the cool water, Chase's arousal was unmistakable, and when he pulled Dani from the water, there was enough force to propel her into his arms. As anticipated, his erection grew hard against her belly, and when he pressed icy cold lips against hers, he felt her arc into him. Kissing her deep, he let her taste the sweet vodka-orange of his tongue and mentally high-fived. "Here, finish your drink," he said, picking up her glass. He ran a hand down her leg. "Then I'll kick your butt."

With the last two swallows of her drink, Dani detected a slight bitterness, but was too delightfully content to pay it any mind. And when Chase put his hand on her belly, she was hopelessly distracted. Patting his hand playfully aside, Dani giggled. "You can't catch me in, or out, of the water; now line up, you call it."

In two races, she beat him soundly, and Chase called for a breather.

"Enough, girl, you're too good for me, I need another drink." He brushed her breast with his hand as he helped her from the pool. And when she didn't protest, he knew she was thawing. After leading her to the chaises, he made more Screwdrivers and set a glass beside her. "Got any lotion?" he asked, lightly brushing her arm. "We could burn something fierce out here."

"Cooler," she slurred.

"Want me to put some on your back?"

Dani flipped onto her belly. "Please, can never reach, it always gets burned."

As he massaged ice-cold lotion into her heated skin, Dani felt his fingers dissolve into her, stroking the very fibers of her being. Then he flipped the clasp on her bra. "Na-ah," she snapped. "Leave it."

"Calm down, little lady," he said smoothly. "Gotta do the whole area. Unless you want a line, which I have to tell you is not attractive." He oiled as much of her back as he could reach. "Okay, you're done, my turn."

Chase lay on his back, encouraging Dani to oil his entire body. And when his muscles corded hard beneath her touch, she was fascinated. She enjoyed the power she had over the powerful sexual creature before her. And without any concern for consequences, she proceeded with confident circular strokes, around and about his upper thighs. Moving meticulously up his hipbones and across his belly, there was no doubt Chase was all man. And while she had deliberately avoided his explicitly aroused area, when she looked at his closed eyes and the dark lashes fluttered, she knew she wanted to minister to a particularly sensitive spot. But that wouldn't be right. Dani withdrew her hand.

"If you don't oil everywhere, I'll burn." Chase took her hand and placed it firmly in his groin. "You don't want to be responsible for that, do you?"

Breathing shallow, Dani's palm encountered the silky, butter-smooth, feel of him. She found it impossible to continue in circles, and moving carefully back and forth, she grasped him around. Her heart raced at his size. And as he continued to expand in her hand, her head became a cotton cloud of possibilities. "Lookin' gooood," she drawled. "Got it'd done."

Chase grasped her wrist. "Keep going, I burn real easy."

"Kay—jus-ist a bid lunger," she slurred, not quite understanding why her words sounded disconnected. Deep in the back of Dani's mind, a muddled series of events collided and vaguely niggled. Nevertheless, she remained diligent in her goal to prevent the sun from causing marks on his perfect Adonis body.

"Come closer," he said, pulling her into a kiss.

When she moved close to him, his hands were like feathers on her body. Ultra-light, delicate and ethereal. And the air that would normally strain through them in flight was oil and her flesh. With her nerve receptors screaming, channeling erotic impulses throughout her system, her desires welled. The air seemed thinner, taking her breath. The breeze seemed sensually probing, making her shiver. And her mind raced, as she fought her way back to the present. "Waiting me to rest," she babbled. "Need a drink, getting dehydra-tay-ted."

Reaching for a drink, Dani took a large swallow. She hoped it might calm her ardor and quell whatever was chasing inhibition from her body. It was the nectar of a rainbow. Light and bright and all things pure. And something hit her with clear unquestioning light, and guiltless unsullied freedom. She was once more invincible, in control, ready for anything. Life was wonderful, and she knew exactly how it felt to be a woman. And as she surrendered to the warmth enveloping her body. She effortlessly floated on one of the clouds that had deserted the sky feeling Nick's hand running down the inside of her thigh. When she opened her eyes, Chase was there. "Silly you," she chided, swatting his arm. "What you doin' with 'em hands?"

Chase smiled. "I know how to beat you. Wanna try racing me again?"

"Course…" said Dani, dropping into the pool. She beat him over two laps.

"Okay, here's the deal," he said breathlessly hanging onto poolside. "I need an incentive. What if...I beat you, the suit comes off."

She knew he couldn't beat her. "Deal."

Chase beat her soundly on the next lap. And when they stopped to get their breath, his hard body pinned her against the pool wall. Immediately recognizing the glazed eyes and enraptured expression, he flipped the clip on her bra, and let her breasts feel the pressure of his teeth. And when he felt her nails rake his back, he ducked under water and removed the bottom of her suit. Knowing she would be irretrievably his for at least forty minutes, Chase devoured her.

All Dani felt were therapeutic waves delicately lapping against her body. With eyes closed arms akimbo, she trailed watery ribbons back and forth. She was motion perfected. Water and sun mingling in time. A basking mermaid. And the passion she felt was the water breaking on her tail. It came up between her arms, teasing and tormenting her, landing with the lightness of vapor on her upturned face. And when it touched her exposed and receptive breasts, she squirmed with pleasure. Rivulets of fire flowed through her. Her skin was so sensitive she could feel the sun's heat through the water. And moaning softly, every scale it touched had the exquisite imprint of the rhythmic waves' assault. Undulating joy, like nothing she'd ever experienced, transported her to another place. And overtaken by a force she was powerless to resist, she surrendered to the mind-numbing sensations the pounding waves created. It flowed delirious this never-ending tide. Back and forth, up and down with rhythmic cadence enough to overwhelm her. And to quell the beating in her bursting heart, she dove beneath the waves, to be uplifted and carried back to shore. And she was a sandpiper advancing and retreating, occasionally touched, but never overrun by the power of the relentless ocean. She simply rose fulfilled, independent, in control of her destiny challenging the power of the water. And as the sun warmed her face, and the breeze ran heavy through her lashes, a whispered voice was smoke ahead of a developing storm. She became anxious. But could not stop. She was compelled to keep running back and forth, matching the tide's ebbing and flowing. Then it surged, increased in strength, and threatened to engulf her. No matter, she imagined—I'm a bird. If needed, I will fly. And she continued running. Ebb and flow, some long, some short, and the waves broke mercilessly. The tide ran stronger, its power biting into her very core. It was faster, deeper, and more intense than she had ever imagined. It picked her up and threw her helpless against the rocks. And still it came. Pounding and building, dragging her back to the rushing waves. It carried her aloft, running swifter and angrier than she'd ever known. Fighting for breath, and weak from running, she could resist no longer. The ocean was too deep. It plunged her downward with a force that near engulfed her. And as the raging torrent lifted her skyward, its dominance terrified her. She could hold out no longer. Vainly clawing at the current, from which there was no escape, she dropped into the abyss.

All seeing, all knowing, Dani's soul looked down. But she wasn't ready to die. Vehemently rejecting the encroaching blackness, her mind concentrated on the deepest point of the enveloping tide. She could feel its power, sense its urgency, and understood what she needed to do. The sea continued its assault. Rising and falling, coming and going. And she answered with stamina and a will to survive, battling through whatever it brought. It bruised and caressed, loved and hated her. By will alone, she broke through the white-capped crest of foaming swell.

She matched the strength of the raging storm. Pushing upward, and back, pulling power with muscle alone. And as she broke through the dark, deep places, the world erupted into monstrous plumes of fireworks.

As explosions reverberated through every inch of her body, Dani heard screaming. It was her voice echoing and she was begging for more. And the most exquisite pain answered her plea. Colors she'd never seen, emotions she couldn't explain, and feelings she didn't want to control, overwhelmed her. She never wanted the explosion to end. Then, as the tide subsided, retreating into the distance, her dream evaporated into clouds. She breathlessly whispered "Nick."

Chapter 21

The sun was setting when Dani woke, and the girls were anxiously milling around the chaise. Horrified that she'd fallen asleep in the sun, she checked for burns. Her shoulders and arms were sore. Her face was on fire, and she had an odd ache in her belly, which she wrote off as hunger. "Silly willies," she said, stroking her canine companions. "Why'd you let me sleep so long, you must be hungry too?" As she attempted to stand, a splitting headache and sweeping dizziness overcame her. "Whoa, Nellie, did I get sunstroke or what? Come on, girls, let's get inside. I've had the dream to end all dreams. It'll take at least five pages in my diary,"

When Dani entered the house, the message machine was blinking.

"Hi, pumpkin," said her Dad. "We'll be leaving Boston around five, so depending on rush hour traffic, we should be home around seven-forty-five."

Dani looked at the clock, it was seven, and damning the sun for giving her such a headache, she put out the girls' food and proceeded to the bathroom. Catching sight of herself in the mirror, she gasped. Her shoulders and breasts exhibited angry blotches and her lips were crimson and swollen. "Good grief," she said, shaking her head. "That's the last time I fall asleep in the sun, I'm a Ubangi." She climbed into the shower and turned on the cold water.

ఌఌఌ

By seven-fifty, Dani had set out a supper of salad and quiche. She was opening a bottle of wine, when her dad and Jo pulled onto the drive.

"Well look at you," said Mark as he entered the kitchen. "You're quite the little hostess, any chicken with that quiche?"

"Yes, Dad. But as you always point out, I'm not leaving it out because we'll all get salmonella."

"Really, right off with sass." Mark shot an exasperated look at Jo.

"Not my fault. Simply responding to conditioning."

"Now, now, team," said Jo. "It's been a long day. Let's have a nice dinner and talk about something non-confrontational."

"I will now bring out the chicken," said Dani as she sashayed to the fridge.

Mark couldn't help noticing her back. "You all right, Dani? You look a bit toasted."

"Fell asleep in the sun."

Jo walked over and touched Dani's lip. "Did you use that sun block I gave you?"

Dani nodded. "Duh, yes. Slathered it all over—several times."

"I think with your fair skin you're going to have to do it more often. That lip looks sore."

"It's fine," said Dani. "I'll put cream on it at bedtime."

"Make sure you do," repeated Jo.

"I said I'm fine, jeez—what is with you two?"

"Dani!" Mark cut in. "Manners."

"It's okay, Dad. Jo isn't offended, we're BFFs."

Jo smiled. "Right, no offence taken."

Mark raised an eyebrow. "BFFs?"

"Best friends forever," said Dani. "Sheesh, you have *got* to get up to speed."

"Well, I certainly thank you for enlightening me," said Mark coldly. "Now, enough of the smart mouth, let's eat."

"So sit," Dani snapped. "I'm ready."

On his way to the dining table, Mark picked up a pill-box on the counter. "What's this?"

"Oh shit," said Dani. "My pills. Damn it to hell and back. I fell asleep, then I took a shower—"

Mark opened the pillbox. "Dani, we've talked about this—a lot. I trusted you to take these as prescribed, you promised me. Without them, you're a harridan."

"I am so not," Dani whined. "You're just being mean."

Mark raised an eyebrow. "Oh, really? Damn it to hell and back? It looks like you have all three doses here. Breakfast, lunch, and dinner. You know what can happen when—"

"Yeah, yeah—I don't need the lecture. For Christ's sake, give them to me. I'll take them now."

Mark pulled the pillbox back. "You can't take them all at once. You know the drill, it's—"

"God, do I ever!" Dani snapped. "I've been listening to it for months."

"Dani, seriously," said Jo kindly. "Just how many doses have you skipped?"

Dani's eyes flashed. "Why do you both assume there's more? I mean, puleez—now you assume the worst of me."

Mark glanced at Jo. "Dani, let's not argue about this. Wait until your evening dose and tomorrow try to keep up."

"I didn't do it deliberately. I fell asleep—sheesh, what do you want from me?"

"I want you to behave like the grown up you constantly remind me you are."

"How can I be a grown up if you—"

"Guys, guys," interrupted Jo. "No harm done. Let's have our supper and change the subject. I'm sure a couple of missed doses aren't going to be disastrous."

Mark took Jo's hand. "Thank you—the voice of reason."

"That's why I'm here," Jo said calmly. "Now, Dani, pour me a glass of wine. We're celebrating my return to the advertising world's 'in crowd.'"

"Can I have one too?" Dani asked sheepishly.

Jo looked at Mark. "She's eighteen. In Italy and France, she'd have one at twelve."

"No meds, alcohol, and, helloooo, this is America."

"I know, darling," Jo said squeezing Mark's hand. "But I think one small glass will be okay."

Dani smirked. "I so love the voice of reason."

℮⁊℮⁊

As the women interacted, it became increasingly clear to Mark that his "little girl" was maturing fast. He suspected the backtalk came from missing her meds. But there were other more subtle changes in her that he suspected had everything to do with Nick. While he knew it would eventually happen, it was hard for him to accept she was no longer a child.

For her part, Dani appreciated how much Jo had mellowed her father. It was so obvious they were crazy about each other. As the trio ate, chatted about her plans for veterinary college, and Jo's latest jingles, Dani could hardly believe it would be a matter of weeks before she was on the first leg of her own career.

Jo could barely stop smiling, and it wasn't the wine. Her career was soaring. She finally knew where to go in her relationship with Mark. And as equally important, for the first time in her life, she understood what it was like to be part of a real family.

Chapter 22

As Chase Markum drove toward Mapletree Rise, he wondered whether he'd have an opportunity to reacquaint himself with the naïve redhead. She'd been a particularly luscious piece of tail, and recalling past conquests, he'd never before had the opportunity to tackle an up-market chick like her.

Stepping from his truck, Chase was delighted to see the young redhead by the pool with an older chick he assumed was the property owner. It would be a while before he would forget the image of the youngster's long legs and hungry suppleness. How she might open up and suck the tar out of him until he couldn't stand. Nevertheless, despite her youthful attributes, the sight of the other woman with the more mature body might be equally as fuckable.

Dani heard a truck swoop up the drive and thought it might be her father. But when the dogs leapt into protection mode, she followed their aggressive barking. She caught her breath seeing Chase swaggering toward them. He was combing his fingers through the length of his shining blue-black hair and his body seemed to radiate an aura of sexual promise. She pulled a towel over her legs, feigned sleep, and hoped he couldn't tell she'd had such a highly erotic daydream about him the day before.

As Chase stepped onto the pool surround, the sound of boots scuffing concrete caused a flutter in Dani's belly. And when he hovered over her in a frighteningly familiar pose, she became surprisingly uncomfortable.

"Howdy, Red," he said boldly. "We meet again." He turned to Jo. "You must be Ms. Weston?"

"Hello," said Jo, putting out her hand to calm the dogs. "Girls, quiet, sit down. Sorry about the noise, they're very protective."

"Yeah, same as last time," said Chase.

"Last time? Can we help you?"

"Name's Chase. Stopped by yesterday. Spoke to Miss Dani here. She said I should come back today. Heard up there at Metcalf's you was looking to have some lumber cut?"

His words flowed into Dani's consciousness, soft and low, like smoke in the wind. They made her involuntarily shudder, and she didn't know why. "Sorry, Jo, I forgot to mention it. Chase stopped by yesterday while you were at your meeting."

"Sorry Mr…er…Chase. I gave the job to someone else. The Donaldson brothers said they'd cover it."

"They's the ones sent me, ma'am," he lied.

"They said they would sub the job out. They also said they would call me and tell me who to expect. Why don't you wait here while I call them?"

Having a penchant for young girls, Chase glanced at the lithe, supple Dani. His mind flipped between the potential delights of the youngster to the more mature woman. And he deleted Jo from his mental screw list. There were too many fresh pieces of tail to bother with that. "Take your time, ma'am, got all day."

As Jo disappeared into the house, Dani squirmed uncomfortably on her chaise.

"Hi, sweet thing," Chase said, dropping down on the

chaise opposite. "Told you I'd be back. And once Ms. Weston checks my bona fides, how 'bout you haul that wiggle in my direction, and we take us a walk to where the job is." His eyes bore into her as his tongue ran lasciviously over his lips.

He was a lot closer than was comfortable, and Dani shrank back in her seat. "Why would I do that?"

"Come on, Red, didn't we have a nice conversation yesterday. Thought we had us a groovy thing going."

Dani was puzzled. "Thing? What thing?"

He ran a finger familiarly down her thigh. "I can feel you ain't no angel, so don't play hard-to-get. We could have us a real nice session right there." He nodded in the direction of the pool.

She slapped his hand from her leg. "Are you crazy? What the hell makes you think I'd do anything with you?"

"Come on, sweet cakes, loosen up. Some booze and a couple of these—" He pulled a small plastic bag of pills from his back pocket. "—and we'll have us a time."

Dani recoiled. He was behaving exactly like she imagined in her dream. But before she could say anything, Jo hailed him from the deck. "Hey, Chase, come up to the kitchen, Snappy Donaldson wants to talk to you."

"Later," Chase said, mouthing Dani a kiss. Then he jogged off to the house.

As Dani watched Chase disappear into the house, she was mortified. She couldn't possibly have done anything with that creep. She had dreamed they had sex in the pool. It was one of those hallucinations that plagued her when she didn't take her meds. Her mind had done that film thing, where she was there, outside her body, watching it happen. Besides, she knew she'd been asleep. She woke suddenly and her head had done that buzzing thing. It was her imagination. It *was* her imagination.

By the time Jo sat down beside her, Dani was deathly white, her mind a whirlwind of confusion.

"Dani, are you all right," asked Jo, dropping onto her chaise. "You look like you've seen a ghost?"

Dani had the feeling Chase wasn't ready to give up on her. And she wasn't keen on being anywhere she might have to see him again. "That man gives me the creeps, Jo. Can you get someone else to cut the lumber?"

"Come on, Dani, you know the score. The Donaldsons arrange things. They send the same bunch of guys from property to property. I'll tell you when he's coming, make yourself scarce, and you won't have to see him. Besides, look at him; compared to old man Benson, he's got to look better with his shirt off."

When Chase came from the house, bypassing them both with a wave, Dani hoped she'd never have to set eyes on him again.

Chapter 23

Jo was still in the throes of arranging her special date with Mark. But it seemed every time she got her ducks in a row, something came up. She tried to take it in stride, but specters of her life with Chris haunted her thoughts. She, Mark, and Dani had just finished dinner when a call from her boss at Bean Town once again conspired to wreck her plans.

Jo answered the call in monosyllabic tones before sharply hanging up the phone. "Dani," she said. "Would you mind clearing away, I want a word with your dad."

Mark raised an eyebrow. "Everything all right?"

"Sort of," said Jo. "Can we go outside?"

As the deck lights popped on, Mark could see she was worried. "I can't make out that look." He swirled his fingers about Jo's face. "Are you annoyed, disappointed, confused, what?"

"All of the above."

"Tricky—who was that on the phone?"

"Marvin at Bean Town. The sponsors want another meeting tomorrow."

"I knew it. We should have stayed over. Sorry, sweetie, I can't drive you tomorrow."

"I don't expect you to drop everything just to chauffer me to the office."

"I guess having no life is the price of success." He ran his fingers down her face. "What do they say? Be careful what you wish for."

"I had such plans for us tonight."

"Really?"

"I was going to ask you to stay over."

Mark pulled her close. "Stay over as in sleep over?"

Jo smiled. "I didn't exactly have sleep in mind."

"Oh, boy," said Mark, smiling. "And that isn't going to happen because…"

"You need to keep an eye on Dani, make sure she takes her pills."

"I can come back after she's taken them."

"You could. But I don't want our first time to be a quickie before the alarm goes off."

He laughed. "Well, never let it be said I have an aversion to the quickie. But I can see, in the larger scheme of things, how it could rankle."

"Dammit, Mark. Now you're making fun of me. How can you be so calm about our sex life? I'd planned to spend hours showing you exactly how I felt about you."

"That's not the sort of thing you should be saying minutes before you kick me off the property."

"I know. It seems we're doomed to failure. I had a plan for wild fun and games two nights ago, and I get summoned to Boston. I reboot my plan for a night of unadulterated bliss and, kapow, Boston calls and I have to dash off again."

Mark laughed again. "Fun, games, and unadulterated bliss…ummm. They sound like terrific plans." He pulled her close. "You know, one more night is still do-able. Besides, if you get called out again, I'll simply bring in the Peter's sisters as back-up."

Jo frowned. "Mark, it isn't funny. This is so what happened with Chris and me. It's taken me a while to work it all out, but basically, I hated his predictability and playing second fiddle to his damn job. Being alone all the time hurt. I felt like a spare part. An appendage to be aired out when there was nothing else to do. Our life as a couple was always mañana, and I don't want that happening to us."

Mark pushed aside a lock of her hair. "Then you need to sort yourself out career-wise vs. us-wise. You can't, in all good conscience, tell Marvin you're back on board if it means you only work when it suits you."

"I realize that," said Jo.

"Nor can you pack me off home whenever you want to avoid the quickie situation. Make no mistake, I'm all over the quickie if it's the only way we'll be a real couple. But remember, I'll be around no matter what. So, decide what you want, and together we'll stick with it."

"I have decided. I want you."

Mark smiled. "An excellent choice."

"But…"

"Dang those buts."

"A career isn't entirely out of my system," said Jo.

"Then we have a little problem, and it involves going down to Boston whenever they call."

"Do you hate me?" she whispered.

"Yes," said Mark, matter-of-factly. "You're right. It hurts not to be the most important thing in someone special's life."

Jo eyes widened. "You don't really hate me?"

Mark smiled and pecked her on the nose. "Of course not. I'm smart enough to let you come to terms with whatever you need to, at your own speed. If I push or pull in a direction you don't want to go, you'll simply end up hating me—"

"I don't think I could ever hate you."

"Then *we* have a splendid start. Go down to the city, do your thing, and tell Marvin to leave you alone for a few days. Plead female problems or something you know he isn't going to question you about. A few days will give us the opportunity to spend some time together and talk about where we realistically go from here."

"When did you get so smart?"

"Oh, it's always been there. You just fought me every step of the way."

Jo pecked him on the mouth. "Thank you for being you and loving me."

"And you would be where on that subject?"

She smiled. "Getting there."

Chapter 24

As Mark loaded supplies into the back of his truck, he couldn't help noticing an alabaster lawn ornament atop the feed store's stoop. It was a child lying on her belly reading a book. Perched on the edge of the book was a butterfly, and the look of wonder on the child's face reminded him of Jo when they talked about something she knew nothing about. They'd never broached the subject of lawn ornaments, who would? But he couldn't resist. "Sara, add this ornament to my tab," he shouted into the store. And after gently placing it on the passenger side floor of the truck, he headed back to the farm.

As the old truck ate up the miles, Mark realized being with Jo had somehow equalized his life. These days, he'd come to terms with not sweating the small stuff and joy came easy. They made time to see each other every day and while he ached to show her how much he really cared, they had an agreement. Of course, there were times when he regretted that decision. No man as in love as he was would be content with a celibate lifestyle. But he understood where she was coming from. For now, he waited, confident of what was in her heart. He had mustered heretofore-unknown patience, to give her the time she needed to get her head together. And it seemed from their conversation, that she might truly be near that point.

Chapter 25

During Jo's meeting, the sponsors were unusually cordial. They suggested a plan for ongoing cooperation and heaped praise upon her for her latest jingles. However, kudos aside, she felt her presence was pointless. She fidgeted constantly, unsure whether her disinterest was due to her longing for Mark, or because she was losing interest in the work. She'd never before allowed anything, or anyone, to be more important than her career. However, now her true allegiance had made itself clear, she couldn't wait to get back on the road and head north. So much so, that when the sponsors offered her a bonus expense-account shopping weekend in town, she declined. Everything she wanted was in Maine.

Chapter 26

When she pulled to a stop at the house, the girls were conspicuous by their absence. And upon opening her front door, all seemed normal save the delicious smell of flowers. Dumping her portfolio, Jo approached the kitchen and found an impressive vase of roses alongside an alabaster statue of a prostrate child reading a book. A post-it was stuck on the counter.

Riding in the woods, took the girls. Dad says dinner tonight. Wear something nice, he'll pick you up at five-forty...love, D.
PS Never seen him give anyone anything like this before.

A perfectly symmetrical arrow pointed to the statue.

Flowers from him too.

Jo plucked one of the thorn-free long-stemmed beauties from the vase, and let its heady perfume caress her consciousness. Mark had never sent flowers before, there were so many in the garden. Now her practical, no-frills farm boy had sent her an adorable lawn ornament as well as the most overtly sensual flowers in the horticultural catalogue. Could he read her thoughts? Did he know that her mind as well as her heart was finally committed to him? Replacing the bloom, Jo removed the standard white card from the plastic florist's fork. There was nothing on it but "M" and a small red heart. She smiled, deciding to abandon her night of unadulterated bliss to assume whatever his plan might be.

⊱⊰⊱⊰

When Dani and the girls returned at three-thirty, Jo realized she hadn't seen the youngster for a few days. They spent a few minutes catching-up, but nothing was mentioned about the dinner.

Then Dani looked at her watch. "Well, gotta go," she said, heading to the field.

Jo was right behind her.

"Shouldn't you be gussying up for the big date," said Dani.

"Na-ah, missy, not so fast. You're being very cagey, which is not at all like you. What's with the dinner?"

Dani shrugged. "Don't ask me, I'm the last to know anything. Naturally, I tried pumping Mrs. A. She flat out denied all knowledge. But I do know he's been wandering around like a lost soul all day."

"Thought the farm was keeping him busy?"

"He had some meeting with a doofus from Portland first thing. Wouldn't tell me what that was all about. Since then he's been pacing and mooning about with a far-off goofy look in his eyes. Don't know what you do to him. But he's got it bad. I'll be glad when he gets back over here and you two do whatever it is you do."

"Excuse me?" said a surprised Jo.

"You know..." said Dani. It was apparent from the youngster's inflection, she thought the adults were sleeping together. "But I understand if you don't want to talk about it. After all, he is my dad."

"Dani!"

"I know, none of my beeswax. I'm going. Don't be late. He's a stickler for punctuality."

"I know." Jo felt a warm glow hearing Mark was missing her as much as she missed him. "Well, missy, if I'm to live up to Graduation Ball standard, I better get going."

☙❧☙

As Jo laid out her clothes, the girls retreated to their lazing places, and a peaceful calm enveloped the house. Ordinarily, Mark arrived soon after Dani's departure, and it was a little weird when he didn't. *No matter*, she mused, *he'll be here soon enough*.

Stepping into the shower, Jo luxuriated in the rivulets of body wash, teasing and tormenting her uncharacteristically hypersensitive skin. Mark had never ventured into the places intimately caressed by the water. But suddenly Jo felt he was there and the realization of the deliciously mysterious vibe almost overwhelmed her. It wasn't just the water. It was something intangible, more intense, an almost karmic inevitability. She felt sure Mark was thinking the same thing as she, at that precise moment. As her mind fought to focus away from the intensely erotic feelings surging within her, Jo knew whatever his intentions this evening, she was going to show him exactly how she felt.

Chapter 27

Dani stood at her father's bedroom door. "This is serious, Dad, right?"

Mark smiled. "Is it that obvious?"

"Haircut, new suit—do the math."

"Smarty pants."

"Okay, Dad...look at me...smile...good...twirl. Yep, excellent," Dani said playfully. "You're ready to go. Will you be home tonight?"

"What makes you ask?"

"You like her, she likes you. You're both attractive and single. It's spring—what's to discuss."

"Nothing, missy," Mark said, tousling her hair. "However, to put things into perspective, spring is over, and you're not old enough to be thinking about such stuff."

Dani shot him a look. "Dad, I live on a farm, I've seen all sorts of animals doing it."

"Hey! This is me—your dad—behave." Mark put a hand on his daughter's head, as he brushed by. "Go to bed early, and don't wait up."

"So, you are staying out." Dani followed him downstairs.

"Quiet!"

"Have fun..."

Mark frowned. "What did I just say?"

"Okay, I'll stop." She threw up her hands. "Do you have—"

"Dani!"

"Handkerchief a clean handkerchief—what did you think I meant?"

Her innocent demeanor didn't fool him. "Cheeky monkey. Have you finished those college applications?"

"I'm only interested in one," Dani said. "And it's already sent. I'm just waiting for my room assignment."

"You shouldn't bank on it, sweetie. After all, it is New Zealand. They'll choose locals first."

"You taught me never to take second best, Dad. I'm destined for the best veterinary college on the planet. And if that's in New Zealand, New Zealand is where I'm going."

He smiled. "Okay, that's your decision. So, Mrs. Ainsworth left you supper, now come here." He pecked his daughter on the cheek. "Goodnight, see you tomorrow."

"Umm, you're pretty confident for an old guy."

Mark shook his head.

"'Night, Dad, I love you."

"Love you too, pumpkin." Mark picked up a box of Godiva chocolates, went to the garage, and got into a navy-blue Porsche Carrera.

⌒⌒⌒

When a Porsche turned into her drive, Jo had no idea who it might be.

She wasn't entirely prepared for the hunk who exited the classic car.

Watching him stride purposefully toward the house, a fluttering tickled everything south of her navel. And she was waiting at the door when he got there.

"Oh my," she said, running her fingers down his cheek. "You do clean up nice."

"Thank you, kind lady, now get a move on, your carriage awaits."

"Would you like a glass of wine before we go?"

"Nope," he said, handing her the chocolates. "Got a plan."

She couldn't help smiling at his textbook prom style overtures. "Well, so far it's all very impressive. But I have to ask—does the rest involve a high-speed police chase?"

Mark smiled. "Where do you get your ideas?"

"Well, look at it from my side. Farmer turns up at my door. I already got the commemorative statue and long-stemmed red roses. Now he hands me a hundred bucks worth of chocolates. He's got a new suit, very *GQ* I might add." Jo ran her fingertips through his hair. "Feels like an expensive haircut, and oh yes, old McDonald is driving a classic Porsche—gotta be a bank robbery in their somewhere."

Mark laughed aloud. "Think you're so smart, don't you?"

"Yup, that would be an affirmative. I most certainly do."

He nuzzled Jo's neck. "By the way, you clean up nice too, and you smell delicious."

Jo pushed him away. "Back off, Romeo, or we'll never make it to the car. I want to see where this adventure ends."

"Works for me."

❦❦❦

It took fifteen minutes to get to The Lakeside Grill, one of the most romantic spots in the area. There, dinner was served inside, on the patio, or on *The Bounty*, a floating restaurant. Mark had made a reservation for the boat. And as the soothing sounds of a classically played grand piano flowed over them, they were shown to one of the five tables on deck. Glasses of wine were waiting.

"Wow, what service," said Jo, taking a sip of the perfectly chilled wine. "Yum, my favorite Chardonnay, how did they know?"

"I told them. Space afloat is limited so you have to order everything in advance. I think you'll like the food as much as the wine. Robyn is the owner and chef, lately of The Four Seasons in Boston. She prepares everything herself."

"Wow, again, who knew? But hang on a minute, you hardly know me, what if I hate what you ordered?"

"Number one, I know you quite well enough. Number two, if anyone hates the food, both the chef and he who ordered get to walk the plank. This is *The Bounty* after all."

All tables were occupied within minutes of Mark and Jo's arrival. And as *The Bounty* staff prepared to get underway, a waiter delivered champagne, and a tray of hors d'oeuvres.

"Oh my, this is yummy," said Jo popping a smoked salmon canapé in her mouth. She took a second. "Well, good sir, so far, you have made an excellent choice on my behalf."

Mark smiled and raised his glass in acknowledgement. "I aim to please."

Each time Jo connected with Mark's eyes, they spoke to her. She adored that. They showed no guile. Did not hint at an ulterior motive. Threatened no deception. What you saw was what you got. It was also comforting to be the focus of his caring and attention. She trusted him implicitly, and this evening she was determined to put herself completely in his hands.

It was precisely six when *The Bounty*, lit by a thousand fairy lights, sedately departed the dock. Lush foliage barriers separated the five tables, so although others were close, it was as if each couple were on their own floating island. And, as their magical evening of good conversation and exquisite food flew by, any doubts Jo might have had about his knowledge of her likes and dislikes were dispelled. His quiet strength and empathic way gave her emotional satisfaction she'd never known, and she couldn't imagine her life without him. And while on nights alone, she'd agonized whether she could completely surrender herself to him, his actions this evening clarified her mind. There was no doubt she should share what she'd held in check for so long. Glancing across the table, noting the tenderness in his eyes, enjoying the way his easy smile made he feel, Jo knew whatever their future held, she could do nothing less than return the devotion of such an extraordinary man. "Why do you stare at me?" she said, knowing the answer.

"Because I love you, and, quite frankly, you're so closed off in some areas, I'm not even sure you like me."

"That's 'cos I hate ya, can't stand ya—"

He reached for her hand. "Serious moment, Jo, do you?"

"Look in my eyes," she whispered. "What do they say?"

"I think they say you do like me, so I guess I'm good."

"That's it—you're good?"

Mark smiled. "Yop, yop, good."

"So, Farmer Newcombe, where do we go from here?"

"Remember I told you in a former life I was a chemist."

"Of course, and you wanted to explore the medicinal secrets of the Amazon rain forest."

"Will you come with me?"

"I thought you put that aside to concentrate on finding better ways to farm organically?"

"I did, but that was before I met you. Now with everything in place and working, I can leave the farm and indulge my other passion."

"It sounds fabulous, but I have a job too. I'm still grappling with whether a life or my job comes first. But I definitely can't just abandon everything and run off to South America."

"Why not?"

"Umm, why not indeed? As I said—you have me seriously thinking about that."

"Take your time," Mark took her hand and kissed the palm, "I'll be here when you decide."

☙☙☙

By eight, dessert plates were cleared and champagne glasses were charged. And with the breeze off the water, cooling the air fast, the waiter handed wraps to the ladies. While the pianist played softly in the background, diners watched in rapt anticipation as the waiter reappeared from below with birthday cakes for two of the tables, an anniversary cake for another, and a single red rose in a crystal bud vase for the other.

In front of Jo, he placed a tiny box of Godiva chocolates.

"More chocolates, are you trying to make me fat?"

"I'm a regular guy," he said, smiling. "I ran out of ideas and had to double up."

Jo noticed a trace of concern wash over his face. "Well, you've done a splendid job. This was all such a wonderful surprise I don't think I ever want the evening to end."

"It's not over yet. You haven't tried the Godiva's. I know you love them."

"I'm not sure I should. I've eaten enough for ten."

"One won't hurt. Besides, I'd like to know what all the fuss is about."

"Okay, but I'm warning you, once you get a taste, it's going to be hard to stop."

"Bit like your kiss." Mark took her hand brushing her knuckles with his lips.

"You're so sweet, why didn't somebody snap you up years ago?"

"I was waiting for you."

"Are you sure about that?" Jo untied the ribbon encircling the box of chocolates and when she removed the golden lid to pluck one out, a large diamond ring nestled between the pieces. At the precise moment Jo thought she could be in no further awe of her highly practical companion, who she never imagined could be so creative, he was making the most profoundly romantic gesture imaginable. Fighting the urge to gasp, she carefully removed a chocolate, bit it in half, and offered him the other half, before closing the box.

Mark ate the half-chocolate. "They're good, but I didn't get enough. I need more."

"You sure?"

"I'm sure."

Jo opened the box where the diamond sat silently taunting her. "We're not talking about chocolates, are we?"

"Would that be a bad thing?"

"Mark, I'm not—"

"Uh-oh, not sounding good."

Jo smiled and took his hand. "I think you know you're

more than special to me, and I want to be everything I can for you. You are the most wonderful, kind, generous man. However, I want to be sure you know what you're letting yourself in for."

Mark smiled. "I'm a big boy. I can handle whatever demons you think you have."

"Of that I have no doubt. But you've said you'd like more children. I can't give you what you need. Are you sure you're okay with that?"

"Dani will have kids one day. Then I'll be glad to have them for a while before I give them back. Jo, I've thought about this—a lot. Every time I leave you, it's like a piece of me is missing. I don't function well. I can't focus on anything a hundred percent. I've been there done that, and frankly the tee-shirt no longer fits." He took her hand. "I need you with me."

She could see hurt in his eyes and felt his pain. She'd always been acutely aware that life had trade-offs. And while her life might be without her own children, wasn't having Mark and Dani in it better than a dozen alternatives she could think of? However, she'd barely come to terms with her feelings for him and wasn't sure she was ready for marriage.

"What if I close the box and think about eating the rest another time."

"I'll throw myself overboard."

"You wouldn't."

As Mark moved his chair to get up, Jo held fast to his hand. And in that instant, something happened. She didn't know exactly what, probably never would. However, a flutter of butterflies erupted in her stomach and the frisson between them was palpable. She'd never felt anything like it before, and her lingering angst, morphed into an intense outpouring of love. It took her by surprise.

But Mark, more than anyone she'd ever known, deserved her love.

"I'd really hate for you to ruin such a beautiful suit," she said, more casual than she felt. "Or your hair, it's so...neat. Besides, there'd be no-one to take me home." She drummed her fingers on the table. "What to do, what to do?"

He pulled her hand to his heart and knelt before her. "Are you going to torture me all night?"

Jo raised an eyebrow. "Would you like that?"

"I think I might. But for now...Jericho Palestine Weston, will you marry me?"

"Can I still torture you?"

"Later...now be serious. I have loved you from the minute the girls invited you to the house. The second you passed the seven-cookie test. The instant you accompanied me to the cemetery under the spreading chestnut tree—"

"Fool, it was a pine." She pushed the chocolate box toward him and when their eyes met, she could tease him no longer. "Yes, I will marry you. Now get up before you ruin those pants."

His eyes, concerned, seconds before, now shone with relief and love. He pulled her to her feet, enveloped her in his arms, and kissed her.

She was breathless when they broke apart. "Can I have my ring now?"

His beaming smile spoke volumes. "Gold-digger!" Taking the ring from the chocolates, he placed it on her finger. It was a perfect fit. "Jo, almost wife. I can't even tell you how much I love you right now. Do you think the rest of the passengers would mind if I kissed you again?"

"It's hard to see anybody through the foliage. I don't think they'll even notice."

When he kissed her and stroked her ringed hand with

intimate delicacy, waves of desire surged through her body. "Darling, you better stop. Much more of that caressing thing, and I'll be doing something that will get us arrested."

Mark smiled. "A night alone in the cells with you? Could I ask for anything more?"

"I think we can do better than that. How much longer 'til we dock?"

∾∾∾

Mark was very subdued on the drive home. And after he pulled sedately to a halt at the log house, he hopped out and opened the door for her. He helped Jo from the car, but instead of letting her proceed, pinned her against the door, and hungrily lowered his mouth on hers.

Jo didn't feel any of his usual holding back. His kiss had none of the control and resistance she'd felt before. And his unexpectedly masterful side intoxicated her. Something had most definitely changed in him, and when she shifted position beneath him, she could feel what his body had in mind. She'd almost forgotten the spine-tingling effects of a man really kissing her. The satisfying weight pressing against her, and the contours of his maleness. He so deliciously fit her she bent herself to his passion. And the tantalizing action of his lips and tongue stirred feelings within her that hadn't surfaced in years. Stunned at how the depth of her respect for him had, in an instant, transformed into white-hot desire, she responded. She was scared and exhilarated at the same time. And when his hands explored where they'd never ventured before, she realized how badly she wanted him.

Then he pulled back. "Jo, we have to stop."

"Why?" She had reached her point of no return, when he could do anything, as long as he made love to her. "I had no idea you could make me feel this way, you've always been so controlled. Do you really want to stop?"

"Of course not, I love you. But I need you to want me, too."

"And you think I don't?" she said, barely able to mask her surprise.

"You always said you'd tell me when you were ready, and you haven't. Besides, in the restaurant, when I asked you to marry me—you hesitated. Am I rushing you? Maybe you really don't want to marry me."

"I was simply surprised."

"Why surprised? You know I'm crazy about you. I'm at the cabin twenty times a day because I can't be without you for longer than a couple of hours."

She smiled. He was worrying needlessly and she had to lighten his mood. "And here I was thinking you're making sure I'm looking after the girls."

"Well yeah, there is that."

Jo ran a hand down his cheek. "You know I love it when you just turn up. It plays havoc with my work. But you know something, I don't care. I never thought I'd actually say that, but there it is. I no longer have this all-consuming drive to work. This head full of deadlines and the need to win 'just one more contract.' You have won me over and turned me into a gal with real emotions and a need for something more." She took Mark's hand and placed it on her heart. "Feel that. It's you doing that. You give me feelings I've never had before. And I really like it."

"So I guess, at the moment, we have no problems," he whispered.

"There is one—we haven't slept together. What if we're not compatible, what if I can't live up to your expectations. Doesn't that matter to you?"

"Not the way you might think. I know it matters when

I have to fight to keep my hands off you. It matters because I can't kiss you the way I want to. It matters because I have to force myself not to get carried away with you. But I respect you and understand where your doubts and anxieties come from. I've spent years conquering all that, and if you need time, if you want to wait until we're married, whenever that might be—I'll wait. *You* are what matters to me. And you have to be a thousand percent sure *we* are what makes you happy."

She brushed her lips against his. "I can hardly believe you're so patient."

"I love you so much. You can't imagine how desperately I want you. But before I eat my words and blow everything, I better leave."

"I don't think so."

"Don't think what?"

"That I want to wait," said Jo quietly.

"Are you sure about this. It's not because you feel obligated now we're engaged?"

Jo laughed. "Got nothing to do with it. I know it sounds crazy, but I was about to suggest what you just did. I was waiting 'til I felt…" No words were adequate, so Jo twirled a finger in the air. "Something I can't explain, and suddenly it was all so clear. I was always attracted to you, but I kept thinking of…"

"Chris."

Jo nodded.

"I knew that," said Mark. "Remember, we're in the same boat. I never thought I could love someone else either. But you can't overthink love. When it happens, you simply have to let it take over. Tell me truthfully. Did you make one of your lists?"

"God, I hate you."

"No, you don't," he said, stroking her cheek.

"No, I don't. But it's scary that you so know me. And, you know where my confusion came from. In retrospect, I was married but love never took over. And I so wanted it to. With Chris, we were always something else. In truth, I don't think I ever loved him. We started off in a whirlwind of mindless sex. It had no substance, no real truth. And once that rush was gone, there was nothing left. What do they say 'marry in haste, repent at leisure'?"

"Good God, that sounds grim," said Mark.

"I know, but it really wasn't. We simply existed as a couple in the same place. Our life was pleasant enough, albeit excruciatingly safe and predicable. Jeez, I could set my watch by him. But when I was in it, I simply saw it as safe and, for me, normal. I drifted through life with no speed bumps, no stop signs, and no road works. It was okay. Life with Chris was okay—and looking back, I hated it."

"Why didn't you simply divorce him and move on?"

Jo frowned. "Why? He was pleasant. He provided. We had good sex when he was home. What grounds would there be?"

"He didn't make you happy?"

Jo smiled. "Jesus, where were you when I needed a friend?"

Mark smiled. "Sounds to me like you may have had your 'light-bulb' moment and are ready to move on."

"Amen, friend. Now put me down for a spotlight." Jo pulled him close and kissed him passionately.

"You have no idea what a kiss like that does to me," he said, voice thick with passion.

Jo kissed him again. "I know exactly what it does— come with me."

❧❧❧

Once they were in her bedroom, any iota of control Jo

may have had over their situation ended. She guessed
Mark would be gentle and thoughtful because that was
his way. But when he laid her on the bed, peeled away
her clothes, and his mouth explored every inch of her
body, she was delighted his measured public side evaporated. Surrendering to his boldness and enthusiasm, she
was quickly hovering in a blissful state she'd only
dreamed about. She hadn't made love in some time, but
Mark's uninhibited actions, and synchronous carnality
spurred her to explore her fantasies. And as she perfectly
matched his rhythm, her muscles pulling the length from
him, his body reacted. As he thrust deep, to the essence of
her core, the intoxicating effect of him deep inside bewil-
dered her. With the breathless abandon of a teenager, she
reveled in the joys of their compatibility. And when, during a heart-pounding orgasm, she screamed that she loved
him— there wasn't a doubt in her mind that she did.

Chapter 28

When Jo woke, she was disappointed. Instead of Mark's lean muscled body next to her, she found a note. It read, *I love you…I love you…I love you, but critters wait for no man.* Smiling, she wrapped a robe around her naked body and patted barefoot to the kitchen.

No sooner had she put on coffee than the girls started making a commotion and, looking out the office window, she saw his old truck trundling up the drive. He jumped out, followed by the Ps. It was so like him to appear, just when she thought she was alone. Jo let out the girls to join their canine friends and was at the door as he rounded the corner. She hadn't thought it possible, but he was more handsome than she remembered. She stepped forward into his arms.

Mark kissed her as if they'd been apart for twenty years, and his passion accompanied a hand to her breast. Her robe fell open, and he kissed her shoulder before pulling the fabric together. "Have I told you today how much I love you?"

Cinching the robe, she giggled infectiously. "Sort of, between milking the cows and shearing the sheep. Good job you don't have any more mammalian commitments, I'm not sure you'd fit me in at all."

"Oh sweet darlin'," he whispered. "I could fit you in anywhere. In fact, right now I have ten minutes—what say you?"

She cuffed his arm. "Animal!"

He ushered her back into the house and closed the door. And when he pulled her close, her leg wrapped about his. "I like where this is going," he whispered. "But I'm not sure ten minutes will do it right now."

Jo had no intention of closing the emotional floodgates of the unconventional man assaulting her senses. "You get fifteen," she teased.

As his lips locked onto hers, Mark loosened the tie on her robe. "You're a good negotiator," he said, running a hand between her shoulder blades and down her spine. He was at her butt when he felt her arch into his hand. "What will it take to get twenty?"

All Jo could think about was what those hands, and his body, had done to her several times the night before. And with feelings hidden so long bursting to the surface, she pushed him back. "Stop wasting my minutes, mister." He so intoxicated her, Jo hardly recognized the sexually charged being she'd become. "We need to hit a bed right now."

His strong arms lifted her and carried her to the downstairs bedroom.

చించిం

Jo watched him undress, and her desire for him was painful. And when he stepped forward and stood in front of her, skin barely touching skin, she felt the mingling of their souls. She shivered as he released her robe and took a breast in his hand. "Pretty sure of yourself these days, aren't you?"

Mark smiled. "I never felt better."

"Well, I have something to make you feel a whole lot better."

"Don't tease me woman," he whispered, voice thick with passion.

Jo locked her mouth on his and maneuvered him onto the bed. Then climbing atop him, she positioned herself so he could enter her. With his first thrust, a satisfied sigh escaped her lips. She took a minute to appreciate his broadness fitting so perfectly inside her, and then began to rock back and forth.

"That is so good," he moaned, matching thrusts with her rhythmic rocking. But when she tightened her pelvic muscles, he was instantly dragged to a climax. With breath coming in satisfying gasps, Mark pulled her down and flipped her on her back. "How did you do that so quickly," he said, raining kisses on her face.

"We agreed you'd only get fifteen minutes."

He grinned. "You agreed on fifteen minutes. I was still mid-negotiation." As he watched her breathing settle, he traced patterns on her body with his finger. "Can I stay with you again tonight?"

"Of course. But what about Dani, is it fair to leave her alone?"

"She loves having me gone. She plays her music loud, talks to her friends on the phone, stays up late. Besides, she has to get used to being alone."

"How so?"

"Wait here." Mark jumped from the bed, went to the living room, and returned with a letter.

"What's this?" asked Jo.

"Dani got a full scholarship to Massey Veterinary College in New Zealand."

"My God, how wonderful. She must be over the moon."

"She is. In fact, when she got this, she let out such a

scream, I thought she was having an episode."

Jo frowned. "I'd forgotten about that. Is her medical issue going to be a problem?"

"We checked with Doc Brewster, and as long as she takes her meds, all should be well."

"Umm, not so good. Her reliability on that subject is iffy."

"I know. But we spoke about it, and now it's real and connected to the college of her dreams. We contacted them, and they don't have a problem unless she fails to take her meds. I know for sure she will not screw up. She knows how important it is to the college and letting her stay to fulfill her dream. At some point I simply have to trust her."

"Whoa. Now that's new. Seems Dad has accepted his maturing daughter and he has to let go."

"It's more like a fait accompli. It's what I have to do."

Jo smiled, and patted his thigh. "So, when does all this happen?"

"Their system is a bit different than ours, and the season is upside down, so she'll be here a few more months. Fortunately, there's plenty of work on the farm, so she doesn't drive me nuts. But in the end, she'll get what she wants."

"Seems the whole family gets what they want." She pecked him on the nose. "Tell her I said well done."

"You can tell her yourself, she'll be over this afternoon. She wants to say hi to her new mom."

Jo smiled broadly. "I like how 'her new mom' sounds. Was that your idea or hers?"

"Are you kidding? This is Dani we're talking about. She doesn't do anything unless she wants to. Anyway, she wants to see the ring. I wouldn't show it to her before I gave it to you."

"Why not?"

"She couldn't keep a secret if her life depended on it. She'd have let it slip while she was over here, and I wanted to see the full surprise on your face thing."

"Instead you got the OMG rejection thing."

"I know. What was that all about?"

"Told you. I was waiting for something intangible. It's a girl thing, you wouldn't understand."

"Try me."

"Not at the moment, mister. That's going to require blankets and chardonnay under the stars."

Mark smiled. "Sounds like a date."

"You got it. However, to maintain my dating promise, I have to conjure up a way to make your toes curl."

Mark picked up Jo's hand, kissed her ring, moved up her arm and landed on her mouth. "Too late. Been there, done that, ordered the ribbon."

"Oh, really."

"Yup, and it's gonna be blue."

"Blue?" asked Jo.

"Hello? Farmer? County fair thing. Blue ribbon is top drawer, 'A' number one."

"Oh, brother," Jo teased. "How can you say that with a straight face?"

"'Cos I love you, and it's true. God, how did I get so lucky? You're so amazing. I have never in my entire life felt this good."

Giggling lasciviously, she kinked her neck expressing an attitude. "You ain't getting no free ride, farm-boy! Tonight there's pay back." She kissed a finger and pressed it tenderly on his lips. "I've heard there's something called Supreme Champion, Best in Show."

Chapter 29

With her dad, and new "mom" on another business trip to Boston, Dani and her friends sunned themselves by the cabin's pool. They had just settled into a conversation on the merits of potential romantic entanglements at one college versus another, when the throaty roar of a motorcycle came up the road. Within minutes, the groaning Hog swung onto the drive.

As the girls took off to check out the intruder, Dani sat up. "Oh, crap, what's he doing here?" She was speaking to no one in particular as she blushed. She couldn't help remembering the daydream she had about him. Or the lurid entry she penned in her diary. Then his lame attempt at seduction during their last encounter. And his assertion that they'd had sex in Jo's pool. His essence seemed to creep toward her like an insidious malignant smoke in dense fog. Like the blanket of his carnal putrefaction somehow permitted him to touch her. And she was disgusted.

"OMG," gasped Becky, reaching for her glasses. "Is that who I think it is?"

"Well, I for one have no idea, Becky," said Dani sarcastically. "Who do you think it is?"

"It's Chase Markum," whispered Becky. "Ladies, watch and learn. I guarantee that the Adonis will, at some point, disrobe and you will see what I can only describe as perfection."

"Puleez," Dani snapped. "You are such a girl. Just how many half naked men have you seen to make an honest assessment?"

Becky and friends ignored Dani and watched as Chase stripped to the waist to begin cutting trees.

"Oh no he didn't," whispered Shelly.

"Didn't what?" asked an exasperated Dani. She turned to find Chase stripping off his shirt. "Now that's a health and safety hazard."

"Uh?" asked her friends in unison.

"Not only is he supposed to wear a shirt and a visor to protect himself from flying wood. But he's also supposed to cover his legs with those steel reinforced chaps in case the chainsaw bucks back." Seeing his perfectly toned and bronzed torso were a vivid reminder of how much she missed, and wanted, Nick. "Not even close," she sniffed, turning her chaise where she wouldn't have to see him. And as the incessant whine of his chainsaw rent the air, she could feel his eyes boring into the back of her head.

Her friends, however, had other ideas and remained standing to better appreciate the view.

"What the heck are you all gawking at?" Dani snapped.

Melissa was transfixed. "Ladies, *attendez-vous*. Get a load of those muscles, if you know what I mean. Can you even imagine what it would be like to have him driving into you like a rampant stallion?"

"Don't be so moronic, Liss, you sound like a dime-store novel," said Alice, pigtails, glasses and way too serious for her sixteen years. "Who talks like that anyway? Even if I wanted to get involved with the hired help, it wouldn't be him."

Melissa snorted. "Huh, says you. Since when did you get any choice in the matter?"

"Since I have a brain. Aside from a pursuit, you bubblehead, do you even know another meaning for the word 'Chase'?"

Melissa stuck out her tongue. "Ladies, pardon the impertinence of the precocious child sitting next to me, because Chase is a perfect name for him." She beckoned her friends closer. "I've heard he chases women and marks 'em. Get it—Chase Markum."

"Jesus H. Christ," Dani said.

"Seems perfect to me," chimed in Shelly. "But I have it on very good authority he doesn't have to chase any woman. He has a dozen waiting to get in his pants. Plus, I hear he uses that drug…ecstasy…or roofies, is it?…or whatever…you know, the one that makes you have sex and you don't even know it. God what a waste. I'd want to feel every inch of a primo scre—"

"*What*?" Dani snapped. "Who the hell told you that?"

"Whoa, Dani—chill. What is your deal?"

"Who the hell mentioned anything about screwing him?"

"Jeez…it was Kathy Martin." Shelly paused for effect. "In church. She told me he was at a party, they got talking, and the next minute bang—she was flat on her back naked in the barn. Didn't remember a thing, said he must have slipped her some of those pills. You know her family is huge at church, and she feared for her immortal soul."

"No way," said Melissa.

"No one's going to tell a blatant lie in a church," Shelly added.

Dani shook her head in disbelief. "Well, I'm not buying it. Any party with Kathy Martin wouldn't attract a guy like Chase Markum. And the only ecstasy she'll ever experience is seven Hail Mary's and an Ave Maria."

"Well, yaboo, smarty pants, that's all you know. She also told me in confidence she was a virgin and when she woke, she had 'seventeen' written in blood on her leg, and some crazy bite mark on her shoulder. Just like they said—Mark 'em—see?"

"God, you are so full of crap," Dani said. "And who the hell are 'they.' You are such a dip. I don't know why I bother listening to you."

Dani's mind had tried to block out him and his proposal. But a trickle of realization quickly became a flood. Had he approached her with pills? He'd definitely touched her with familiarity. Like he'd done it before. She'd thought that afternoon when she'd fallen asleep in the sun was a daydream. But, in truth, she now wasn't sure. Did she have marks on her body? Were they merely the result of being too long in the sun? Her jaw tightened. She should tackle the miserable slime. Find out if he plied her with drugs and alcohol to have sex. But what good would that do? Would it stop him? Probably not. Would it make her feel better? Doubtful. And if anybody found out and gossiped—like her bubbleheaded friends— it would ruin what she had with Nick. Confrontation was not an option. She was furious at what might have happened but wasn't prepared to risk everything in order to prove it.

♥♥♥

The girls talked non-stop about their experiences after that. But Dani didn't say much. She wanted to block out all knowledge of Chase Markum and what he may have done. All she cared about was what was between her and Nick. Only *that* made her feel warm inside. Only *that* made her feel truly wanted, loved, and needed. She couldn't tell these girls anything that was between them. What they had was so un-sharable, so precious, and private, she could only tell her diary. That was where her mind's freedom lay.

"What you thinkin' about?" Becky cut in.

"Nothing," said Dani. "Why?"

"You have that far-away look on your face again. Clearly, a man like the Adonis in the field is the last thing on your mind. College in New Zealand and never getting involved until you've established your career is about your speed."

"That's all you know," countered Dani.

"I know," added Melissa. "You can be so borrrrring."

"Yeah, boring, that's me," said Dani.

⌘⌘⌘

As shadows lengthened, Chase Markum packed up and left. And Dani said goodbye to her friends. It was as she entered the cabin that she saw her pills on the counter. *Shit a brick,* she thought. *What is it with me and these freaking pain-in-the-ass pills?* A little voice in her head whispered that her father was spot-checking the vial and would surely give her grief about her irresponsibility. Something she absolutely didn't want after she'd made a promise about New Zealand. *Well, fuck that. I'll soon be in college and will come and go as I please. I'll decide what I do and do not want in my body.* As a spontaneous wave of anger washed over her, Dani lobbed the vial into the sink. It hit the stainless steel, and being unscrewed, popped open. Several pills tumbled down the disposal. She smiled. *Good, don't need to worry about taking the useless crap for a couple of days.*

Chapter 30

Dani hadn't been feeling well for a few days, and by the time she picked up a new batch of meds, she was completely off her schedule. And while the pharmacist pointed out the dire emotional consequences that could arise from not taking her meds, Dani simply smiled and said, "I'll be more careful in future."

Mental aberrations were not something she was particularly concerned with at that time. She'd spent the last few mornings queasy and disoriented, with gut-wrenching heaves going nowhere. She'd never been particularly regular, because of her bi-polar disorder. But the absence of a most important female function left her praying the worst thing possible hadn't happened. Nick had been meticulous about using a condom during their lovemaking, which was one of the responsible adult things she loved about him. So, what was happening? The only thing she could conclude was that Chase Markum actually did violate her that afternoon, and she might be pregnant.

Chapter 31

October surrendered to solemnity. Trees dripped steady from overnight rain, and deep carpets of formerly vibrant leaves rotted silent beneath their hosts. After an agonizing September wondering whether she was pregnant, the tender fullness of Dani's breasts and her plump rounding belly confirmed the worst had happened. Beside herself with anger, she was unable to accept the challenge fate had presented to her. In a couple of months, she was boarding that flight to New Zealand, and nothing, short of death itself was going to stop her. There were tangible goals at stake. So, applying the sort of logic, only another desperate teenager would understand, she determined to find a way to abort the dream killer.

Chapter 32

In the mountains of Maine, the ripe beauty of fall was fleeting, and was quickly eclipsed by winter's chill. Paralyzing snow deeply blanketed the resting land beneath, and as Jo looked out over the pool, winterized two months since, she missed seeing the area filled with the rambunctious Dani and her friends. And as the heavy half-lit sky replaced bright azure days, Jo wondered if she'd ever see Dani or the sun, again.

Lately it seemed it was just her and Mark. She smiled, that was not a bad thing. But being snowed in, even with him, was something she found difficult to deal with. Today as yesterday, and the day before, he was outside plowing back and forth up her driveway. And as she watched the tunnel he made grow higher and narrower with each pass, she wondered how long it would be until there was no way in or out at all.

As Mark completed his task and walked toward the house, she waved. He seemed to take it all in stride. She guessed that was the difference between being raised in Maine and moving there.

Mark banged his boots on the doorjamb before entering. "So, Ms. Adventuress," he joked, pulling off his balaclava and gloves. "How'd you like Maine now?"

"Not so much. But it's not like I wasn't warned," she answered. "You look like a crazed ninja in those things, where'd you get them?"

"Dani bought them at one of the Lords Ladies bring and buy sales."

"Recently?"

"No, she hasn't been out much of anywhere lately."

"I noticed. In fact, I don't think I've seen her since the snow started to fall."

He stripped off his coat and draped it over the back of a chair. "That first lot was pretty heavy even for us, and we do have a hell of a drive. By the time she clears it each day, she's pretty bushed."

"She plows the drive?"

"Sure. A farmer's gal does anything necessary to get to the livestock. You get special dispensation 'cos you're from the city. But next year look out, I'm getting you out on that tractor."

"Well, I have to tell you the snow is pretty to look at. But being trapped here gets old real fast."

"Get used to it. It might be here 'til April."

Jo frowned. "Yikes. There must be something amiss in the cosmos allowing that to happen."

Mark looked up from stripping off his boots. "Excuse me?"

"Here you are plowing snow like a thing possessed, and within a couple of hours, it'll need doing again."

Mark grinned. "That's the nature of the beast."

"Precisely, so I think there should be some cosmic rule that says snow-plowing, grass mowing—" She paused. "—and dusting for that matter, should be good for a month or two. Now wouldn't that be nice?"

He smiled and shook his head. "Where do you get these ideas?"

"I'm a quirky, outside the box sort of gal."

"That you are," he said, reaching for her. "So come here, I have something inside the box for you to think about." He kissed her deeply.

"Well, that's certainly food for thought," she said. "But seriously, at what point does that roadway close completely trapping me in here?"

"With my plows, I doubt that will happen. Unless you want to be shut in the house for weeks." He kissed her again.

"Umm, forced incarceration with a handsome sex machine. It's sounding better every minute."

"I thought as much," said Mark. "You're a closet nymphomaniac, and *that's* sounding better every minute."

Jo smiled and returned to preparing dinner. "So, Mr. Intrepid Snow Shoveler, before you started on this Herculean task, what had you been up to?"

"Mostly repairs inside the barn and log splitting. Another of those cosmic things. Weather gets bad, people want to stay warm—ergo, I get more orders for firewood."

"Is Dani helping with that too?"

"Not much. Its heavy work and really dangerous if you're not concentrating. She continues with her routines, but concentration doesn't seem to be her thing of late."

"Is she taking her meds?"

"I assume so. We've had words, now it's up to her. She has to get used to taking responsibility for herself. After all, I won't be with her in New Zealand."

"Then could her difficulty concentrating be Lackofnickitis?"

"Excuse me."

"Lack-of-Nick-itis."

"Oh, right, I've been so focused on us, I forgot about their budding romance. It's been a while since he's been able to break away from school, and he does have his job at The Coop. I guess it's a case of out of sight out of mind. Funny thing is, she doesn't seem to mind him not being around. At first, she was all moody sitting by the phone waiting for his call. Now it seems to be 'whatever.' You think she's cooling on him."

"Not a chance," said Jo. "Did you see them last time he was here, love's young dream. I remember it well."

"You do?"

"Yeah. Last night. The night before…er…and then there was…"

"Nympho." He grinned, pecking her on the nose. "So, I can stay again tonight?"

"Of course, isn't that what almost husbands do?"

"That's exactly what they do. Now, almost wife, get your priorities straight. What's for dinner?"

"Typical. Good thing I have proof to the contrary, otherwise I'd think you had a one-track mind."

Mark pulled her into his arms. "Glad you realize this mind has two tracks, my love."

"Oh, yeah." Jo smiled. "Definitely two."

Chapter 33

Dani was missing Nick, but his school commitments and part-time job turned out to be a godsend. Winter allowed her to revert to her tomboy persona with lumberjack shirts, dungarees and voluminous down jackets. She'd never have hidden her rounding belly from Nick. It was easy with everyone else, because nobody questioned her shapeless, baggy clothes. And as long as she continued to deal with the animals and kept out of her dad's way until he went over to Jo's, she could retreat to her room in the evening and maintain her secret.

She hadn't hesitated a second in her resolve to abort her baby, and while her dad questioned her a couple of times about borrowing his chemistry books, Dani was able to divert his curiosity under the guise of being a budding veterinarian.

Only she and her diary knew she was researching chemicals to get rid of the child she was carrying. But as she compiled a list of possible curatives, most everything she came across was only available on special order at Metcalf's farm supply. That route was most definitely not an option. Word would quickly spread about what she was buying, and her father would have questions before she put the goods to use. Nevertheless, Dani was determined not to let an unwanted pregnancy ruin her or

Nick's life. In the absence of store bought aborting agents, she'd resort to herbal methods.

A microsecond after she abandoned her father's books, Dani was on the internet. Tansy and pennyroyal were known agents she could use. However, she passed on both. Not only were there documented deaths of women using those plants. She had no idea where she might get them. On the other hand, her interest peaked upon finding value in a mixture of brewer's yeast, slippery elm, nutmeg, and saffron. They were probably all accessible in Mrs. A's pantry. And if she mixed them with a copious amount of alcohol, violent heaving and straining enough to abort a fetus was pretty much, guaranteed. Dani smiled, she had her "abortifacient."

With her mind set, Dani made sure the ingredients for her potion were indeed in Mrs. A's pantry. Then she checked the liquor cabinet. Her dad drank very little, but they always had bottles of spirits left over from parties. She identified everything she needed and planned to use her concoction on one of the frequent nights her dad stayed with Jo. He normally returned at first light and got straight to work on his animal rounds. That gave her until noon to deal with the hangover she knew was possible. Covering all bases, she would fain having cramps for the rest of the day. No one need know she suffered through anything more than a severely painful and unusually heavy period.

సౌరస

Friday was a bright, brisk day, and when Dani came in from her chores, Mrs. A informed her Jo was coming over for dinner. Then she and Mark would spend the night at the log house. It amused Dani that her dad and Jo only slept together away from the farm, as if their lovemaking might offend her youthful sensibilities. However, nothing could be farther from the truth. Her dad had blossomed since the engagement, and she loved Jo. Moreover, knowing once she was in college, they'd embark on his Amazon dream trip, what she planned was more necessary than ever.

അഅ

At four o'clock on the dot, Nick called. As usual, his enthusiasm for medicine and the college experience burst from him. He enthused how great their life together would be, once their schooling was over. They even talked about whether Jo would sell the log house to them once she and Mark were married. And as always, his call ended with him professing his undying love for Dani.

Thoughts of the perfection of their life together strengthened Dani's resolve. And when she made the inevitable notes in her diary, her writing confirmed why she had no regrets about what she must do.

Chapter 34

As soon as her dad and Jo left for the log house, Dani washed the dishes and tidied the kitchen. Then taking a deep breath, she took a tumbler from the cabinet, gathered ingredients, and mixed them into a paste. She'd purposely eaten little at dinner, anticipating an empty stomach would make the potion more effective. And armed with her curative, a half-full bottle of vodka, and a bucket from the scullery, Dani retreated to her bedroom.

The paste Dani made looked disgusting. And after half-filling the tumbler with vodka and mixing it thoroughly, it looked like the worst kind of cow deposit. She brought it gingerly to her nose and it had a strangely pleasant fragrance. However, bouquet notwithstanding, when she sampled a little on her tongue, the mixture was so vile she gagged. Disgust was not an option. She had to swallow it. So, taking a deep breath, Dani chugged it down. The job was done.

As Dani sat quietly atop her quilt, waiting for something to happen, she unconsciously ran a hand over the beautifully constructed throw. Her focus seemed to blur around the ancient cotton triangles, poignant reminders of the Newcombe women sadly lost to childbirth. And while the family's history showed there had been many, she only grieved for her mother. A solitary tear rolled down Dani's cheek, and she felt ashamed. Ashamed that, unlike her mom, who had lived life nobly and died so her daughter could live, here was that daughter taking a life. Then she remembered why she was taking such a drastic measure. Notwithstanding the possibility that Chase Markum had created the abomination within her, it was vitally important to her happiness that she have a career and live her dream. It was crucial that Nick, her dad, and now Jo, see her achieve the goals she'd set for herself. So, she swiped away her tears. This was for Nick. For the Newcombe legacy. And for herself. Suddenly, any guilt she had about aborting the fetus disappeared. She knew she was doing the right thing.

As she lay down, the clock beside her bed had an almost imperceptible tick. But as she drifted to a place unknown, it grew louder. Her room seemed to have become a cave. A cave where sound bounced from the walls and echoed deep in her soul. A soul that had no doubts about the outcome of her action. An action that for a moment would hurt. But would cleanse and settle, allowing her to move on and relive her life.

Then a pounding began in her head. A pulsing, vessel-bursting rhythm that had her gasping for air. Then came churning, burning waves of nausea. And as Dani awaited the inevitable, her hands clutched at the quilt. *What if I'm violently sick,* she thought. *I don't want to risk soiling the quilt that means so much.*

Rising slowly, Dani neatly folded the heirloom, and placed it on the dresser. And as she ran her fingers across the fabric, a wave of something bright and pure washed over her. The pounding in her head stopped, her stomach settled, and the only thing she felt was an overwhelming sense of well-being. Whatever straining and heaving was supposed to happen, didn't. And as she stared at herself in the mirror, the face of the mother she never knew smiled back. Then she saw her grandmother, in a stream of faces she'd only seen in photographs. And her tears fell. Hot tears of disappointment. Burning tears of failure and not living up to her potential. And her resolve hardened.

Returning to the kitchen, Dani emptied most all of each of the cartons of ingredients into a larger bowl, and using gin instead of water, remade her herbal paste. Then returning to her room, she chugged it down, and continued sipping vodka until the bottle was empty.

As she lifted the bottle aloft, Dani felt lightheaded. But her stomach exhibited no ill effects from the aborting mixture or the alcohol. It was clear she had done something wrong. Her body must have assimilated and compensated for the deadly concoction. And she felt nothing but frustration. Her carefully researched plan was so much smoke and mirrors. And as she swung her legs over the side of the bed, she hurled her tumbler against the wall. With a shower of glass bouncing toward her, Dani stood her ground. Her head felt foggy, but she remained gynecologically sound.

Staggering downstairs to the liquor cabinet, Dani selected a bottle of gin and, stopping at the bathroom, palmed a bottle of aspirin. She wasn't entirely sure how she'd explain the missing alcohol to her dad. But she'd think of something later.

As Dani sat on her bed, she washed down the bitter taste of aspirin with gin.

Within minutes, the intensified combination had her feeling nauseous. She continued swigging gin until she threw up violently. And when her stomach was empty, the gut-wrenching dry heaves began. But nothing gynecological happened. With alcohol impairing her judgment, she continued drinking the gin. Then she passed out.

Chapter 35

Mark had been at Jo's for twenty minutes, sharing wine and talking about a honeymoon in the Amazon rain forest. However, he couldn't settle. "Sweetie," he said, arm around her. "Have you noticed something odd about Dani?"

"She misses Nick, that's pretty clear."

"Nah, it's not that," said Mark. "These days, she barely even talks about him. She's *off* somehow."

"Has she been taking her medication?"

"God, I hope so. I told you, I can't make her take it."

Jo smiled and patted his thigh. "I know, but you can *suggest*."

"I don't mean to be rude, Jo. You might *be* female, but you've never had to raise one. I know what to expect from her and, frankly…enough with the rebellion. My gut tells me it's more than missing Nick or skipping her meds. She's not in any way herself lately."

"How not herself?"

"She's withdrawn, secretive, and uncharacteristically moody."

"Sorry, Dad," said Jo, smiling. "She sounds like a normal teenage girl. All those things sort of come with the territory."

"I know that. We've had our share of head butting

about it. This is different. Whenever I broach any subject relating to her health, she's almost paranoid. I've never seen her like this before."

Jo took his hand. "So, time for a reality check—"

"Uh-oh," said Mark.

"Relax, you can handle it."

"I can?"

"Let's say, she and Nick are definitely sleeping to-gether—"

He took his hand away and stuck his fingers in his ears. "La, la, la, not listening."

"Mark, stop. It's two thousand fourteen. Kids are more advanced than we were."

"Jeez, what are we…sixty."

"You know exactly what we are. Remember how you felt before we…" Jo swirled a finger in the air. "You felt disconnected, couldn't focus, stuff like that. She's going through all that with bi-polar and PMS thrown in. Dani's simply a woman missing having her man around. And to make you feel better, I'm banking she misses his friend-ship as well as the intimacy."

"So, you're saying my baby is simply growing up?"

Jo smiled. "Catches up with you fast doesn't it, old man?"

"I'm still not convinced. These past few days she's spending less time with the horses and is flat out ignoring the Ps. Those animals are her kids. Hell, she's going to be a vet. Nothing has ever diverted her from that path be-fore."

"You could have Doc Brewster review her meds. But for me, it has a lot to do with sex. It too is a powerful drug. Once you have a taste, it's hard to do without."

Mark smiled. "You don't have to remind me. Come here." He pulled her into his lap and kissed her passion-ately. However, when Jo's hands ignited flames near the surface, Mark couldn't get Dani out of his mind. "Something's wrong."

"So, let's go upstairs."

"Not us, you goose—Dani. I'm getting weird vibes and they're driving me nuts. Sweetie, I'm sorry, would you mind if I ran home and checked things out?"

"Call her," said Jo, motioning toward the phone.

"Duh…" Mark dialed. There was no reply. He tried again. And again. "Darling, I'm sorry, she's not answering. I have to check things out. I'll be right back, I promise."

"Okay, Mr. Worry-wart, drive carefully. Call me when you get there."

He stroked her cheek and kissed her affectionately. "God, I love you so much. I'll be back in twenty-five minutes—tops."

∽∾∽∾

Pushing his old truck to a speed it hadn't reached in a couple of decades. Mark was at the farmyard in ten minutes. There, much to his surprise, the Ps were patiently sitting on the front porch. Something was definitely amiss. Dani would never leave them outside in October. And if they wanted out, she always made sure they were back in the house before she went to bed.

After greeting the huddled canines, Mark tried the door. It was unlocked. And when he stepped inside, all the lights were out. The kitchen sink light was always left on. When he called Dani's name, his voice echoed. The house radiated an uncharacteristic emptiness. It was cold, frightening, and uncomfortably silent. Mark sensed something was horribly wrong.

As the Ps charged to Dani's room, Mark switched on the upstairs light. And then the dogs began howling. Taking the stairs two at a time, Mark reached the landing and saw why they were fretting. Dani's bedroom door was always left open for them to come and go. It was shut. Mark knocked the door and called her name. Hearing nothing, he pushed it open. The Ps rushed past him and leapt onto the bed. Mark saw Dani face down, hanging over the edge. The Ps snuffled and butted around her. She didn't move. He stepped into the darkened room and gently shook her. She didn't stir. And when he flipped on the bedside lamp, she appeared comatose. Then he saw an empty bottle of vodka, a half-empty bottle of gin, and an open bottle of aspirin on her nightstand. From the bucket beneath her face, it was clear she'd thrown up.

Mark shook Dani vigorously. He couldn't wake her and knew her bi-polar medication and an excess of alcohol could be deadly. He had to get her to a doctor immediately. He also knew the local ambulance volunteers would take at least an hour to assemble. Moreover, a Portland locum was standing in for the doctors Brewster who were away at a conference. He could be at the medical center by the time anyone got to the farm.

Scooping up Dani in his arms, Mark carried her downstairs. Deciding it would be quicker to take the Porsche he flipped the keys from the rack. Then staggering out to the garage, he dropped his dead-weight daughter unceremoniously into the deep bucket seat.

Mark cursed loudly as he slammed the car in gear and sped off. Miss Dani was going to have a boatload of explaining to do after the hospital pumped out her stomach.

En route to Portland, he called Jo, briefly told her what he found and advised her where he was going.

എന്

With the night roads free of traffic, Mark ignored the

traffic lights, and made the journey to Maine Medical Center in under an hour. There, he pulled the Porsche into an ambulance bay and carried Dani into emergency. The staff immediately descended on him and placed Dani on a gurney. He briefly explained to the doctor about her bi-polar disorder and the empty bottles he saw by her bed. He was directed to the waiting room.

છે૦૯૦

Mark was pacing when the doctor rejoined him. "Well, Doctor," Mark nervously asked. "Is she going to be all right?'

"Thanks to your quick thinking. You were absolutely right to bring her straight here, another hour and I hate to think what may have happened."

"So, was it alcohol poisoning?"

"Not entirely," said the doctor. "The initial toxicology report indicates she had no bi-polar meds in her system. However, she had ingested aspirin and a bunch of herbal substances."

"You mean marijuana?"

"No, nothing like that." The doctor consulted his pa-perwork. "You're lucky it's the middle of the night. The lab is quiet, and we can get an analysis quickly. That said, this is still a preliminary finding. They are suggesting she may have swallowed a concoction of brewer's yeast, nutmeg, saffron, and something akin to slippery elm."

Mark looked surprised. "They can be that specific this early on?"

"They've seen the combo before," said the doctor mat-ter-of-factly. "I'm assuming you have these things in your pantry."

"I'm sure my housekeeper has all that stuff. She bakes—a lot."

"Quite. But the slippery elm was the decider."

"Decider?" asked Mark. "My housekeeper gives it to us when we have a cough."

The doctor smiled. "These ingredients are common homeopathic remedies in many country kitchens. Thing is, ladies generally put them together with aspirin and alcohol for a purpose."

"And that would be?"

"It seems your daughter may have been trying to fashion an abortifacient."

"An abortifacient, are you sure?"

"You know what that is?"

Mark nodded. "Jesus, I was a chemist in a former life. I should have recognized the combination of ingredients as soon as you said them."

"Sometimes we're too close to these things and our emotions shut off our brain."

"So, you're saying she's pregnant?" asked a shocked Mark.

"Yes. Can't be precise at the moment. I'll leave that to the OBGYN team. But I'd guess between twelve and sixteen weeks."

"*Is*, so whatever she tried to do didn't work?"

"Correct. Getting rid of a baby is a lot harder than most people think. Mother nature has her way of protecting the species."

"Thank you, Doctor, can I see her now?"

"You can. We've pumped her stomach, and she's drifting in and out of sleep. Might be best to look in quickly, reassure yourself she's on the mend, and come back later."

ඏඏඏ

When Mark entered Dani's cubicle, it was hard for

him to believe the pale, drawn, rag doll before him, was his vibrant daughter. "Hi, pumpkin," he said gently. "How're you feeling?"

She turned her back on him.

"Okay, you don't want to talk right now. I understand. Anyway, you're probably going to have a sore throat for a while. They had to pump out your stomach."

Dani said something to the wall that came out a hollow rasp.

Mark sat behind her and stroked her hair. "The doctor told me about the baby, Dani. You didn't lose it. It's going to be okay."

She remained facing the wall, and when he pulled the hair off her face, she sobbed uncontrollably.

"Sweetie, it's okay, really. Whatever problem you think you're having, we can work it out. A baby happened sooner than I expected, but it'll be fine. Try and sleep now, when you wake up, you'll feel much better."

No amount of consolation would make Dani face him, and a nurse advised Mark to go home and give his daughter time to adjust to her situation.

ভ৩ভ৩

Mark drove home, his mind in turmoil. He dialed Jo's number, and she picked up right away. "You were right," he said coldly.

"About what?"

"Dani and Nick are having sex. She's pregnant. The doctor thinks she was trying to abort the baby."

"Oh my God, is she all right?"

"I got her there in time. I'll be home in a while. Can we talk?"

"Of course," Jo said. "My place or yours?"

"I have all sorts of things going on first thing in the

morning, do you mind meeting me at the farm?"

"I'm on my way over."

"Thank you, I love you."

"I love you too, drive carefully."

cಶಿ

Mark cut through the pitch dark of rural Maine, wrapped in a cocoon of solemnity. Memories of his last trip to Maine Medical flooded back. And as a tear slid down his cheek, he remembered he'd lost his wife and gained a daughter. This time, he'd almost lost it all. As he swiped away the regretful tear, he couldn't help thinking of Dani and Nick being intimate. Jo had called it. Had almost made their coupling seem right. And while he thought he was okay with it, now he knew for sure, he was angry. He wasn't sure why. Maybe it was because his daughter's uncompromising goal to have a career and see the world had distorted her attitude to the sanctity of life. He wasn't against abortion, for the right reason. But this wasn't that reason. Maybe it was because she hadn't even discussed the situation with him. Given him a chance to help, make her see that she wasn't alone and things would be all right. Or maybe he was simply mad because of his own need for more children, knowing the woman he'd fallen in love with, couldn't have any? Mark cursed. Whatever his personal feelings might be, the time to explore them wasn't now. But of one thing he was certain, whatever difficulties the young people faced, together, they would work them out.

cಶಿ

Jo was standing in the doorway when Mark arrived back at the farm. "Is she really okay?"

"Sleeping."

"And the baby?"

"Fine too, although when I told her I knew about it, she became hysterical. I've never felt so useless and so in need of cussing someone out. What the hell is going on?"

"You're handling the situation a lot better than some fathers."

"Do I have a choice? I mean, I've always thought marriage and a family was inevitable for them. And we guessed they were having sex. But accidents happen, why would she feel it necessary to kill the baby? She used to tell me everything. Why didn't she come to me? We could've worked things out."

Jo stroked his back. "Some things you don't tell your parents, no matter how close you are."

"Did she say anything to you?"

"Nothing. I'm as shocked as you are. Besides, they're so grounded. I can't imagine why he wouldn't use a—"

"Jo," Mark snapped. "Too much information, right now. I don't want to hear any more."

"So, you're not as open-minded as you think."

"It's hard. I don't know whether I'm on my ass or my elbow. One day she's in my arms asking me to fix a boo-boo. Now she's all grown up in a place where I can't fix anything. Why didn't she trust me enough to say something, ask for help?"

Tears filled Mark's eyes, and Jo saw a side of him which tore at her heart.

"Will you come to the hospital with me this afternoon? Maybe she'll talk to you. Tell you what's going on."

"Of course, I will. Remember, now they're my daughter and grandchild too."

Chapter 36

When Mark and Jo returned to the hospital, the doctor pulled them to one side.

"Mr. Newcombe, your daughter is in a state of extremely high anxiety," he whispered. "She hasn't said much. However, I gather she's adamant about aborting her baby. She's physically fine. It's her mental state that bothers me. We need to keep her under observation until tomorrow. In the meantime, I've set up an appointment with Dr. Raina Bliss. She's one of the center's psychiatrists and specializes in adolescent issues."

"Whatever she needs, Doctor."

"One more thing. When you talk to Dani, try to avoid bringing up the subject of the baby. Let her deal with it in her own way, until Dr. Bliss can see her."

Mark and Jo nodded.

They found Dani propped up in bed staring blankly at a TV screen showing one of the soap operas she hated. And while Jo filled a vase for the flowers they brought, Mark approached her bed.

"Hi, pumpkin, how're you feeling?"

Dani didn't look at him. "Why did you do it, Dad?"

"Do what, sweetie?"

"Save the friggin baby. The nurse told me but, for you, and all your money, it would be gone. But no! You have to charge out of nowhere, meddle in my affairs, and now I'm stuck with it."

Mark looked at Jo and finding support in her eyes, took Dani's hand. "Sweetie, let's not talk about that. We can deal with it another time."

Dani snatched away her hand and, with malice in her eyes, turned to face him. "Another time? I want to say my piece now. I had it all planned. I knew what I was doing. I had things under control. But you couldn't leave things alone. Now I'm going to have this bastard child or die in the attempt. My life is ruined because of you."

"Dani, stop, you don't know what you're saying. We can deal with this together. And Nick's a good kid. He wouldn't want you to get rid of his baby."

"What's Nick got to do with anything?"

Mark looked at Jo and back at Dani. "Isn't it his baby?"

"This is my body, and I decide what I want, or don't want, in it. You're to say nothing to Nick. Do you hear me, Dad? Nothing! You too, Jo. Do you understand me? If he gets to know about this, I will never, ever, speak to either of you again!"

As Dani burst into hysterical tears, Jo called a nurse, who administered Ativan. With the medication kicking in, Dani settled.

Jo touched Mark's arm. "Let's go into the corridor," she whispered. They stopped where they could see Dani but were out of earshot. "Go easy on her, darling. She has to be in some sort of shock."

Mark paced. "What does she mean—it's her body. And why wouldn't she want Nick's baby? I don't understand any of this, and it's my fault. I've been leaving her alone too much. I was with you instead of watching her."

Jo brushed a hand down his arm. "Mark, we've had this conversation. She's an adult. You can't be expected to watch a teenager twenty-four-seven. And let's get one thing straight. You're a wonderful father. None of this is your fault."

"You don't understand, Jo. I told you after Dee died, it took me awhile to realize I was all Dani had. I made it my business to be unconditionally there for her. And until I met you, there was just her and me. I knew what she wanted before she did. I was there whenever she needed me. We spent time together as a family. Now I barely see her."

"So, what are you saying?" asked Jo softly. "That this situation is my fault."

A shadow clouded Mark's eyes. "I don't know what I'm saying. I can't make sense of anything."

"I think that's going to be the way of it for a while. But you can't punish yourself, or me, because we want to build a life together. Whatever *you* might want, Dani is growing up. It was always just a matter of time before she left you to make her own life. However, *we* are different. You and I are going to build a life together. You're stuck with me." She took Mark's hand. "Let the psychiatrist do her work. And once she tells us what's going on, we'll make whatever adjustment is necessary and go on with our lives."

Concern shadowed Mark's eyes. "Are you really ready to take that on?"

Chapter 37

When Mark and Jo arrived at Dr. Bliss's office, Dani was already there. She was staring from the window, rocking back and forth. The psychiatrist invited them to sit.

"Dani," the doctor said quietly. "Turn this way, your dad and Ms. Weston are here."

"Jo," Dani snapped. "Her name is Jo."

"Okay, your dad and Jo are here."

Dani turned, aiming a beaming smile at Jo. "Thank God. I have at least one friend in the room."

Jo moved her chair next to Dani and took her hand. "Don't worry," she said. "Everything will be all right. The doctor will get you back on track, and together we can handle the rest."

"Nothing to handle, Jo, I'm dying. Remember, I told you when we first met. You said you couldn't have kids. And I said the Newcombe women didn't do childbirth either. This baby has sentenced me to death—"

"To death?" Dr. Bliss interrupted. "What do you mean Dani?"

Dani exhaled impatiently. "Well, it's clear neither your medical team, nor my father, have fully grasped the big picture."

The doctor shot a quizzical look at Mark before refocusing on Dani. "And what is the big picture in your mind?"

"It's not in my mind. It's fact. Why are you all ignoring the obvious?"

"Dani, listen to me," Dr. Bliss said. "Years ago, it was supposed a woman with bi-polar might have difficulty with a birth. Times have changed. We have other methodologies now."

"I'm not talking about the bi-polar. Newcombe women die in childbirth, plain and simple."

Mark ran his fingers over an eyebrow. "Dani, that's not entirely true, and you know it. I have a brother. What you're saying isn't logical."

"You're not logical. I'm not talking about boys. Grandma had you two then when she got pregnant again, with a girl, she died. Mom just had me and died. Girls are killers. Go on, deny that if you can."

"I can't. But times were different then," Mark said. "There were circumstances beyond anyone's control."

"And they died," said Dani emphatically.

"Yes, but—"

"In childbirth."

"But—"

"But nothing, Dad. They died giving birth, you think about that."

A cloud shadowed Mark's eyes. "I can't help but think about it. Every time I look in your face, I see your mother and think of what might have been."

"And, yet, you want me to have this thing, knowing it will kill me."

"You have no grounds for—"

"I have plenty of 'grounds,' Dad. It's genetic. You took genetics in college. You have medical knowledge. Do the math." Dani jumped up from her seat and began to pace. "Go on, Doctor, tell him. Genetics is all about mitochondrial DNA and stuff we can't control. I'm predisposed."

Mark reached for his daughter's hand. "Dani—"

"Don't say anything else, Dad. You're ignoring me because you think I'm an hysterical kid. Well, I'm not. I know I'm going to give birth to a daughter, and I know I'm going to die. Tell him, Doctor, go on, tell him."

The doctor scribbled on her pad. "Let's just all take a step back and calm down. Mark, you're right, we've done enough tests to confirm Dani is perfectly healthy. It's highly improbable anything will happen to her in childbirth. And, Dani, in a sense, you too are correct. Genetics can do strange things. However, the issues you are referring to, mostly happen in boys. In your mother's case, she had other issues. Rare issues we're still working on understanding."

"Am I, or am I not, carrying a girl?"

"We've had no reason to establish that," the doctor said.

"So now you do, point me toward the test, right now."

"No," Mark snapped. "Absolutely not. This whole thing is a silly fixation, which will only get worse if you know for sure you're having a girl. I won't hear of any test. We have to work through this."

Dani turned on her father. "You won't hear of it—*you*. What about me, and what I want? I thought I'd made it clear. *I* decide what I do with my body, and somehow, some way, I'm getting rid of this baby."

"Dani, please, you're not thinking clearly," Mark said. "All you need is time to get your head together."

"Get my head together? Are you serious? I had my head together. I was taking personal responsibility for a pregnancy I neither expected nor wanted. But for your interference, I'd be on a plane to New Zealand and train-ing to be a vet."

"Okay, Dani, let's calm down," the doctor said. "Your father is right. From a psychological perspective, this is not the time for you to know the baby's sex. When we get you back on an even keel, I'll—".

Dani pointed at the doctor, eyes black with anger. "Just do the friggin test. Isn't that what my father is pay-ing you for?"

"Dani!" Mark snapped. "Remember your manners."

"Oh, knock it off, Dad. But for you, none of this would be happening. Now, I'm stuck with a baby that's going to kill me."

"Okay, missy, that's quite enough. Sit down, right now, and stop talking nonsense."

Dani slumped into a chair. "Not nonsense, it's fact. Fact you won't face up—"

"Mark, Dani, please, this isn't helping." The doctor pulled out an order slip. "Dani, I'm going to have you see someone who specializes in genetics. He'll establish the baby's sex and do some more tests. Let's put your mind at ease on that side of things. Then if everything checks out, we can move on with the pregnancy."

Dani turned away from everyone. "Don't want to move on. Given the first opportunity, it's gone."

✑✑✑

After a genetic evaluation that proved negative, two weeks of observation, and psychiatric intervention, Dr. Bliss was unable to make headway with Dani's fixation. She adjusted Dani's medications, so her outbursts of an-ger were less frequent. Nevertheless, Dani made it clear that, given an opportunity, she would harm her unborn child. However, when Dr. Bliss suggested Dani's state of mind warranted some time in a psychiatric facility, Mark wouldn't hear of it. He insisted that he, Jo, and Mrs. Ainsworth could take care of Dani as well as anyone. And when he assured the doctor they would monitor her closely and keep her occupied, she was released into Mark's care.

As days turned into weeks, the happy-go-lucky youngster they'd known became a morose depressive. Mark took on the role of vigilant protector, and he spent little private time with Jo. He blamed himself for everything that had happened to his once-radiant daughter. And though he found Jo a supportive, caring partner, guilt consumed him every time she appeared at the farm.

Chapter 38

Nick was frantic. Dani wouldn't take his calls or answer his emails. First, he'd been told she had the flu then strep throat and she lost her voice. Now she was experiencing some sort of psychotic break. Flu and sore throats certainly happened. And being bi-polar, Dani had experienced her share of emotional ups-and-downs. But a psychotic break? He needed to find out more about that and dialed the Newcombe farm.

"Hi, Mr. Newcombe," Nick said, frowning. "I'm sorry to be a pain. I know you keep saying don't worry about Dani, but I can't help it."

"I know, Nick, but you understand how Dani is. She says she looks like she has the plague, blotches, swollen face, and all, she doesn't want to see anybody right now."

"I don't care how she looks, I love her. I want to be there for her."

"I know, son, but she won't see you. She's worried you'll get sick, miss school, and fail a course, and it'll all be her fault. You know women, they have these ideas."

"Okay, sir, I understand about the risk of contagion. But does whatever ailment she has include a hand inju-ry?"

"Excuse me."

"I really don't mean to be rude, but I've sent dozens of emails. She hasn't answered one."

"I didn't know that," Mark said. "Why don't you give me some time to find out what she's up to, and I'll get back to you?"

"You said that last time and didn't call back."

"I know. It's been a bit hectic here. You know how farming goes. I'm cutting and splitting wood twelve hours a day. Maybe she's just in one of those girlie moods. She'll come out of it soon."

"You'll call and let me know, right?"

"Yes, Nick, I will."

Nick solemnly replaced the phone. He'd spoken amicably with Mark on many occasions. However, this time he detected a difference in the way Mark answered his questions. He'd even attempted to question his parents, doctors to the Newcombe family. But they cited patient confidentiality and would tell him nothing about Dani. Nick's only bright moment had been whispered words from Mrs. A before Mark picked up the phone. She emphatically stated that he and Dani were destined to be together. And if he found a way to confront her, they would work out whatever was wrong.

Mustering control from deep inside, Nick returned to his studies and counted down the days to Thanksgiving. At that time, nobody would prevent him from seeing Dani.

☙❧☙

When Nick pulled into Limerick, snow lay in neatly plowed roadside banks. He smiled. It always cheered him when he left the city's urban sprawl and emerged in the fresh clean air of the village. He looked up. No more snow for a while. The absence of even a wisp of cloud in the glacier blue sky boded well for him to sort out what was going on. As he entered the general store, the old boys who normally sat out front, nursing smokes and righting the world, were jabbering around the fire. They basked in the heat of the potbelly stove and grinned as Nick removed a bunch of flowers from the bait fridge. They knew for whom the expensive blooms were destined. However, as Nick spent a few minutes, catching up with local goings on, no mention was made of Dani's absence from the town's hub.

The Newcombe farmhouse was about a mile out of town. And as Nick formulated what he'd say to Dani, it seemed the longest distance he'd ever driven. He wanted to be sensitive to whatever she was going through. However, he knew he'd have a hard time masking his disappointment at her, seemingly, callous dismissal of their understanding.

As his truck razzed over the grid, he saw the Ps and the girls gathered on the porch. And when he pulled to a halt, they rushed deliriously forward. At least they were as crazy about him as they'd always been. There was no sign of Jo's SUV, and as all the dogs were present, he hoped the adults were out on errands. That would give him a fighting chance of pleading his case with Mrs. A and seeing Dani. Dogs tangled around his feet as he knocked on the door.

Mrs. A answered, and hugged him around the waist, as high as her diminutive stature would allow. "Why, Mr. Nick," she gushed, pulling him inside. "We weren't expecting you. I suppose you're up for Thanksgiving with your family."

Man and dogs spilled into the warmth of the farmhouse's kitchen. "And to see Dani."

She gestured for him to sit and produced cookies and milk. "Oh, my dear, I'm not so sure that's a good idea right now. She's not quite ready to see you."

"Not ready?"

"It's only my opinion, Mr. Nick, but she's struggling with something. It's going to take some time. She'll come around eventually. I know my girl."

"Struggling with what Mrs. A? Nobody is telling me the truth about her, what's going on?"

"Not my place to say. But I've nursed that young 'un since her mom died, and I know what she's about. Got a will of iron when she puts her mind to it, and right now she's being obstinate and doesn't want to see you."

"But you said if I faced her, we could work out whatever is bothering her."

The old housekeeper couldn't miss the pitiful sadness in his eyes. "I know, dear. And don't you worry. I know, deep down, she loves you. You simply have to be patient."

"Then I'll come back later."

"It's too soon. She won't see you, or anybody else for that matter. Things will work out, mark my words. She'll come around."

"Will you tell her I stopped by?" Nick held up the flowers. "Tell her I love her. Please, Mrs. A. she'll listen to you. Convince her we can work out whatever is wrong. I'll do anything to make things right, will you tell her that for me?"

"Of course, I will," said Mrs. A, tears welling.

⁃⊰⊱⁃

Nick called the farm every day he was in Maine. Dani wouldn't speak to him, and when he again stopped by unannounced, she wouldn't leave her room. Everybody was supportive and appropriately sympathetic, but with his hopes of seeing her dashed, he prepared to return to Harvard.

Feeling like he'd spent a Thanksgiving with nothing to

be thankful for, Nick waved goodbye to his parents. He was relieved to be away from their constant attempts at cheering him up. And though he knew they were trying to help, their concern made his isolation and confusion more acute.

The drive back to Boston gave Nick time to think, and one thing was clear. Neither he nor anyone else could force Dani to marry him. If she'd changed her mind, so be it. However, they'd known each other for so long, and had shared so much. If Dani no longer wanted him, hearing it directly from her was the only acceptable end to what they had together.

Chapter 39

As Jo joined Mark on the sofa, there was a thousand miles between them. She hadn't felt so isolated since her first night alone in Maine. At that time, it was he who helped her make sense of her feelings. Now, she had to try to help him out of whatever abyss he had fallen into.

She took his hand. "I can hear the cogs turning. None of this is your fault—so whatever is going on in that head of yours, you and I have to talk about it."

"I should have spent more time with her, Jo. Until recently, I had no idea childbirth frightened her so much."

"That's not the sort of casual conversation a daughter has with her dad."

"You were a complete stranger and, after a couple of hours, you knew all about it."

"It's a girl thing," Jo said. "I'm sure all her friends knew how freaked out she was."

"They did."

"How do you know that?"

"We talked about it."

Jo raised an eyebrow. "Good grief, how did that conversation come about?"

"They came by with some gifts. She wouldn't see them. However, we got talking. One of them said some-

thing like, 'God I haven't seen her this freaked out since
Kathy, whatever her name, I forget now, got pregnant.'
Then the floodgates opened and they told me quite a few
things about my own daughter I didn't know. I should
have approached her fear differently, but I brushed it under the carpet."

"We're all wise in hindsight. But in the big scheme of
things, it's not you who has the communication issue."

"Excuse me?" asked Mark.

"You talk. You get people to open up. You're willing
to share your experiences, no matter how painful. It's
Dani who has trouble."

"She's bi-polar. Withdrawal and paranoia are part of
the deal. Why do you think I get so crazy when she
doesn't take her meds? Besides aren't young people re-
luctant to listen to their dad's opinion."

Jo grinned. "Well, there is that. But seriously, darling,
can you set Dani aside for one second? Because we have
another issue that needs attention."

"Us?" asked Mark.

"Bingo," said Jo. "I know you feel guilty about what
happened, but I'm here to help you sort out the demons.
Since we met, you've been my rock and sounding board.
You've taught me more about myself, my feelings, and
how to truly love someone than I've had hot dinners. I
have *never* felt more safe and secure in a relationship,
and I know I will spend the rest of my life paying you
back for that. You don't have to deal with any of this
alone. However—"

"Uh-oh, I hate the 'however.'"

"*However,* lately there are light years of distance between us. I'm afraid part of you is unconsciously shutting
me out."

Mark smiled.

"Why are you smiling?"

"Funny you should say light years. I remember my first foray into bringing you from the darkness was a lesson in star-gazing."

"So, it's fitting, because I intend to drag you kicking and screaming from the dark place you've parked yourself. I want my carefree, adventurous, spontaneous cavalier back. This gloomy Gus, who, might I add, is losing his healthy outdoors tan, is not at all my style. So, having said all that, where do you want me to start?"

"I have no idea. Do you really want to do this now?"

"Yes," said Jo emphatically. "Although it sounds like it could be a bumpy road. How about I just talk and see where we go. That okay with you?"

"You know, I might be a little confused at the moment, but I'll eventually sort everything out."

"No doubt. However, being an impatient, in-your-face, make-it-happen kind of gal, I'm forging ahead."

Mark smiled thinly. "There's absolutely nothing I can do to stop this, right?"

"Nothing."

"What if I'm just not in the mood to discuss it?"

"Simply listen. I'm saying my piece no matter what." Jo waited for Mark to reply, but he did not. "So, we both know from experience that dark places are tough. When you're there, they seem impenetrable. Until something happens to point you in the right direction. With me, it was my boss telling me I'd lost my mojo. Next thing I know, I'm in Maine buying a house on the say so of a trio of dogs."

"Think I had a little to do with that," said Mark quietly.

"I know, but let's go with the dog thing for a moment."

"It's your 'piece.'"

Jo smiled. "We both agree that Dani is in her dark

zone right now. Nevertheless, I'm confident something will happen to point her where she needs to go. But why, to put it bluntly, are you?"

"I don't follow."

"You're going to be grandfather. Something I know is right up your alley. You should be ecstatic, making plans for tea parties and such with your daughter and her little princess. Instead, you're pussyfooting around Dani's emotions, and it's dragging you into her darkness. You're not supporting her, or helping her get out of it, like you helped me. You're enabling her."

"It's not like that at all. Besides where are you going with this?"

"Look over there." She nodded toward the corner where the dogs were lying. "I have never seen all six of them so subdued, so sad, so off their game. And do you know why?"

"Why?"

"They feel it from you, and they feel it from Dani and Mrs. A. I don't think any of you has a right to visit darkness on the Ps, let alone the girls, 'cos they're mine now. Those dogs brought this family together, and you shouldn't set them aside because you all have an issue. An issue none of you chooses to deal with."

"Yikes, that's quite a speech," Mark said. "Have we really been neglecting them?"

"*You*—for the sake of this speech—have been neglecting all of us." Jo squeezed his hand. "As you can tell, I've been elected spokesperson for the combined pack. And between you, me, and the gatepost, you need, and I emphasize *need*, to snap out of this funk. Whatever you do, be sure the dogs and I will love you unconditionally. However, we much prefer our old master."

Mark smirked. "I'm your master?"

"Yeah, absolutely, all the way." Jo pulled his hand to

her lips and kissed his knuckles. "I'm serious, Mark. I hate seeing you this way. It tears me apart. If this hole you've made for yourself is our new norm, I'll make that adjustment you and I talked about—"

"You remember that?"

"Of course I do, which is why I've given you some time to sort out how best we can help Dani. However, I'm now officially over that portion of the adjustment schedule. If Dani is to flourish, we *both* have to put a positive spin on whatever is happening to her. We have to give the Ps access to her room, whether she wants it or not. We have to stop allowing her to cut herself off from everything and everybody. We have to get her life back to as normal as we can make it. And finally, we have to find a way to clue in Nick."

"That's not going to be easy," said Mark. "You know he's worried sick about her. If we told him the truth, he'll insist in seeing her *and* getting involved. And remember what Dani said. My daughter means what she says. We'd lose her entirely."

"How would you feel if right now, for no reason, I cut off all contact with you?"

"I'm with you in spirit, and I take your point about Nick. But telling him makes me really nervous."

"I don't advocate a party, but baby steps are most definitely in order. We know he's been by and, without doubt, he'll be back. Let's not be so diligent in keeping him from her."

Mark squeezed Jo's hand. "When did you get so smart?"

"Oh, it's always been there, you just fought me every step of the way."

"Hey, aren't those my words."

"I'm a quick learner. So, what do you say? Can we please get back to some semblance of normal and that includes you getting away from this farm now and again?"

"Can I really leave Dani alone?"

"Number one, you have Mrs. A. Number two, we can hire a nurse. Number three, you've left me alone for weeks and, hellooo, I'm over that too. I'm your fiancée, but about now I feel like your maiden aunt."

Mark smiled. "Jo, I'm so sorry, I had no idea this business was consuming me."

"I know. That's why we're having this conversation. We have options in regards to Dani and her ongoing care. We'll explore every one of them to get what's best for her and us. But right now, I want my man, and I want him bad."

Mark smiled. "You really are special, you know that?"

"You better believe it, buster." Jo took a list from her pocket. "Now here are the local home health nurses. We are going to get one, or more of them, over here. We are then going to spend several hours at my place proving how much we love each other. Then we are going to reintroduce Dani to her family, four-legged and otherwise. You up for that?"

Mark stroked her cheek. "Have you any idea how much I love you?"

"Not at the moment, but I figure after several hours at the cabin I might."

Mark smiled. "Now there's the nympho I know and love."

"Welcome back, fiancé," she whispered. "Now come here." Jo pulled him close and kissed him as if her life depended on it.

Chapter 40

Nick had spent the weeks between the Thanksgiving and Christmas breaks trying to work out how he would see Dani. Once he'd seriously begun to think his situation through, the solution to his dilemma wasn't difficult. The answers he sought, though protected, were right under his nose—in the files of the clinic attached to his parent's house. His mother had been Dani's doctor since her birth, and whichever specialist she might have seen would generate a treatment plan in her medical record. He simply had to wait for the clinic to close, borrow his mother's keys, sneak in, and pull Dani's file. It was of no consequence that his future would be in jeopardy if he were caught breaching a patient's confidentiality. The most important thing was to bring back the smart, vivacious spirit he'd pledged his life to. Nick smiled. Forewarned was forearmed, and when he actually faced Dani and brought all their obstacles into the open, he had no doubt they'd work things out.

❧❦❧

As he left the confines of the city, whose grubby slush-filled streets displayed the unpleasant face of a New England winter, Nick couldn't wait to see the pristine snow-blanketed meadows of rural Maine. And driving north, Massachusetts and New Hampshire flew by all but unnoticed. His spirit soared as he hung a right off the turnpike and the White Mountains rose unyielding and resolute ahead of him. It hadn't snowed for a couple of days, and banks of snow reflected dangerously blinding, contrasting the precisely plowed ebony road, slick wet, and refreshed from snowmelt.

He arrived in Cornish around noon as the sun's unfiltered rays radiated through an ice blue sky. Ice-clad tree limbs sparkled like silver ribbons, dripping a steady stream of water into swollen ditches running fast on the Indian summer day. But Nick knew such respite would be short lived. When the sun sank powerless beneath the evening's frigid air, the melting waters journey would halt, freezing black and treacherous in the night. At such a time, when nature was at her most unyielding, and all sensible folk sought shelter, he determined to reach his goal.

ᥱᦺᥱᦺ

When Nick's parents closed the clinic and entered the house, aromatic drafts of garlic and basil indicated their son was home. "Ho, Nicko," said his father. "Seems we have our master-chef back. Things must be A-Okay in your world."

"Hi, guys, I guess they are."

His mom stepped forward and pecked his cheek. "Good, now did you get the—" She looked in the dining room. "Yes, you did, table laid, and wine poured."

"Early Christmas gift, mom," said Nick. "All you have to do is sit and enjoy a family evening."

Nick's dad patted his shoulder. "It's been a long time, son, we missed them."

"I know, Dad. I'm sorry for being such a brat on my last couple of trips up. But it's all good now, let's eat."

⌀⌀⌀

Nick's parents hung on every word of their son's Harvard experience at the hands of this or that tutor who was still in-situ so long after their education. And though they didn't ask, it was assumed his lack of conversation about Dani meant Nick was at peace with her absence. By eight, the family had settled into playing after-dinner board games.

"So, Nick," said his mom. "You'll be joining us at the mayor's Christmas Eve Ball tomorrow."

"I don't think so, Mom. It's always so adult and stuffy."

"Excuse me, did you just call your dad and me stuffy."

"Not you two, silly, the others. You know, the Barkers, Parkers, Lurkers, and Jerkers."

His parents laughed.

"Besides I'm bushed from studying as well as working. If it's okay with you, I'd just like to get in some early nights."

"Of course," said his mom, patting his hand. "We'll bring you home some goodies."

"No, Mom, please. You know the only thing left will be Mrs. Riley's fruitcake. You're a doctor, you know it's gonna kill someone one day."

"Fresh mouth—it most certainly will not."

"Oh, I don't know, Emily," said his dad, refilling wine glasses. "I think he's got something there."

"You're incorrigible, both of you." Emily pointed at her husband. "You, drink your wine in the kitchen as you load the dishwasher." She turned to Nick. "You, get to bed, you look about beat."

"Yes, Mommy, fank oo," joked Nick.

Emily smiled. "You really are getting a fresh mouth, young man. And I'm certain Harvard didn't teach you that."

∽∾∽

As Nick lay in bed, only he knew that while his parents were at the ball, he'd be in the clinic interrogating the file of the woman he loved. Content with his decision, and warmed by thoughts of Dani, he drifted into a dream of them together.

She rode, burnished copper billowing behind like lava flowing from a fiery volcano, and he chased the beacon of her light across lavender fields. He rode fast but couldn't catch her. Then she was waiting on a distant knoll. And even as she dropped from her horse and beckoned him forward, he couldn't reach her. He was outside her dream-space looking in, mesmerized by her green eyes and blush-pink lips inviting a kiss. But he was paralyzed beneath her outstretched arms. Dodging and ducking he crawled, fooling the protective powers. But within an arm's length of her feet, a torrent of water gushed between them. And though swim he might, he could not forge the raging river that divided. Ethereal and angelic, she silently watched his despair, willing him to triumph and make love to her. He ached to feel her skin beneath his fingers, spend his passion, and refill his heart with her love. But no matter how he tried, she remained out of reach. In half sleep, he tossed, frustrated and helpless, and all he felt was the agonizing need for her. And his agony was the key. Now he felt her skin beneath his fingers. Now he smelled the perfume of her hair. Now he lay naked and open beside her. He craved the melding of her body with his. But when he tried to sink within her, mak-

ing love the way he remembered, she pushed him away. And his voice whispered, thick with anguish and unrequited love. He wanted to taste her skin and feel her legs about him, and he pleaded to be heard. But his plea fell on deaf ears. She would not listen. And as she drifted away, he could do nothing. Rooted to a spot not of his making, he watched helplessly and she drifted far. He fought to stand. Scratched at the air in an attempt to rise. But it made no difference. He could not reach her. Then he was standing, transfixed and impotent, head bowed with shoulders caved from despair and pain.

And she felt his loss. She waved and moved toward him. She reached out and begged him to forgive her. And as glossy pearls flowed translucent over her alabaster skin, his heart filled with love. But when he raised his arms to comfort her, and brush away her tears, she dissolved into a sweetly perfumed kaleidoscope haze. And in the haze was a beautiful girl child with blue-green eyes and a shock of strawberry-blond hair. She smiled with an innocence he would forever remember.

ಞಞ

Nick woke with a start, perspiration beading his brow. His breath came in short sharp gasps, and he knew what was wrong. It was all there in his dream. He loved her more now than he could ever imagine because he knew Dani was pregnant. Pregnant with his baby. And for some reason, she didn't want to tell him. Was it because it might prevent him from continuing at Harvard or her going to New Zealand? How silly was his goose of a girl.

With his mind a whirlwind of emotions, he sat on the bed. Did she think he wouldn't stick by her and make things work? Was the child he saw not their baby, but a facsimile of her, indicating she was too young to be making love? Did the child with the blue-green eyes represent both of them? Was he the one too young to be serious about her? Did dreams mean anything anyway?

For his peace of mind and her ongoing sanity, it was imperative he see her file, talk to her, and convince her how much he cared.

Chapter 41

On Christmas Eve afternoon, Nick called at the farm with a gift for Dani. He wanted to make one last attempt to see her, before resorting to invading her privacy.

Mark answered the door. "Hi, Nick, I heard you were home. Your parents must be excited to see you again."

"Yes, sir, they are, I made dinner, haven't done that in a while...er...could I see Dani?"

"She's not..."

"Just for a minute, I won't put any pressure on her, I promise."

"She's not here, Nick."

"Not here? But it's Christmas, she loves Limerick at Christmas, she wouldn't want to be anywhere else."

"Things change," Mark said calmly. "People change."

"Not Dani, where did she go?"

"To spend Christmas with her uncle in upstate New York."

"Upstate New York, she has an uncle in New York? I thought he lived in Arizona?"

"Did...moved...recently. Wanted to be back in the pines."

"They have pines in Arizona. Up north, Flagstaff, and such."

"He...er, he had some medical issues. Wanted to be nearer family too."

Mark looked uncharacteristically flustered and Nick frowned. "Dani never mentioned anything about that."

"It seems you don't know her as well as you think."

"I don't know much of anything right now." Nick handed Mark a small exquisitely wrapped gift. "You better hold on to this then. It's her Christmas gift."

"I'll give it to her."

Nick retreated to his truck. It had been some time since he'd cried about anything. He'd always been taught to cope with whatever came his way. Nevertheless, as the truck ate up the frosty miles back to Cornish, tears of frustration freely flowed.

❧❧

Jo arrived at the farm a few minutes after Nick left. "Was that Nick I saw tearing off toward Cornish," she asked.

Mark nodded. "I hate lying to that boy. He's so decent and honest."

"I know, darling. But we agreed, baby steps. They need to get together but after Dani screamed at Mrs. A. this morning for hanging Christmas stockings, I don't think the time is right. It's too overwhelming. You did right saying nothing."

"Nick reminded me how much Dani used to love Christmas," said Mark. "The caroling in Limerick, the lights and all. God, will we ever get that back?"

Jo ran a hand down Marks arm. "Yes, we will. But for now, we bite our tongue and let things play out. I feel sure Nick will be back while he's on break. But we're agreed right? Adding him the mix now might push Dani over an edge we don't want to re-visit."

"Right." Mark put an arm around Jo. "If we've come to terms with her situation, why can't she?"

"Don't have an answer. We simply continue letting her know that no matter what, we love her, and one day, she might come back into our world. And talking about coming back, that goes for you too."

"What does that mean?"

"Have you looked in the mirror lately?" Jo pulled him in front of the hallstand and ruffled his hair. "This normally shines like copper, and I can practically braid it. I already told you how pale you were, and you've lost weight. I like your muscles, so you're going to have to do some serious log splitting. And I just noticed the dark rings under your eyes, which means you need a good night's sleep."

"It's not easy maintaining the GQ look when you have a daughter driving you nuts."

"Maybe, so I will make it my job to ensure you are the best-looking nut around."

Mark took her in his arms and pecked her on the nose. "I'm a mess, why do you bother with me?"

"Now that's a phrase I'm familiar with. Because I love you, and, unlike your daughter, I will always tell you everything." She pecked him on the lips. "Now, part deux of the Newcombe recovery plan involves a change of venue."

"For whom?"

"Me. I'm moving in so you can resume your work on the farm and at the cabin. Just between us, the guy you sent to plow my drive doesn't do anywhere near as good a job as you do. And my thank you smooch on him isn't nearly as satisfying as with you."

"*What*?"

Jo giggled. "Gotcha. Just wanted to make sure you were paying attention. After Christmas, we should increase the nurse from just days when Mrs. A is gone to include nights. That should allow you to get some decent sleep. I will be here and available whenever, for whatever you desire in the way of emotional and physical support."

"Oh, really, we talking days and nights?"

"Animal. So, what do you think?"

"Personally, I think it's a great suggestion." He nuzzled her neck. "I can see how you moving in will allow me to get more sleep."

She smiled and pushed him away. "It will only work if you actually sleep. Jeez, and you wonder why I'm a nympho. You do nothing to discourage the idea."

"And aren't you glad?"

Jo smiled. "Yes, sir—yes, I most definitely am." She kissed him hard. "Now, that's your quota for a while. I have my clothes in the car. It's Christmas Eve, and if we're going to get back to some semblance of normalcy, I intend to start at the mayor's ball. Mrs. A should be here any minute to watch Dani."

☙❧☙

When they were set to go, Mark was still nervous about leaving Dani. He vividly remembered two weeks previous when she was in Mrs. A's care. Apparently, the farmhouse turned strangely cold, and the old lady went down to the cellar to check on the furnace. When she returned, Dani was sitting in the middle of the kitchen floor with a pair of scissors. She was staring at the wall, with a strangely peaceful smile and had hacked off her hair. When she got up, leaving a haystack of Titian locks on the ground, she put the scissors back in the drawer. Then, after kissing the old lady said, "Sorry, Mrs. A, it's just too much trouble."

Chapter 42

When Nick pulled onto his parent's drive, he didn't want them to see him upset. He sat quietly for a moment and focused on the conversation at the farm. Putting aside the actual words, Nick felt Mark Newcombe looked uncharacteristically uncomfortable. He definitely sounded different. Tight, pinched, his answers too pat. Nick felt sure Dani would have mentioned if her uncle was so sick, he had to leave Arizona. Especially when part of his reason to go there, was to escape New England's crippling winters. Moreover, when he handed over Dani's gift, Mark said, "I'll give it to her." Not, "I'll keep it 'til she gets back," or, "I'll send it to her." "I'll give it to her." Those words rang true. Dani was still at the farm. Nick smiled. He thought he felt her presence. Could smell her perfume. Could hear her breathing nearby. Now his mind was set. He'd tried to do it the legal way, the moral way, and it failed. Now he was going to break the law, and he didn't care. Tonight, come what may, he was getting the information he needed. Then he was going to confront Dani.

Chapter 43

As the elegantly dressed doctors climbed into the limo, Nick was relieved to see them go. He watched the car leave the drive, returned to the kitchen, and pulled his mother's keys from the cabinet. He paced anxiously for five full minutes, counting down the last seconds. Then he dashed across the breezeway connecting his parent's house to the medical center. The outer door's key was familiar and he let himself into the waiting area. Then taking a deep breath, he crossed his fingers and approached the inner office's security keypad. Hoping the code hadn't changed, he tapped in the numbers he'd used at his last stint as a clinic volunteer. When the green light blinked, he mentally high fived and slipped silently into the records area.

Banks of lateral files sat front and center. However, he headed off to the right where a small wall-cupboard hung behind the office managers desk. He selected the smallest key on his mother's key ring and slipped it into the lock. With a triumphant, "Yes," Nick opened the key cupboard.

The daunting collection of identical keys hanging before him momentarily squelched his enthusiasm. Fortunately, he'd worked with his parents' well-organized officer manager. He knew exactly what to look for. Setting aside a pile of identity blanks on the cabinet bottom, he found the key ID card she'd made. Within seconds, he was holding a pair of small silver keys marked *M/R-MNO-5/3*.

Turning back to the files, Nick stood before medical records file number five, knowing somewhere in the third drawer down he'd find Dani's record. He didn't entirely know why, but he hesitated as he opened the drawer. Turning back wasn't an option. It was too late, he'd broken in. He'd already compromised his integrity. With nothing to lose, he flipped the folders, until he reached Newcombe, D.

With trembling fingers, Nick pushed the files before and after it aside. He hesitated again, but not for himself, for Dani, knowing how fiercely independent and private she was.

So, is this really it, he thought, taking out the file and placing it on the cabinet's pullout countertop workspace. *Is invading the privacy of the woman I love something circumstances dictate I may do. Or is it something I absolutely have to do.* He flipped open the file. *Will knowing this medical information change how I feel, or will not knowing it drive me mad?*

Nick set his flashlight to shine directly on the neatly catalogued pages, and silently thanked his mother for her fastidious attention to administrative detail. And while his immediate question was quickly answered, when he delved deeper into the file, concern clouded his face. A tear slid down his cheek as he replaced the file, retraced his steps to the house, and returned his mother's keys to the kitchen cabinet. All he could ask himself was *Why*?

એએએ

As Nick followed an evening snowplow along a deserted RTE 160, nothing stopped the mammoth machine from throwing its burden aside. And as the snow set hard into banks of pristine simplicity, Nick wondered if the knowledge he now possessed would wipe his and Dani's slate as clean.

When he arrived at the farm, Mrs. Ainsworth answered the door. "Why young Mr. Nick." She smiled. "How nice to see you. What're you doing here on Christmas Eve, aren't you supposed to be at the mayor's ball?"

"Not my style Mrs. A, besides I'd rather be with Dani." He stepped past her into the house. "May I come in a minute?"

"Why of course, where are my manners? Come into the kitchen, I'll get you some hot chocolate, and a couple of those almond cookies you love."

"That's all right Mrs. A, I'm not hungry. I just need a few words with Dani, and then I'll go."

"She's not here, Mr. Nick, gone to relatives in New York for a bit. Change of scene don't you know? Doctor said it would be good for her."

"Then why are you here?"

"Watching all them dogs for Mr. Mark and Ms. Jo."

"No you're not, they don't need watching. Mrs. Ainsworth, I'm sorry to sound rude, but I know Dani is here, and I have to see her. I'm going crazy with everybody telling me stories about her being sick. I'm not a child, I know what's going on, and I know she's not sick. If she doesn't want to see me again, it's her choice, but I need to hear it from her. Please, it's Christmas. Don't make me go through this torture. I need to see her just once. I can't bear not knowi—" Nick detected a change in the housekeeper's expression, and turned to find Dani standing in the doorway.

"What do you want, Nick?" Dani said coldly.

He rushed forward, taking her in his arms. "I've been so worried. Why won't you talk to me?"

Dani pushed him away. "Got nothing to say."

"We've got plenty to say." He glanced down at her belly.

Mrs. Ainsworth clattered some pots. "Why don't you two go into the parlor, I'll bring you a nice cup of chocolate."

Nick clasped Dani's hand. "Thank you, Mrs. A., and I really would love a couple of those cookies."

"Go away with you now. I'll be right along."

The two sat silently side-by-side until Mrs. Ainsworth had deposited the hot chocolate and cookies.

"Why did you come, Nick?" Dani asked. "I thought I'd made it clear I didn't want to see you."

"I came because I love you. And since when are we a one-sided affair? How come you're the only one who gets to decide whether we continue seeing each other? We had an understanding."

"I changed my mind."

"And didn't have the guts to tell me to my face?"

"Wasn't like that."

"Wasn't like what, Dani? I thought you cared for me. What we did—didn't it mean anything to you?"

"You mean making love."

"Of course, I mean making love. Why are you being so weird?"

"Things have changed."

"You said that already, though God knows what you think could change to make me stop loving you. What did I do that was so awful you couldn't at least discuss it with me before saying you don't want to see me."

"Don't want to talk about it," said Dani.

"Well, damn what you want. You're going to talk

about it. We had plans to get married and spend the rest of our lives together. You can't simply tell me to go to hell without an explanation."

"Can and will."

"Okay, so now we've straightened out what you want, let's discuss what I want. We'll start with my baby!"

He might as well have slapped her in the face.

"Yes, I know about the baby. How long did you think you could keep that a secret in such a small community?"

"You don't understand."

"I'm trying, Dani. I love you, and nothing will change that. I want us to be together. I want you. I want to be part of my baby's life. Please don't turn me away. Whatever we need to do, we can work this out."

"You have to finish college, I have to go to college. This is not what we planned."

He took her hand in his. "Life doesn't always work out exactly the way you plan. It doesn't mean what happens instead is any less important. I love you, and I want our baby. What I don't understand is why you tried to kill yourself."

"Didn't plan to kill myself—just the baby."

"Goddammit, Dani, why? Did you think I would abandon you? Didn't you for one minute think this might happen when we made love?"

"We used protection."

"So what? Condoms aren't fool proof. You get what you get. Besides, if you remember, I told you I'd been carrying around the first one we used for years. It could have been broken or perished. You probably got pregnant that very first time."

Dani hadn't, for one second, imagined that could happen. All she could think about was a day of stupidity by Jo's swimming pool, the nightmares of an assignation with a rake like Chase Markum, and the probability that the baby wasn't Nick's.

"Look, none of that matters now," Nick said. "What matters is I want you to be my wife, and I want our baby to have a real family. I love you with all my heart and soul. How many times do I have to say it before you believe absolutely nothing will ever change that?"

"Nothing?" whispered Dani.

"You really know how to drive me nuts, don't you? Absolutely nothing. Now stand up and let me see you."

"Won't—I'm fat."

"You're not fat, you're pregnant, there's a difference." Her voluminous dressing gown was obscuring her belly. He loosened the ties, and ran his hands over her rotund belly. "You're beautiful."

Dani stroked his mass of blond wavy hair. And feeling the tenderness of his hands on her body, she realized how much she loved him and missed having him close. "I'm ugly, and what you don't know is that this thing will kill me."

He held her at arms-length. "What're you talking about?"

"You know about my mother and grandmother. I'm not supposed to have children."

"That's nonsense, and you know it. You've had every test imaginable, there's nothing in your records to indicate—"

Dani backed out of his hands. "My records. You've seen my medical records? How did you get those?"

Nick flushed beet red. "I borrowed my mother's keys."

"And what else did you see?" Dani snapped. "That I'm crazy and need to be put away?"

"Does it matter?"

"Yes, it matters. That stuff is my business and you had

no right to pry. Now you need to leave. I don't want your pity."

"There's no pity. You're carrying my baby."

"Says who?"

"God, you *are* crazy. What is going on in your head?"

"Nothing that need concern you."

"Everything you do concerns me," said Nick.

"Well, I've certainly heard that before. Have you and dad been conspiring? What's with you men? You all want to control me."

Nick couldn't hide his shocked expression. "That's more nonsense, and you know that too. Your dad could've put you away but he didn't—because he loves you. I know he believes that together we can make things right."

"We?"

"Yes, 'we.' I believe that too. I could've taken your 'don't want to see you' for a final answer. I could've continued college, met someone else, had a big fancy wedding, and given her babies. But I didn't. Doesn't that say something to you?"

Dani pouted. "Says that everyone thinks they know my business better than I do."

"No, it doesn't. It says that many people love you, Dani. Whatever lunatic things are in your head, we'll deal with them. You're not crazy. You're simply confused about your situation. And what you really need right now is me. So here I am, and here I'll stay until you tell me to my face that you don't love me."

"You have to promise not to do that again."

"Do what again?"

"Look at my private stuff without permission."

"Why?"

"Because I'm asking you, that's why."

"Okay, if it makes you feel better, I promise," Nick

said tenderly. "But there shouldn't be any secrets between us. You can tell me anything. It won't change the way I feel about you."

Dani frowned. Everyone had secrets. But hers was so monumental nobody could know. Having another man's baby was the worst kind of betrayal, and she had no clue how she could tell him. But it might not come to that. What would Nick know if she "lost" the baby a little farther down the line? It would simply confirm what she'd told him. Newcombe women don't do childbirth well. She would sort things out. There was still time to make things right. For now, however, she was content to bask in his attention. She had missed him. And was glad he was here, loving her still. Just as she wanted. The true test of his love would come later.

"Are you sure?" she asked, running a hand down his cheek.

"I'm absolutely, one hundred percent, rock bottom solid, sure. But I do have a question."

"Which is?"

"What the heck did you do to your hair?"

Dani ran her fingers through what was left of her fiery tresses and smiled nervously. "It was too girly."

Nick's heart melted. "You are such a goose. We really need to discuss your doing daft things and acting like a crazy person. However, right now, I desperately need to kiss you. I want to hold you, and feel you care. You do still care, don't you?"

A tear formed in the corner of Dani's eye, and she nodded.

He chucked her under the chin. "Say it."

"It." She smiled. "And I love you."

"That's all I needed to know."

Chapter 44

The most prestigious gathering of the season was the mayor's ball. It is an opportunity for everyone to catch up on good, and bad, news in Cornish, and the surrounding villages. The most exciting happening this year was not the abundant harvest or early onset of snow. It was the engagement of Mark Newcombe, the most eligible bachelor in four counties, to a woman from away.

Mark warned Jo she would be the unwitting guest of honor. Therefore, she wasn't surprised half the county wanted to talk to her. By mid-evening, Mark was surprised at the number of crest-fallen available women who wanted to have him confirm he was really off the market. And as his amusement turned to irritation, he imagined the only way he could quiet tongues was to enlist the help of a town crier. He'd schmoozed and danced his way around the ballroom, and by the time he made it back to Jo, it was ten-thirty. He approached her with a tray of champagne.

"Good grief," she said. "Are we that desperate?"

"Mrs. Nelson waylaid me and ordered me to pass them around. But dammit, I think I am that desperate."

Jo took a sip of wine. "Wow, I'm impressed. This is the real stuff."

"Always is," said Mark. "Don't let the country bumpkin demeanors fool you. These people are smart cookies with money who know how to throw a party."

Jo smiled. She was warming to the different social pace. The city people she knew had seemed shallow and grasping compared to the folks she was discovering in the village.

"It's actually quite nice to be an object of curiosity. Except when it got a bit creepy."

"What do you mean?" asked Mark.

"The guy over there in the pale blue tux asked me so many questions I thought he was going to propose."

Mark smiled. "Being from the city, he was probably checking your bona fides."

"Excuse me?"

"That's Mac, our local state trooper. He keeps an eye on all of us. Likes to know who he's dealing with. Knows more about us than we know about ourselves."

Jo raised an eyebrow. "That's a bit scary."

"Won't be if you ever need him. He's a lousy dresser but a first-rate cop."

"I'll remember that."

Mark put down his glass and ran his fingers down Jo's face. "So, I don't know about you, but I'm about ready to call this a night."

"Old man can't keep up, eh?"

Mark smiled and pecked her on the nose. "I can keep up plenty, just not in a roomful of people watching us like hawks."

"Okay," said Jo. "Given this is your first foray, into the land of the living, since Dani got sick, I think you've done your bit. Come on, let's get home and put our feet up."

❦❦❦

On the drive home, Mark was very subdued. He pulled the Porsche off to the side of the road.

"You okay?" asked Jo.

"Fine."

"So, we're stopping here because…" When Mark leaned across and kissed her, Jo felt the same hunger as when they made love. It was several minutes before they broke apart. "Now *that* I don't mind stopping for," she said. "I have so missed my spontaneous cavalier. Welcome back."

"Darling, I'm so sorry. I haven't had much time to think about anything but—"

Jo put a finger on his lips. "I know. It's all right, I understand."

"You won't leave me, will you?"

She giggled. "Leave you—whatever gave you that idea?"

"I saw the way some of those guys were holding you. You were smiling and happy and—"

"You're jealous."

"It's that obvious?"

"Oh, yeah, come here, fool." Jo locked her mouth on his, and as her hand traveled down his body.

His response was instant, and he gently pushed her back. "Darling, I love you so much, I desperately need to make love to you. If we go back to the farm, we have to have hot chocolate, eat cookies, and talk to people. All I want to do right now is make you scream."

"Mark, be serious you're six-three, I'm five-eleven. We're in a Porsche—do the math. We could injure something, and I don't mean the car."

He'd almost forgotten her wicked sense of humor and, smiling, he realized how much he'd missed it. "I don't mean here. I can turn this car around and we can book into The Farrington Inn."

"Mrs. A's nephew is picking her up at twelve-thirty, the cabin is nearer."

"I need more time than that. I want to make love until we can't stand. I want to tease you until you beg for mercy. I want to do things to you no man has ever done."

Jo moaned softly. "I'm not sure I can handle that in the time allotted, but an extended quickie would be very much appreciated."

"I'm serious. Jo. I am so over nurses, helpers, and all manner of strangers in our house. I'm sick of listening for a knock on our door, or a call for help. Dammit, I want to stay in bed all day making love and drinking champagne. I want us to be *us.*"

"I know, sweetie. But let's get Dani better, and then we can spend all the time we want. We'll make love until we're sick of each other."

"And when will that be? What if its months, or years. What if she never gets better?"

"It doesn't matter how long it takes, I'll always be here for you."

"Well, I can't wait. I've racked my brains about what to do and I keep coming back to the nursing home we talked about. I can't do any more for her here, and guilt is consuming me. I haven't done any of the things I'd planned for the farm. I'm constantly lying to Nick, the poor kid calls every day hoping to speak to Dani. He's obviously crazy in love with her." He ran his hand lightly down Jo's cheek. "And most important, I'm neglecting you. You've been so patient, but I simply can't do this any longer. We have to send her away to recover. I know it'll hurt for a while, but I have to do what's best for everyone."

Jo squeezed his hand. "Whatever you decide, I'm a hundred percent behind you."

"I know, and I thank God every day you're here." He

kissed her again, and his hand moved to her breast. "Now, I'm really desperate. Are we on for that quickie, or what?"

෴

It was approaching one o'clock when they pulled into the farmyard and the first thing they noticed was an unfamiliar vehicle.

"That must belong to Mrs. A's nephew," Mark said. "We owe them big time for waiting." Moving quickly to the farmhouse, the door opened before he and Jo reached it.

It was Dani with one hand on the door and the other holding a large kitchen knife. She had an extraordinarily contented smile. "Hi, you two," she said. "Have a good time?"

Given what he knew of her mental state, Mark feared something had happened. "Yes, pumpkin, we did." He kept Jo behind him. "Why are you answering the door with a knife, and where's Mrs. A?"

"Gone."

He moved cautiously. "Gone where, sweetie?"

"Home," said Dani matter-of-factly.

"Home where, pumpkin?"

"Home where?" Dani asked. "Why are you being so weird, Dad? Perry Corner, second house on the right. We took her home hours ago."

"We?" Mark turned back to Jo, worry in his eyes.

Dani reached behind the door. "Nick and me."

As Dani stepped aside, Mark breathed a sigh of relief.

Nick fanned his fingers at the adults. "Hi, Mr. Newcombe, Jo."

"Is that your car?" asked Mark.

"Mom's. My truck is in the shop."

Mark held Jo's hand and took a step forward. "What's with the knife, Dani, you scared the beejezus out of me."

"Making sandwiches."

"God almighty," he said, exasperated. "And why are you here, Nick?"

"I'm sorry, Mr. Newcombe, I know you said I couldn't see Dani, but I was desperate."

Jo squeezed Mark's hand. "Darling, I'm freezing out here, let's talk inside."

As she walked past the teens, Jo ran her hand tenderly over Dani's shaggy head and smiled. In the kitchen, to-mato soup and cheese sandwiches were waiting.

Mark undid his tie, took off his jacket, and sat at the table. "You did this for us?"

Dani nodded. "Jo did it for us when we were at the cabin. I remember it made me feel so...well, she knows what I mean." The women exchanged a look of under-standing. "Dad, we have something important we need to talk about." Dani scooched closer to Nick and entwined her fingers with his.

"Pretty much figured that out," Mark said, grinning.

After doling out soup and sandwiches, Jo sat next to Mark, making sure her leg touched his.

"It seems you two worked out whatever was bothering you," he said.

"I'm so sorry I've put you and Jo through hell," Dani said, pulling Nick close. "Nick and I talked. I think I'll be able to get it together now."

Nick kissed her cheek.

"Thank God," Mark said. "Does that mean I get my little girl back?

Dani rubbed her belly. "Dad, I'm more pregnant than Nelly Ratson's mare. Little is not exactly my current state."

"You know what I mean."

Dani smiled. "Yeah, I do."

"So, come here." Mark held out his arms.

Dani moved around the table and buried her head in his shoulder. "Nick has something he wants to ask you," she whispered.

When she returned to Nick, he laid an arm protectively over her shoulder. "Mr. Newcombe," he said confidently. "I know, under the circumstances, it's a weird question, but would you allow me to marry Dani?"

Seeing his daughter's face as radiant as it had ever been, Mark grinned. "You don't need my permission?"

"Yes, sir, I do," said Nick. "It's the right thing to do."

"Is this what you want, pumpkin?"

Dani smiled. "It's what I want, Dad."

"That's all I need to know."

⋐⋐⋑⋑

The conversation that followed revolved around school studies, the continuation of Dani's dreams to be a vet, albeit in an American University. And who would care for the baby while the kids were in school. Mark suggested no decisions be made without the Brewsters, and the four agreed that a New Year's Eve party would be ideal to finalize wedding and childcare arrangements.

And when at two a.m., four happy people were ready for bed, Dani addressed her father. "Dad, one more thing. I know this is sort of, er, sensitive."

"This doesn't sound good."

"It depends which way you look at it, because it will benefit all of us."

"I'm listening…" said Mark.

"Okay, deep breath," Dani said to no one in particular. "Can Nick stay with me, here, until he goes back to Harvard?"

"You mean, upstairs?"

"Yes, Dad—upstairs—with me—in my room."

Mark looked quizzically at Jo.

"Daddy, please, don't get all square on me, after all I'm already..." She rubbed her belly.

Mark turned to Jo who was trying not to laugh. He hadn't realized it, but as far as his daughter was concerned, he really was more old-fashioned than he cared to admit. "What do you think, Jo?"

"Why're you asking me?"

"'Cos you're the closest female she's got to a mother at the moment."

"Oh, right, yes, forgot about that." Jo winked at Dani, causing a fit of giggles the men would never understand. "Well, I figure since Nick will be here, you, should be over there." She nodded in the direction of the log house.

Mark beamed. "That means we'll be alone at last."

Jo smiled and rubbed his back. "Sounds very much like it to me."

Mark addressed the kids. "Your mother has spoken, and as always in matters of the heart, her solution is perfect. You'll be okay alone? You can cook and stuff, right? Tend the animals, feed the Ps?"

Dani gawked at her father in disbelief. "Dad, puleez, this is us. We've been doing all those things since we were ten."

Mark grabbed Jo's hand and headed for his room. "Then we'll collect our stuff and get out of here."

eɔeɔ

Nick had left his mother a note about borrowing the car to see Dani, and knew despite the late hour, she'd be waiting up. So, when he called her to say he was staying over at the Newcombe farm, all she wanted was a word with Mark to ensure that he approved. As Nick hung up the phone, a sense of wellbeing flooded over him. Everything had finally turned out the way he'd hoped.

Chapter 45

The journey to the log house was ten-minutes of wordless, electrifying anticipation. Jo hadn't felt such sexual tension since she was a teen on her first date. Like then, she knew the male next to her wanted her body. But unlike then, when she was determined to run into the protection of her parent's house. As soon as this car came to a halt, she was giving this man every inch of her. This night would be one he remembered for a very long time.

When Mark removed the key from the ignition, he lingered in the car, and brought Jo's hand to his lips. "Do you think we did the right thing?"

"Absolutely, now let's go inside."

"What if they—"

"Hellooo," said Jo, smiling. "They're already having a baby, what more is there for you to worry about. Let's go inside."

"I wish we could have a—"

Jo put a hand on his thigh. "I know, darling. I thought I'd come to terms with not being able. But now I have you, a baby would have made *us* perfect."

"I'm sorry to open an old wound."

"You didn't. It is what it is. Besides, we'll be grand-parents soon. We can spoil Dani's baby rotten and give it back when it gets cranky."

Mark smiled. "Best of both worlds, eh?"

"Exactly. Besides the nympho in me has morphed into an eternal optimist. Therefore, I can see absolutely nothing wrong in supporting that age-old adage—if at first you don't succeed, try, try, again."

Mark lifted her hand and brushed his lips across her knuckles. "You got my vote."

"Good, however, in order to consummate the deal, we have to go inside."

Mark smiled. "So, let's get going before I forget my manners and take you right here in the parking lot."

"It's ten degrees below out there."

"And your point is?"

"Won't the cold impede your performance?"

Mark roared with laughter. "I swear you are the most provocative female I have ever known. You really have no idea what you do to me."

"I have a pretty good idea." She kissed him passionately, and described the same things he'd suggested to her, a few hours earlier.

"God, woman, get out of the damn car. I'm so charged right now, I could keep going for a week."

She pecked him on the nose and opened the car door. "Now that, I want to be part of. Come on, stud. I want to know just how long you can keep up with me."

Chapter 46

In November, the holidays had promised to be a somber, low-key affair. However, as Christmastime saw Nick living at the farm, it once again became a tranquil haven of love and belonging. It was due, in no small part, to Nick's religious monitoring of Dani's medication. And while she might have been careless about taking it alone, under his care, she thrived.

❦❦❦

When Nick returned to Harvard, Mark worried Dani might revert to her former state of depression and self-destruction. However, he hadn't counted on the intensity of love and commitment between his daughter and the young man who'd saved her from herself. Each day, as Dani grew stronger, a little more of her formerly outgoing and vivacious self, emerged. Her outlook on life resumed along positive, optimistic lines, and the sallow skin and dull, lifeless hair of the former depressive, once more radiated her overall health and wellness. She dove back into the plan for her life, learning housekeeping skills from Mrs. Ainsworth while continuing to tend the animals, which were a huge part of who she wanted to be. Every spare minute she'd write in her diary, documenting her thoughts on motherhood. She outlined her progress toward being a veterinarian. And penned romantic tomes to Nick predicting the perfection of their life together. She couldn't help missing him. Any woman in love would. But she dealt with his absence by pigeonholing her feelings into a chapter in her diary labeled *necessary for our future*.

ෞඌ

As the weeks passed, Dani was not the only one to regain energy and enthusiasm for life. Mark split his time between his and Jo's property, vacating the farm when Nick managed a weekend home. And to Jo's delight, at those times, she and Mark retreated to bed, for what she comically referred to as their "lust weekends."

Jo's business in Boston eventually took a back seat to whatever was going on in Maine. However, when she couldn't get out of a meeting and had to venture south, she took the driving time to reflect on what it was that made her feel so alive. It wasn't a single event, but the convergence of a million little things. How Mark had worked his magic, making her feel so cherished. How being with him, made her life more complete than she'd ever imagined. And how a job really wasn't the be-all-end-all of her life.

She hadn't quite realized how content she was until one of her colleagues commented on the change in her demeanor. How calm she seemed, how at peace, and glowing with good health. Jo simply smiled. She could never explain how her life had become everything she'd ever wanted. How blissfully happy, and crazy in love she was. And how ecstatic she was about the prospect of becoming a grandmother.

Chapter 47

Western Maine's snow drifted deep and crept across desolate fields, piling high in sound-proofing banks against the farmhouse walls. And as the mournful howl of the wind flowed about the eaves and spandrels, it wrapped the century old house in an eerie shroud. When the wind died, and a clear night of myriad stars hung sharp in an ink-black sky, no sound penetrated but the brittle scratching of tree limbs against windowpanes. Jaded by too many horror films introducing window-scratching abominations, Dani focused her consciousness on the snow. The zillions of fat cotton-balls, delicately dropping on the roof atop her. And as they piled layer on layer, she anxiously anticipated the rushing avalanche when it flowed headlong down the steeply pitched roof.

For a pregnant teen without her mate, or benefit of parents in the house, some nights were almost too quiet to bear. To chase away the loneliness demons, Dani would gather the Ps on her bed, put on her headset, and drift to another place with the music she loved.

It was one such night, with melodic dubstep filling her senses, that Dani could almost feel Nick's hands caress-ing her body. And as she drifted in thought, that hand locked, and she hurt. Sitting up with a start, Dani tore off her headset. The baby kicked her again, hard. She rubbed her distended belly. "Don't worry, baby," she whispered. "Daddy will be with us soon enough." Then she lay back, realizing that the house, so warm and welcoming by day, became darkly brooding and frighteningly silent at night.

She couldn't settle after that, and as she gazed from the window watching the driving snow mount the barn roof in a high drift, a hint of her former darkness overcame her. *Don't be silly*, she told herself, *a twinge of pain now and again is normal; Doctor Brewster said it would happen.*

Returning to bed with her music, she found no solace. The soaring sounds simply transported her to places too painful without Nick. And when her baby kicked again, it reminded her how close she was to being a mother. When a rolling, convulsing, jarring occurred, a frightened gasp escaped her lips.

Dani had been to classes and knew what to expect. Nevertheless, the intensity of the baby's movement surprised her. She immediately focused her eyes on a point ahead and breathed deep and steady to de-escalate the rolling pain. She felt better. However, in the instant oxygen flooded her brain, she looked from her darkened room to the dimly lit hall.

There was no mistaking the shadowy figure of a man. He was medium height with the body of an Adonis. And in his dark nakedness, she knew he had ebony hair flowing well beyond his shoulders. The vision was Chase Markum, and she knew his heart was as black as his eyes.

Shaking uncontrollably, Dani clutched the belly Nick had encouraged, and convinced, her to love. But now, as tears of pain overshadowed his words, she couldn't get the specter of Chase Markum out of her mind. She hadn't hallucinated for some time, but this one was different. The illusion was so real, her confusion concrete and scary. And as she dropped into an abyss of doubt, her mind was in turmoil. Did the womanizing lothario appear now, because he was the sort of man she really wanted to be with? Was her love for Nick an illusion? A convenience, because of the baby? And as her delusion intensified, she fancied only a monster like Markum could father the child kicking so viciously inside her. A scream escaped her throat as her world went black.

꒰ꔷ꒱

When Dani awoke, Mark and Jo were beside her.

"Hi, pumpkin," Mark said gently. "You gave us a little scare there. What's going on?"

"Had a really bad nightmare, Dad. What are you doing here?"

"I had one of my feelings, and we came over to find you passed out. I called Doc Brewster, she should be here in a few minutes."

"Don't need to bother her. I'm okay."

"Let her check you out. After all, she has a vested interest in this baby."

Chapter 48

Dani's nightmare episode and her approaching due date prompted Mark and Jo to move back to the farm. She was comforted having them there. But as the baby became more active, she couldn't escape being morose and fretful. Blinding headaches, and spikes in her blood pressure also plagued her. On several occasions during high moments of anxiety, Jo had transported her to Dr. Brewster's clinic. However, the doctor suspected hormonal changes were causing an adverse reaction with her bi-polar medication, made the necessary adjustments, and sent her home.

She continued to note such events in her diary because writing things down seemed to clarify her feelings and set her mind at rest. However, her ease was momentary. After one painful episode, Dani took Jo's hand.

"Thanks for being there," she said. "I hate these false alarms."

"I told you, whatever happens, you can count on me."

Dani smiled. "It's so good to know you're reliable and cool under pressure. Nick and Dad will be safe in your hands."

"Safe in my hands?" Jo said. "Whatever do you mean?"

"When I'm gone. You have enough love and caring for both of them."

"Dani, stop right there," Jo said. "Dr. Brewster said your blood pressure is a little high now and again, and you need to rest more. And if you take your new medication properly and stop fretting about the actual birth, you have nothing to worry about."

"She doesn't know everything."

"She knows a lot more than us. Besides, if you're worried about the pain, she's already agreed to give you an epidural."

"Pain won't bother me," Dani said. "I won't be there."

"Now you're not making any sense."

"Makes perfect sense. Pain meds or no, I won't be around to argue the point."

"Dani, please stop. I thought we'd moved beyond this. You need to think positively for the baby's sake as well as yours."

"Won't make any difference."

"Okay, missy, enough of that nonsense," said an exasperated Jo. "Let's refocus. I have some lovely things on the way from Boston. And your dad thought he'd punch out the wall in the bedroom next to yours. You'll have a completely private area for you, Nick, and the baby."

"Whatever."

"Well, miss 'whatever,' with the hormones raging. I will choose to ignore your rudeness."

"Sorry."

Jo patted her hand. "Accepted. We should also start thinking about your wedding dress, who's getting an invite to the reception, the flowers, and the caterers. Good grief, we have enough stuff to keep you occupied until next Christmas, let alone April."

"Whatever."

"Dani!" Jo snapped.

"I know I'm being an ungrateful brat," Dani said. "You've been wonderful to me, and you're the best thing that ever happened to Dad. Really, I'm truly sorry. I can never thank you enough for what you've done."

"Say that when I drive you mad picking at the wording on the wedding invitations."

"I don't think you'd drive anyone mad," Dani whispered. "You're a wonderful, special person. I'm so glad to have had you in my life."

"Had?"

"Yes, you know, because of—"

"Actually, I don't know," Jo snapped. "What I do know is that I can only bend over so far backward in the be-sensitive-to-Dani's-emotions game. Which means it's truth time. Can't you see how all this negativity about the baby is morbid? Morbid and cruel. You're speaking to a gal who can't have kids. A gal who would give her right arm to be in your position. This should be one of the happiest times in your life, ergo mine, because I'm the grandmother. But you're spoiling it for me and everyone else."

"Jo, I'm so sorry," Dani said quietly. "I completely forgot. Really, please forgive me. I'll try and cool the gloomy Gus-ness." She flung her arms around Jo's neck. "Please, I wouldn't intentionally hurt you for the world. Friends?"

Jo smiled and kissed the youngster on the forehead. "What am I going to do with you? Let's think happy thoughts, like Nick getting permission to come home for the baby's birth. And how we're going to persuade your dad to pay for a wedding table ice sculpture, after he's spent half the winter digging out nature's masterpieces from the cow troughs."

Dani smiled and winked. "I'm sure you'll think of something."

Chapter 49

In the early morning hours of the first week in February, Dani was woken by an excruciating pain. Her head was pounding and a gripping cramp pulsed through her right side. Flipping on her bedside light, she dropped her legs over the side of her bed. However, when she tried to stand, the pain in her head made her dizzy, and she pitched forward.

Dani screamed as her face connected with the wall and blood gushed from her nose. As she was on her knees, watching a pool of blood form, she began to scream hysterically. Her screaming whipped the dogs into a frenzy, and, as they charged back and forth, she clutched at her side in an attempt to stop whatever was happening. She again tried to stand, and she blacked out.

Dani's scream and dogs' howling woke Mark and Jo. He was the first out of bed. He rushed to her room and almost tripped over her body, lying face down. When he shook her, he couldn't rouse her.

"Try her pulse," Jo said, right behind him. "Is she breathing?"

"Dear God, I don't…where am I supposed to?" He felt around her neck but couldn't find the pulse. "Where is all this blood coming from?"

"Looks like she fell face first," Jo said. "It's her nose.

Go get some pants and shoes on." Jo bent down and felt for Dani's pulse.

"Shouldn't I call the fire department?"

"No time, she has a pulse, really faint. We'll put her in my SUV and take her directly to Doc Brewster. I'll call and say we're on the way."

"My God, look at all the blood."

"Mark! Focus—you've seen blood before."

"Not my baby's, what if she's—"

"She isn't. Now get going, there's no time to waste."

છ૭છ૭

As Jo used towels to staunch the flow of Dani's blood, Mark carried his prostate daughter to the vehicle. The car started immediately and he drove gingerly from the garage through a deep blanket of snow. He set off down the farm's long drive, picking his way around drifts and an area he knew was unstable at the best of times. And while he'd driven the distance a million times, he'd never negotiated such deep snow without a plow. Though the SUV was four-wheel drive, he couldn't risk anything more than first gear. And as they chugged along, his knuckles glared white on the steering wheel.

"She okay?" he whispered anxiously.

"Holding her own. The bleeding has stopped. Can you go any faster?"

"Not if we want to stay on the road. Hopefully, when we get to the highway, I can kick up the pace."

"Do your best," Jo said, worry shadowing her eyes.

As they hit the main road, it stopped snowing. Nevertheless, several inches of heavy wet snow lay slick on the road. "What did the doc say?"

"Said it sounded like she was in labor. They'll be prepped by the time we get there."

"Okay, clinic half-a-mile ahead," Mark said. "I can see lights on. Call 'em and tell 'em we're here."

Jo engaged Mark's cell phone and spoke to Dr. Nathan Brewster. "Okay," said Jo to Mark. "Nathan said use the side door. He's got a gurney waiting."

"I see him."

Dr. Nathan was beside a gurney as the SUV skidded to a halt. Jo exited first, covered in blood. "Stand back, Jo," said Dr. Nathan. "Let Mark and I get her out."

"Is she having the baby?" asked Mark.

"Let's just get her on the gurney, Emily's prepped inside."

Mark stepped forward. "I got her, Doc." Despite Dani's dead weight, Mark easily lifted his daughter onto the gurney and set to push her inside. However, he'd barely set his feet when he slipped on the slick ramp, fell forward, and propelled the stretcher into Nathan, almost knocking him off his feet.

"Whoa, slow it down," Nathan said. "Not going to help us if you crack your skull open and bust my leg. Emily's in the second room on the left."

As they entered the surgical area, Mark stepped forward to lift Dani onto the operating table.

"Leave her on the gurney, Mark," Doctor Emily said. "I need to take a closer look at her. Now, out you two go I've got this." She pulled on her mask and nodded toward the door.

"Can't, Emily," said Mark. "Have to stay with her in case she wakes up."

Dr. Emily looked at her husband. "Okay, go with Nathan, scrub up, over there—masks and gowns—and next time I tell you to leave, no arguments."

Emily had completed her cursory examination as Mark and Jo took up a position at Dani's head.

"What's happening, Emily?" asked Mark.

"Something isn't normal. Things don't feel right."

"What do you mean?"

Dr. Emily turned to her husband. "Nathan—call Portland. Have them send a Medivac."

Mark had never seen either doctor in emergency mode. And the precise responses to each other's instructions, using language he barely understood, made him extremely nervous. "What's happening, Emily?"

"Mark, you have to leave—wait outside."

"But I—"

"Outside—now! Nathan, need you back in here."

"Come on, Mark," Jo said, pulling him toward the door. "Let them work,"

"What if she—"

"She won't. Now come on, we're in their way."

Dr. Nathan was instantly at his doctor wife's side. "Speak to me, Em."

"Her notes mention epigastric pain, which at the time, I ruled as heartburn. Nothing in her urine then. And even if I set aside the swelling on her face—looks like she broke her nose when she fell—look at her hands and feet. Pitting edema. Now I'm thinking pre-eclampsia. Run an IV line. Pulse one-fifty-five—convulsing. Let's get in some magnesium sulfate. Temp one hundred four…BP one-sixty over one-ten—I'm losing her!"

⊱⊰

When the helicopter landed amid a blizzard of swirling snow, Dani's condition was critical. Without wasting a second, the medical team exchanged information and swiftly loaded her into the aircraft. Dr. Emily jumped in and, with limited space, only Mark was able to strap in behind her. The noise was deafening as the helicopter lifted off. But all Jo could hear repeating in her head was Mark saying, "Not again, please God, not again."

As Jo's rear view mirror captured the noisy bird's flight into the frigid air, she continued home to change out of her bloodied clothes.

It took her nearly twenty-five minutes to make contact with Nick. Jo gave him her credit card details and told him to rent a helicopter and get to the hospital as quickly as possible. Then she woke Mrs. Ainsworth, and asked her to come in early with her nephew, to feed the animals and hold the fort until they got home.

Satisfied everything was in good hands until she and Mark returned from Maine Medical, Jo showered and dressed. Then, she stuffed a change of clothes for Mark into a rucksack and climbed back into her SUV.

Chapter 50

By the time everybody had assembled at the hospital, Dani was in intensive care, hooked up to a dozen machines. The doctor had briefed them on her condition and it was grave.

"Dani, it's Nick. Talk to me, baby. Come on, open your eyes."

Dani slowly opened her eyes, dull from trauma. "Nick?" she whispered. "Why are you here, what happened?"

"You're having a little problem, baby, but don't worry, I'll take care of you." He lifted her hand and brushed it with his lips. "You have to stay in bed, but soon everything will be back to normal."

"Go back to school—don't want to—" Dani's eyes closed, and her face contorted. "Feel bad…inside." She gripped her side. "Told you this would happen—die now."

"No, you're not," Nick said, stroking her hair. "Don't even think like that." A tear slid down his face and dropped, leaving a small gray blemish on the stark white sheet. "You're going to be fine. You had a little setback. But we're having our baby, and we're getting married. Then you're going to college, and—"

"Please don't hate me."

"Hate you, why would I hate you?"

"Leaving you with a baby."

"Dani, we've been over that. I want you to focus on getting better."

"Where's Daddy?"

"I'm here, pumpkin," Mark said.

"Not your fault." Dani's face, devoid of color, contorted with pain. "See Momma now. Forgive us—sleep now."

As Dani's eyes closed, a doctor entered and with her charts. "Would you all step outside with me, please?" They moved to the corridor. "Mr. Brewster, I'm told you and Miss Newcombe are to be married. If that is your wish, I suggest you do it now. As soon as an OR is ready, we need to carry out a C-section to save the baby. I'm afraid we may not be able to save Miss Newcombe."

"No, Doctor. Do something, increase the medication—"

"I'm sorry. We've done everything we can."

"You can't mean that. It's not possible. This can't be happening."

"Mr. Brewster. I would normally only share this with relatives, but under the circumstances, I'll assume you're the husband. I'm also told you're planning to be a doctor so I want you to step back and put on your doctor hat." He motioned for the group to look at Dani's charts. "Miss Newcombe has full blown eclampsia. See the numbers here, and here. We can maintain her at this level until an OR is free. But the balance is way off, and we can't bring them in line. Her blood pressure is impossibly high, and her systems are shutting down. If we refer to Dr. Emily Brewster's notes—oh, Brewster?"

"My mother," said Nick woodenly.

"It's good she was on hand. I know living out there in the country can sometimes be a trial when it comes to an urgent medical issue, but she got it all right. See here, she notes convulsions present, intravenous magnesium sulfate. More seizures may occur, it happens. But be sure, coma is inevitable. Your baby may already be in distress so we have to do the C-section. And if you mean to get married, I suggest you do it right now."

The weight of inevitable defeat cast its heavy burden on the young man's heart. But there was no arguing with the numbers. His beloved Dani couldn't last much longer. As tears slid down his face, Nick sent for the hospital chaplain.

えうえう

Outside the OR, Mark and Jo watched in stunned silence as the medical team brought Dani to consciousness long enough to become Mrs. Nickolas Brewster. Then with fortitude, which defied understanding, she propped herself on one arm and leaning heavily upon her husband said to her dad, "Now you."

As the hospital chaplain pronounced Mark and Jo man and wife, Dani smiled. Nothing more needed saying, for she finally understood what it was to be part of a complete family. And with her last ounce of strength gone, she sank back onto the soothing coolness of the hospital pillow.

Dani felt Nick kiss her lips, felt his spirit flow into her, and as he caressed her hand with blissfully indescribable tenderness, she couldn't help shedding tears for what might have been. She so wanted to live, to cherish the endless love of the old man Nick would become. And though her heart cried, she knew she'd lived as much time as she was allowed. Her mind drifted somewhere looking for a purpose to it all. She couldn't imagine what it might be, but she gained comfort from the realization that there had to be something. Breathing shallow, Dani forced her eyes to open and there were his. As blue as she remembered them. As true as they'd always been. As devoted and loving as any woman could wish for. And they were married. She had given him what he'd dreamed of. She was at peace.

"Okay, Mr. Brewster, we're ready," said the nurse who wheeled Dani into the OR.

భాసి

The wailing monitor signaled what Dani had known her entire life. Relentless and unyielding, the machine emitted its head-splitting shriek. Nick watched in abject silence as the medical team tried to revive Dani. But when they backed away from their patient, he understood the action. Dani died at six-oh-six a.m. An almost palpable wave of defeat radiated around the OR. Seconds later her baby was born.

Nick could watch no more. Hunched and inconsolable, the full measure of his grief took hold. What did anything matter now that she was gone? What he'd most wanted in life was to marry Dani and live happily ever after. A dream maybe. But one he'd devoted his whole being to making happen. Now just as that dream was reality, a nightmare took over. With his heart torn, Nick swiped tears from his eyes. Then he saw a vision of Dani floating before him.

The ethereal vision smiled sweetly and touched his face. "Dear husband," she whispered. "Never forget, I have always loved you."

భాసి

When the startled cry of a newborn diverted his attention, Nick took a deep breath. He watched as the baby voiced irritation with every wrap of the delivery blanket. Turning to face him, the nurse, in mask and scrubs, gently rocked the tiny bundle against her ample bosom. And while Nick thought it a disproportionately noisy bundle, who wouldn't be irritated at being unceremoniously plucked from the warmth of a mother? He smiled thinly. As long as the baby was healthy, Dani had not died in vain.

The nurse handed the baby to Dr. Emily, who brought it to Nick. "You have a beautiful and very noisy baby girl, Nick," said the proud grandmother. "She's a bossy one that's for sure."

"You're going to have to loosen that blanket, Mom," Nick said. "Dani hated being confined. I guess her daughter is the same."

As Emily loosened the birthing blanket, a tiny fist punched the air in a show of freedom and tenacity. "Well, Dad," Dr. Emily said, smiling. "You already have the knack. She's a fine healthy baby. By the tightness of that fist, and the efforts she made to escape, she's going to be a very determined little girl."

"Thanks to you, Mom."

"Here, you take her."

"Er, can I take her to see Mark and Jo?"

Nick's mother smiled. "Sure, they're grandparents too."

As Nick took the baby, the fretful infant immediately ceased screaming.

"Well, look at that," Dr. Emily said. "She's your girl, all right. Makes you feel pretty good when just a cuddle can quiet them down. Get used to the feeling, son, because from this point forward, she's gonna be hollering and using those crocodile tears to wrap you around her little finger."

Nick smiled and stared into the face of his angelic little girl. With a shock of strawberry-blond hair and deep blue-green eyes, she could only have gotten from him and her mother—she was the child of his dreams. With grief momentarily forgotten, love for the baby girl utterly consumed him. And when his cooing armful focused her huge eyes on him and extended a pudgy hand to touch his face, he was lost.

ᏇᏄᏇᏄ

Mark stood in stunned silence as he looked from Nick and the baby to Dani. He had hoped never to see that impenetrable stillness again. Never wanted to witness the lifeless pallor or the absence of a spirit he so cherished. But the choice was not his. He simply shook his head as he brushed a lock of hair from his daughter's face. And bending low, he kissed her tenderly. "Go find your mom, pumpkin," he whispered. "She's waiting." And as he reached back and took hold of a crying Jo's hand, nothing could stop the tears rolling down his face.

Chapter 51

When the families returned to the farm, Mark recounted the past hours to a tearful Mrs. Ainsworth. And while a quiet resignation, borne of Dani's own feelings about giving birth, descended over them all, they sat down for a late breakfast. But nobody ate.

"The doctor said I can bring the baby home tomorrow," Nick said quietly. "And I'm certain her mother wouldn't approve of us calling her 'the baby.' We never discussed a name."

"Why not?" asked Jo.

"Dani felt it would jinx things. She believed once I saw her, a name would come to me. But frankly, I'm at a loss. She's a beautiful tiny version of Dani, and all I can think of is naming her after her mother."

"Sweetie," Jo said, touching Nick's arm. "I mean no disrespect to carrying on a family thing. But Dani told me many times she hated her name. I know she wouldn't want you to call the baby Dolores."

Mark smiled. "You won't get any argument from me. It seems that name has its own kind of jinx. So where do we go from here?"

"Here's the thing," Jo continued. "When I first met Dani, she thought my name was cool. She said she'd like to be named after the place she was conceived. Maybe you could start there. Hopefully Kezar Falls wasn't where it all happened." She put a hand over Nick's. "Only you would know that."

"It was here," he said nervously.

"So, we're in Victoria Falls, York County, Maine. How about…Victoria?"

"Victoria Brewster," said Nick thoughtfully. "Yes, it sounds good, and feels right. Thank you, Grandma."

Jo smiled, that sounded good and felt right too.

᪣᪣᪣

Soon after Victoria came home from the hospital, Nick was due back at school. They had told him to take all the time he needed. But he knew Dani would want him to get back to school and do what they had planned. Nevertheless, Victoria's care required some discussion. Jo happily volunteered for the job. It was further decided that Jo and Mark would retreat to the log house when Nick was home, leaving him to maintain the baby's routines, under Mrs. Ainsworth's capable tutelage.

Nick came home as often as his studies allowed, but he was unable to entertain sleeping in Dani's old room. So, Mark had a door cut between two of the farmhouse's other bedrooms, creating a second master suite for Nick that included a nursery.

Before long, everybody fell under the spell of the powerful little person who had so tragically entered their lives. And though Dani's absence was felt in a thousand ways, one clasp from the determined hands of the exquisite strawberry-blonde left no one in doubt, to whom she belonged.

Chapter 52

April saw the earth barely softer than granite. However, as the sun warmed, melting the property's snow walls, Nick was able to bury Dani. He chose April twenty-first—the day they would have been married.

Family gathered around the perimeter of the cemetery behind the log house. And as Nick held his daughter close to avoid the constant drip from overhanging pines, he saw Dani's friends standing at a necessary distance from the plot.

Because of the cemetery's limited capacity, it had taken more than the usual amount of paperwork to get permission to bury Dani there. Town officials, now discretely present, had initially refused to allow another burial in so crowded a resting-place. But Nick knew how important the cemetery was to his wife. When her demons raged, she had sat amongst the moss-covered gravestones, regaining perspective from their tactile strength. She had called the cemetery her quiet zone of peace—a place where she reflected on what might have been, communed with the spirits of her family, and found her way back to the present. As a silent tear dripped from his eye, Nick thanked God he had Mark for a father-in-law.

It was he who petitioned to bury another Dolores beneath the pines. And when his request was rejected, Mark
wouldn't be denied. Citing the years of attention both he
and Dani had given the cemetery, he rallied influential
friends in Portland. Anyone who knew Dani's history
couldn't help but be affected by Mark's plea. And, after
receiving letters of support from all living members of
both the Newcombe and Lord families, he convinced the
historical authorities that a new burial wouldn't compro-
mise any of the existing interments.

Dani's draped coffin sat on planks above the excava-
tion. With no room for bearers who would traditionally
lower the casket to its resting place, only two men stood
by the grave. Reverend Wilson, and Nick, holding Victoria. And as the reverend asked Nick if he was ready to
begin the service, he glanced back at Mark clutching Jo's
hand. When he smiled thinly, a wave of understanding
passed between them. Dani would rest, as she had wanted, next to the mother she never knew. In a place, he and
Victoria could visit every day.

Surrounded by the tall pines, in a glade where lady's
slipper, iris, and trillium were waiting to emerge, Nick
whispered to his daughter. "The flowers will soon be
back, Victoria, and I'll show you where they're hiding
just like Mommy showed me. She always loved this
place, and I know you'll love it too."

As the service got underway, the damp and dismal
morning surrendered to the sun. Shafts of light filtered
weakly through the pines to linger on the coffin draped in
the quilt sewn by Newcombe women long since dead. It
had been on Dani's bed for the entire eighteen years of
her life, and she, like all those who had gone before, added to its bright primary colors. Nick knew Dani's contribution was a series of appliquéd animals. She'd spent
weeks attaching each with a precise blanket stitch, but the

vibrant patchwork was more than simply a quilt. It was an inspiration. It had survived the generations. It told stories of the love and strength of those who had sewn it. And for Nick, it offered comfort in more ways than could be counted. Soon, he would place it on Victoria's bed, so she'd feel its warmth enfolding. Just like the arms of the special women, she'd never know.

As Dani didn't like overly formal church doctrines, Nick had asked Reverend Wilson not to dwell on her loss. He gave an uplifting sermon about the promise that was Victoria.

The ceremony ended with Nick removing the quilt from Dani's coffin. And as he walked toward the berm surrounding the site, the congregation then let fly their offering. A multitude of baby pink roses rained down on Dolores Ann "Dani" Brewster's casket and fell about the graves of her mother Dolores Elizabeth, and her grandmother Dolores Constance.

෪෪෪

When all but husband, daughter, and grandparents had left the site, Nick ran his fingers over Dani's gravestone awaiting positioning. It was at the base of the berm, propped against the weathered dry-stone wall. The words inscribed were from a poem Dani loved, attributed to one of her long dead relatives. Nick looked down at Victoria and whispered the words.

> "'Cherish love in good times
> To sustain you through the tears,
> Because when angels call
> And they will, for us all,
> Lonely hearts cry…'"

Chapter 53

When Nick returned to college, Jo settled easily into her role as grandmother. To that point, she knew little about caring for a baby, but it seemed her organized and calm approach to whatever came up had her coping like a veteran. It helped that she set her work aside and was able to concentrate, and she was thankful on a daily basis that Mark's wealth allowed her to do that.

Mark, however, was having a harder time dealing with Dani's loss. He was beside himself with joy watching Jo care for the child and become what she had always wanted to be. But his thoughts invariably returned to the sadness that plagued him the last time a baby was in the house.

༒

Rain poured down as Mark and the dogs tumbled into the farmhouse vestibule. And as the canine family milled around, waiting to be toweled off, the smell of beef stew wafted toward him.

"Smells good," he yelled, into the kitchen.

"Beats wet dog any day," Jo replied. "Mrs. A also made some of that cobbler you like. It'll be done in thirty-five minutes so get a move on."

As Mark strode into the kitchen, the dogs rushed forward to take up positions in front the fire.

"Put your slippers on," said Jo. "You'll catch your death of cold on these flag-stones."

Mark smiled. "That's exactly what Mrs. A. always said when I came in out of the rain. She taught you well. You're beginning to sound like her."

"Oh, really," said Jo, transferring baby Victoria to her other hip. "Come over here, you big lug, and plant one on me. I've got skills Mrs. A never even dreamed about."

Mark smiled and smooched Jo. "Now that I know," he said. And with sorrow etched in his face, he ran a hand gently over Victoria's head. He was having a hard time adjusting to the baby amid another devastating lost.

"Is having a baby in the house still making you nervous?" asked Jo quietly.

"It's not that, she's just so small. I'm afraid my big man hands will hurt her."

Jo smiled. "Don't you worry about that, I can positively attest to their gentleness."

"Am I being an awful granddad?"

"No, I think you're being a sensitive granddad. We all miss Dani. But I think her death has hit you so hard because you blame yourself for not listening to her."

"I should've, plain and simple. She told me from the beginning a baby would kill her. I ignored her, I'm to blame."

"Well, I certainly don't blame you for anything. You followed your heart, and nobody could ask for anything more. And for the record, nothing about this pregnancy was plain or simple. Not even the doctor knew about the quirk Newcombe women have. In Dani's case, her bipolar masked it."

"That's easy to say. However, it doesn't make it any easier. I should have done some research. God, I'm such an idiot—the web is full of medical information."

Jo ran a hand down Mark's arm. "Yeah…that can lead you into a minefield of alarming misdiagnosis. And what if you had done that research? Or blindly listened to Dani? What if you had been sure of this outcome up front? Would you have wanted her to get rid of this beautiful little creature?"

Mark's eyes clouded. "That's an impossible question to answer. All I know is she was right. Something genetic killed her, and I have to bear responsibility for that."

"And to balance that crazy hypothesis, you're distancing yourself from Victoria? Don't you remember how needy Dani was? Why should Victoria be any different?"

Mark turned away.

"Ah, the truth will out," Jo said gently. "We all wish this had ended differently. But you must listen to what she said in the end. Her death is not your fault. And given what they knew, the doctors did everything they could. Their focus was managing her bi-polar during the pregnancy. And minimizing the medical issues associated with her erratic use of the medication. Medicine is not an exact science, darling. Not everything runs according to the book. Tragically, some things just *are*."

"That's supposed to make it easier?"

"No, but it gives you leave to accept that you are not to blame. Besides, Dani would be the last person to want you unhappy. Ever since I knew her she was mentally preparing a life for you after she moved on."

Mark stirred the stew, his tears welling. "To veterinary school, not the great beyond." He had never imagined he would have to go through such sorrow again. However, as he watched Jo rock Victoria in her arms, it warmed his heart.

"What?" asked Jo.

"You look so natural doing that."

"It feels right too, I'm not sure why. I guess there really is such a thing a motherly instinct. You want to take her?"

"No...I'm good."

Jo frowned. "Well, at least you're not drinking."

"Excuse me?" Mark asked, puzzled.

"You told me when Dee died you were drunk for a week. And you couldn't even look at Dani, let alone hold her." Jo smiled. "Only when your brother intervened, did you take any notice of your daughter. Am I to assume this is a pattern? Do I have to send for your brother?"

Mark frowned. "Not this time. But hell, what is raising kids all about? You spend your life caring for your child, teaching them about life and living. And just when they come into their own, putting the stuff you taught them to good use—they're gone. Whether it's dying like Dani, going away to college like Nick, or moving away with a family of their own. What's the point of it all?"

"Circle of life, darling. I really think you're dwelling on the negatives and over thinking this."

"Now you're being flippant."

"Not so," Jo said. "Right now, your whole attitude is colored by Dani's death. But Victoria needs you just as much. You can't cut her off because she's the one left behind."

"Every time I look at her I see Dani."

"Do you see Dee?"

"Not really."

"And why do you think that is?" Jo asked.

"I don't know. But you have *that* look, so I'm guessing you have a theory."

Jo smiled. "It's because I'm your wife now. You'll never forget Dee, but I've sort of filled that void. And in the not too distant future, Victoria will fill the void you now feel with the loss of Dani."

"Maybe," Mark mumbled.

"So, here's my last point on the subject, then I'll quit."

Mark threw his hands in the air and looked up. "Thank you, God."

"Okay, Mr. Sarcasm. What would be happening if I weren't here? Would Nick give up on school, put Victoria in day care, and work on the farm to ensure she had someone here?"

"No," Mark said emphatically.

"So, who'd be looking after her? Don't say the Brewsters. They're both busy doctors who work long hours."

Mark looked smug. "Mrs. A just like she did with Dani."

"Think again. She's in her late seventies. That's not exactly a prime age to be toting around a baby."

"With the economy the way it is, plenty of grandparents have to pick up the slack."

Jo smiled. "I know. That's why *we* are. I rest my case."

Mark ran a hand through his hair. "Have I ever beaten you in an argument?"

"Are we arguing?"

Mark smiled. "Quietly."

"It is what it is, darling. We're Victoria's grandparents, and she's our responsibility for now. In addition, I'm not about to go back on a promise I made to Dani."

"What promise?"

"She was having one of her down days, and said she was glad I was around to look after you and Nick. At that time, she'd pretty much convinced herself, she was going to die and the baby along with her."

"That's so sad, why didn't you tell me any of this?"

"There are some things it's best a father—"

"Doesn't know—yeah, I got that some time ago."

"So, my darling, we both know from experience it's going to take some time to move on. But finding and accepting a new normal is vital. And you know—this isn't the eighteen hundreds. Today, husbands, fathers, even grandfathers, chip in and do their bit with the kids. It's been weeks, and I'm still waiting for your contribution to begin."

Mark moved toward Jo and ran a hand down her cheek. "Yikes, that told me. Since when did you get so equal-opportunity focused?"

"Since you began to slide into a hole. A hole you told me you'd never fall back into. Wasn't it you who said, 'the pain of the why-did-this-happen-to-me, and the what-have-I-done-to-deserve-this, consumed me. And I came up with same answer every time—I have no control over this, and the decision is not mine. Somehow, some way, I have to get past this'?"

"Do you remember absolutely everything I say?"

Jo thought for a moment. "Say and do. I remember the despair I felt after Chris died. The questions and the impossibly absent answers. And I remember meeting this great-looking farm boy who led me out of my particular hole. A guy who seemed to have the grieving process worked out. A thoughtful romantic who made me see what life was really all about. I also remember how he doted on his daughter—an astonishing young woman who has since entrusted me with the most precious things in her life. Her father, her husband, and now her baby. Yeah, I remember the important things. Do you?"

Mark smiled. "I do now."

"So, we need to eat dinner. But first, the diva, Miss Victoria is ready for bed. You want to bring up that basket of laundry? Mrs. A is having a problem with the stairs."

"Ah, now I understand that part of the speech, the ancient one is ailing. Do I have to put the laundry away too?"

Jo smiled. "Do you know where it goes?"

"Sort of."

"Sort of ain't cutting it, mister. We have a system."

"So how about you take care of the laundry and give me Victoria. I know where she goes."

Jo handed over the sleeping baby. "Have I told you today how much I love you?"

Mark grinned. "Thought that was my line."

Jo kissed him on the mouth. "I don't seem to remember that."

Chapter 54

On his first free weekend, Nick returned to the farmhouse. He could hardly believe how Victoria had grown. And seeing her so content with Jo and Mark, he knew Dani would have approved of his decision to finish school and leave her in their capable hands. His visit home, however, was not simply to see Victoria. He had agreed with Mark that before he returned to Harvard, he should be the one to sort through Dani's things. He dreaded the task and had put it off as long as he could.

Nick climbed slowly up the stairs. Dani's room was at the end of the corridor, on the corner, where a huge oak framed the window and gave a view spanning uninterrupted acres of Newcombe land. It was a place he had been a hundred times, to finish homework or tutor Dani in some aspect of math she didn't understand. But being in Mark's house with unspoken romantic feelings for Dani, it was a place he never felt entirely comfortable.

Pausing in front of Dani's door, Nick took a deep, composing breath. And, as he pushed the door open, a draft of her perfume washed over him. It was a silent affirmation of her being. That she had existed. Concrete proof that his dream was real. Then the emptiness that was her loss overwhelmed him, and his tears were instant and unstoppable. He would have liked to turn tail and simply return to Harvard. To being, but not being her husband. But he'd made a promise to complete the task he'd been assigned. So, he took a deep breath and stepped inside the room.

As he walked around, hand outstretched, running his fingers over her things, Nick felt a palpable presence, as if she were there. "Hi, baby," he whispered, knowing that somewhere in the cosmos she could hear him. "So here we are. The point I dread. Your dad says I'm to go through your stuff. I'm supposed to set aside things for Victoria and donate the rest. We talked about you thinning out the basics before going to college, so I've pretty much got that covered. But I'll need some hints on what to keep for Victoria. You gonna help me with that?"

When a breeze from the hall kissed his face, he knew she would.

Moving from one area to another, Nick was surprised how organized Dani had been. Clothes hung in like-colored hues. Or sat neatly folded in drawers. Her books were alphabetized. And boxes upon boxes of school papers sported neatly printed labels, in her tidy teenage hand. She was always late and in a state of disrepair when she met him, and he smiled at experiencing a new side of her. For the first time, he felt comfortable in her room.

Though Nick hated the thought of disturbing anything, let alone dispatching even the smallest piece of her from his life, he opted to start with the massive oak tallboy. He tugged open the first of seven drawers.

Tears rolled down Nick's cheeks as he went through her things. He couldn't help bringing this or that sweater to his face to breathe in her perfume and remember how she looked wearing it. And while he kept a couple that prompted vivid recollection or he knew Dani particularly cherished, he bagged the bulk of her clothing. After three hours, many of the trappings of his best friend, and beloved wife, sat in a string tied block of shoeboxes and four large trash bags.

With step one of his herculean task complete, Nick sat back on Dani's window seat. Almost immediately, he became aware of the oak's branches scratching against the window. He'd never noticed that before. But in the silence of her room, it seemed to speak to him. Looking from the window, he saw St Joseph's Church in the distance and knew where Dani would want her possessions sent. She had always favored the church group called the Lords Ladies. Not only because many were distantly related, but because they distributed donated items locally. Nick smiled. If nothing else, his beloved's passing would benefit young women less fortunate than she had been.

The last thing Nick tackled was an ornate wooden chest, sitting atop the dresser. He guessed it wouldn't contain jewelry, because Dani never liked that sort of thing. However, after lifting the substantial piece, a shake indicated it contained many small objects. Nick flipped the toggle, but the attached locking clasp would not yield. He spun the box and came across a piece of scotch tape under which he found a small key. Its diminutive size proved somewhat of a trial for a man's fingers. Nevertheless, he pushed it into the clasp's opening and, after some jiggling, finally connected the grooves into the locking mechanism. The clasp sprang open on the half turn.

When he lifted the chest's lid, Nick was surprised to find several trays filled with jewelry. A cursory look revealed that most of the necklaces, brooches, bracelets, watches, and rings were gold. Many were heavy, intricately set Victoriana, sporting ostentatious clusters of garish gems. Absolutely not Dani's taste. Nick smiled. Clearly, he had come across heirlooms handed down from grandmother to mother to daughter. Others however, in platinum and silver set with onyx and lapis lazuli, were sleek, elegant, art deco inspired, and smooth to the touch. He was thumbing through the items when Mark came up behind him.

"How's it going, Nick?" asked Mark.

"Painful," Nick whispered, swiping eyes reddened from tears. "Her whole world is in this room."

"I know. I remember after her mom died, it took me months to get motivated to sort out her things." Mark laid an arm around Nick's shoulder. "I'm so glad you're family and can do this. I'm not sure I could handle it again."

Nick smiled thinly. Mark had always made him feel welcome, but he had never before alluded to Nick as being family. "It's not so much what she had that's getting to me, it's the things I didn't know about her. We've been together since first grade, and I never knew she was so meticulous. Everything's in order. I mean everything— folded, labeled, categorized, I had no idea she was so…"

"Obsessive? Yeah, given her oft times cavalier attitude to most everything, I had a hard time reconciling that. It was, in part, how her bi-polar manifested. The rest is from her mother. I remember Dee's first week here. She completely reorganized the place. From the kitchen to the cellar then the barns and even the garage. It got so bad I couldn't find a thing. I ended up with two of everything, the one she organized somewhere, and the new one I had to buy."

"Women," Nick said.

"You know, Nick, I don't know whether I actually said it. But I'm so pleased you and Dani finally got married. I got caught up in deceiving you for a while because I didn't know exactly what she was going through. And I certainly didn't know how to deal with her emotions. Once you got here, you seemed to have a better handle on her moods than I did."

"You're her father. I loved her in a different way than

you did. I could see things you couldn't."

'That's true. Jo always says 'sometimes it's best a father doesn't know certain things.' Either way, you know you two together was always in the cards."

"It seemed touch and go for a while. It's moot now, but I wish she'd have let me know what demons were plaguing her. Maybe I—er, we—could have helped. Despite her independence, she always bragged on you as her dad. I just hope I can match up."

The men smiled together.

"But enough of the mushy stuff," Nick said. "It won't finish the job I need to do here. What do you think about all the items in this chest? For a neat-nick, it's remarkably disorganized."

"All that jewelry is from her mother, grandparents, great grandparents, aunts, cousins—who even remembers where it's all from? With her red hair and green eyes, they felt she was born to be a girly girl, model type, glamorous, fancy clothes, and expensive jewelry. So, when ladies died, she got their baubles."

"I can see that."

"Dani called that lot the 'dead chest,'" Mark said. "We both know dressing up was not something she had much interest in. Her mind was set on things more practical, and that lot was one of the reasons she hated jewelry. Said she didn't want her life remembered through baubles and trinkets." Mark picked up one of the gem-encrusted bracelets. "I know for a fact, a lot of this stuff is very valuable."

"Then all of it should be kept for Victoria," Nick said. "When she's old enough, she can decide what to do with it—except this." Nick picked up a heavy gold chain on which a square masculine looking locket hung. "This looks like a watch chain of some sort."

"It is. It was my father's. I have the watch on another chain, and use it when I wear my Sunday best. Open it up."

Nick opened the locket carefully. On one side, there was a picture of three Labrador puppies, the other a baby, exactly like Victoria. "Well, these are unmistakably Faith, Hope, and Charity. Is this Dani?"

"Yup, my dad said he kept the most precious in his family with him at all times."

"Would you mind if I replaced the girls with a photo of Victoria? I'd like to wear this around my neck."

"It's all yours now, go right ahead," Mark said. "Do you want to take the boxes and bags to church, or shall I do it? It'll be no problem. I have to pick up Jo from your mom's in a while."

"Mom? Mom or doctor mom?"

"Doctor."

Nick looked worried. "Nothing serious, I hope."

"Routine girl stuff," Mark whispered.

"I'm an almost doctor, Mr. Newcombe, you can say Mammogram and OBGYN."

Mark smiled. "Okay, and it's Mark or *Dad*."

"Right, though that might take a bit of getting used to. Would you mind taking the stuff? I'd like to finish here and head back to Boston before the weekend crowd hits the turnpike."

"No problem. And by the way, being a single dad of a girl isn't easy. Believe me, it will get rough. But remember, Jo and I are here for you. And when Victoria turns out to be bright, independent, and smart like her mother, it'll have been worth every sleepless night."

❦❦❦

As Mark hauled the boxes and garbage bags downstairs, Nick finished sifting through the jewelry box. He was about to replace it on the dresser when his finger caught on a sliver of metal at the bottom. It was a small slider. He pushed it left, and was so startled when a drawer popped open, he almost dropped the chest. The cavity hid a diary.

Recalling giggling conversations between Dani and her girlfriends, Nick realized this must be the infamous diary she was mercilessly teased about. It was rumored Dani hid her most personal secrets within its pages, and Nick's curiosity was peaked. He wondered how much more he might learn about his wife by reading its pages. And see what sort of space he'd been assigned.

As he flipped the fat leather bound volume with its sturdy gold clasp, Nick smiled. He'd discovered another thing he didn't know about Dani. She seemed to have a thing for clasps. He sat on the edge of the bed with the diary and depressed the clasp's concave button. The heart-shaped fastener fell aside. However, before he could open it, the Ps and girls hurtled into the room and jumped up beside him. They jostled his arms seeming to want to play.

"Not now, hounds," he mumbled, trying to push them aside. "Got things to do—scat."

The dogs milled around for a few seconds, but when it was clear a short roughhousing was all they were going to get, Charity led the charge back downstairs.

Repositioning the diary, Nick opened it to the cover page. The writing was neat and precise. He read aloud. "'Secret, personal, and very private thoughts of Dani Newcombe—Volume Seven. Do not read on peril of a gory and untimely death.'"

Volume Seven he thought. *Good grief, she really did write in this thing every day. But where are the others? Would it be wrong to find them and read them all? Might*

*I find out when her bi-polar kicked in? Understand what
she was thinking and when her demons took hold?*

As Nick looked around the room, he mentally checked
off all the places he'd been through. All the boxes he'd
checked. He'd found plenty of books, school papers, and
assorted projects. But nothing resembling a diary. *Maybe,
she got rid of them as she replaced them each year.* No.
That was totally illogical and canceled out any purpose in
writing the thing in the first place. He was about to give
up and simply read the one he had when he again heard
oak branches scratching at the window. And with his attention drawn to the window, he realized the seat might
also be storage. Quickly removing the cushions, he found
the seat did have a lid. And when he lifted it, he found
within, six clasped diaries.

It appeared Dani had started writing the diaries when
she was ten. That was about the time he and his parents
moved to Cornish from Boston. He smiled again. He remembered the exact day he had seen the freckled redhead
ride up to school on a pony. It would be nice to see when
she first noticed him. He was sure she would record
something as important as that. But these were private
writings. Should he put the books back in their hiding
place unread? Even though he so desperately needed
something more of her to make his pain go away?
Wouldn't knowing her innermost thoughts offer him a
crumb of consolation when his life was so empty without
her? Besides, what could she possibly have done that she
wouldn't want him to know about? Might the diaries
document a crush on the captain of the football team?
Might she describe stolen kisses with another guy?
Would she admit to a flirtation with whomever? And so
what if she did? Did any of that matter? They were meant
for each other, and in his heart, he knew, he was the only
man in her life. All the rest was part of Dani's past—a

past that, years from now, might interest Victoria. Might give her an insight into her mom growing up. Nick by-passed the early diaries and replaced them back in the window seat.

As he replaced the cushions and sat, Nick knew Dani's recent writings were of importance to him. He picked up the most recent diary. *This is where Dani's demons will be laid bare. Where her paranoia and angst will be manifest. Where she would have documented why she did what she did. This is of extreme importance.*

As he opened the dairy, Nick's hands began to shake. He so wanted to know what had prompted her to attempt an abortion. Was desperate to know what nightmares had clouded her thinking. However, as quickly as the thought came, a pang of guilt told him he didn't have any business prying into her personal thoughts. He vividly remembered that while they'd agreed to have no secrets, he also promised he wouldn't look at anything private of hers, without her permission. Silly really, she was dead now, so were those pacts still valid? And if they were, which one overruled. Was the secret paramount, or was he bound by the more recent promise? In reading the diary, would he find something he'd rather not know about? Or by not reading them, might something comforting about their relationship be withheld? He was torn. But was he more curious than was good for him? He had never experienced such a dilemma, and as he pondered what to do, Mrs. Ainsworth's voice interrupted.

"Mr. Nick, you come down for lunch now."

Snapping the clasp, Nick took the diary downstairs. When he got to the kitchen, the table was set for two. "Aren't we waiting for the others?" he asked.

"I thought you wanted to beat the rush back to Boston," Mrs. A said. "Mr. Mark called to say he was leaving the church, and then he was heading to Cornish to pick up Ms. Jo. Goodness knows how long they'll be."

"I can wait a while."

"Best you don't, Mr. Nick. You know what they're like. They have a habit of getting sidetracked. Don't know what those two do when they're together, but time always seems to get away from them."

Nick smiled. He knew exactly what they did. They were hopelessly in love, and every second they spent together, was special time, for them alone.

With the dogs settled in their respective corners, and Victoria sleeping soundly in the warmth emanating from the ancient stove, Nick knew why Dani had loved this kitchen. There was always something aromatic cooking, the fire made the whole room cozy. And Mrs. Ainsworth always made you feel right at home.

He vividly remembered the countless hours he and Dani spent at the ancient oak table, doing homework, playing board games, swapping sob stories, and being children. Now, here he was with their child, and even though Dani wasn't there, as he set her diary next to his place setting, he felt her presence.

Mrs. Ainsworth brought over a steaming bowl of beef stew and dumplings. "You get that down, Mr. Nick. I've got some cookies and things for you to take back to school. I don't suppose for one moment they feed you right down there."

He smiled. "Thanks, Mrs. A."

"I see you've got Miss Dani's diary, don't let her catch you with tha—"

Nick stopped mid-forkful and looked directly at her.

"Oh, Mr. Nick, I'm so sorry, I forgot for a moment she wasn't…" Tears filled the old lady's eyes as she turned to fuss with her stewpot.

"It's okay, Mrs. A I do it all the time. I still can't believe…" He left his stew, and stepping to the stove, he wrapped his arms around the old lady. "We all miss her dreadfully but thank God we have Victoria. Dani left us a beautiful gift."

"Right you are, Mr. Nick. She's a beauty, all right. Maybe one day she'll enjoy reading her mother's diaries and finding out what she did when she was young."

"I thought that too, which is why I left the others in the window seat. This one is the most recent. And I'm not sure Dani would like anybody reading it."

"What makes you say that?"

"Something she said before she died. Made me promise I wouldn't look at her private stuff. Silly really, but I get the distinct feeling she made me say it, because…well, something doesn't feel right. I think I should burn it."

Mrs. A raised an eyebrow. "Aren't you curious what's in it?"

"Yes and no. I knew Dani for years and am just now finding out so many things I didn't know about her. What I know I like, and right now, when Victoria asks me about her mom, I can tell her things from the heart. This diary has to contain all the evil things she'd been going through these past months. I'm not sure I'm comfortable introducing a side of Dani I might not be able to explain."

"Oh my, now I can see why you're going to be a doctor. You think a lot about things most of us don't even understand. It's your property, so you can do with it as you please. Now, get along and eat your stew before it gets cold."

Nick returned to the table and picked up the diary. And in a gesture, he didn't entirely understand, he kissed the soft well-worn leather that Dani probably touched a million times. He smiled. She may even have kissed it the way he had done. Then he walked deliberately to the stove, opened the lid, and dropped the diary into the flames.

Tears welled as Nick watched the diary's hide toast from brown to black, and blister and buckle. A faint whispering sound accompanied a haunting squeal as the last drop of moisture left the leather. Then the chronicle of a tortured young woman's life burst into flames. As solemn and dedicated as any confidante might be, Nick closed the stove lid. "Your secrets are safe, baby," he whispered.

As he turned back to the table, he passed Victoria, whose eyes were following him. His mom had been so right about the power of his daughter, and his heart melted as she reached for him. He put his hand down and, when her pudgy fingers wrapped tightly around his, it was clear she wasn't going to let go. He picked her up and rocked her gently. Within seconds, her eyes closed, she fell back into sleep, and he returned her to the crib. "How easily she falls asleep, Mrs. A. Must be all the formula you give her."

"It's not that," Mrs. A. said confidently. "She has a pure heart and clear conscience. You lose it when you grow up, that purity and innocence—unless you do the right thing. Do you sleep good, Mr. Nick?"

Nick smiled to himself. "Yes, actually I do." Selecting a spoonful of the rich vegetable and meat mixture, he took a mouthful. "Excellent stew, Mrs. A."

* * *

After lunch, Nick returned to his room to gather his things. It was becoming harder to leave Victoria, knowing he was missing so many things as she grew. But he'd made a promise to Dani, which he wouldn't break.

With pack strapped on, and books in hand, Nick re-entered the kitchen to say goodbye to Victoria and add Mrs. A's food parcel to his load. But as he stepped toward the door, it opened. Mark and Jo were back, looking like they'd won the lottery.

"Hello, you two," Nick said. "What've you been up to? You're grinning like cats that got the canary."

Mark's arm slipped around Jo's waist. "Back inside, son. Mrs. A., break out the champagne."

"Champagne, in the middle of the day?" asked the old lady. "My Lord, what's going on?"

Mark and Jo looked at each other and burst out laughing. Then Mark moved behind his wife, kissed her neck, and placed his hand gently on her belly. "Make that three glasses, Mrs. A. because by some miracle we're still not clear on—we're going to have a baby!"

About the Author

Born and raised in Warwickshire, England, Anji Nolan began her adult life in the Women's Royal Air Force and left the service to join British Airways at London's Heathrow Airport.

Immigrating to the United States in 1986, Nolan worked in the human resources field, writing manuals, training courses, and the like; ran a seniors' apartment community; and—during her last employment as marketing director for an adult care service—wrote a monthly column on Alzheimer's issues. She has lent her voice to local radio commercials, and participated in the veterans video project held in the Library of Congress.

Nolan is a world traveler who now resides in Northern Arizona. She has written five novels. She is a member of the Mystery Writers of America, Romance Writers of America, the RWA-Women's Fiction, NARWA, RWA-Kiss of Death, and the Chick-lit Writers of the World.

www.ingramcontent.com/pod-product-compliance
Lightning Source LLC
Chambersburg PA
CBHW070533260626
47161CB00002B/365